DREAMING IN CUBAN

DREAMING
IN
CUBAN

CRISTINA GARCIA

ALFRED A. KNOPF   NEW YORK   1992

Grateful acknowledgment is made to the following for permission to reprint previously published material:

William Peter Kosmas, Esq.: *"Poema de la Siguiriya," "Gacela de la Huida,"* and *"La Casida de las Palomas Obscuras"* by Federico Garcia Lorca from *Obras Completas* (Aguillar, 1987 edition). Copyright © 1986 by Herederos de Federico Garcia Lorca. All rights reserved. For information regarding rights and permissions for works by Federico Garcia Lorca, please contact William Peter Kosmas, Esq., 25 Howitt Road, London NW3 4LT.

Pantheon Books: English translation of *"Poema de la Siguiriya"* by Federico Garcia Lorca from *Federico Garcia Lorca: A Life* by Ian Gibson. Copyright © 1989 by Ian Gibson. Reprinted by permission of Pantheon Books, a division of Random House, Inc.

Peer Music: Excerpt from *"Corazon Rebelde"* by Alberto Arredondo. Copyright © 1963 by Peer International Corporation. Copyright renewed. Excerpt from *"Tratame Como Soy"* by Pedro Brunet. Copyright © 1956 by Peer International Corporation. Copyright renewed. All rights reserved. International copyright secured.

Library of Congress Cataloging-in-Publication Data
Garcia, Cristina.
Dreaming in Cuban : a novel / by Cristina Garcia. — 1st ed.
p. cm.
ISBN 0-679-40883-5
I. Title.
PS3513.A587H43   1992
813'.54—dc20   91-20755
                                                    CIP

Manufactured in the United States of America
Published March 9, 1992
Reprinted Once
Third Printing, March 1992

For my grandmother,
and for Scott

These casual exfoliations are
Of the tropic of resemblances . . .

—WALLACE STEVENS

Contents

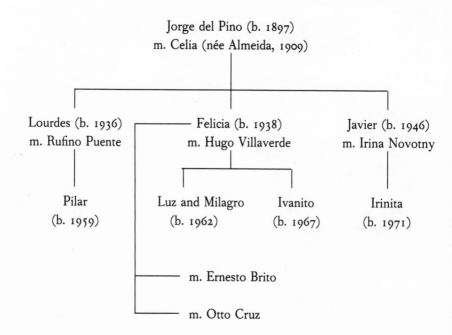

Jorge del Pino (b. 1897)
m. Celia (née Almeida, 1909)

Lourdes (b. 1936)
m. Rufino Puente

Felicia (b. 1938)
m. Hugo Villaverde

Javier (b. 1946)
m. Irina Novotny

Pilar
(b. 1959)

Luz and Milagro
(b. 1962)

Ivanito
(b. 1967)

Irinita
(b. 1971)

m. Ernesto Brito

m. Otto Cruz

ORDINARY SEDUCTIONS

(1972)

Ocean Blue

C elia del Pino, equipped with binoculars and wearing her
best housedress and drop pearl earrings, sits in her wicker
swing guarding the north coast of Cuba. Square by square, she
searches the night skies for adversaries then scrutinizes the
ocean, which is roiling with nine straight days of unseasonable
April rains. No sign of *gusano* traitors. Celia is honored. The
neighborhood committee has voted her little brick-and-cement
house by the sea as the primary lookout for Santa Teresa del
Mar. From her porch, Celia could spot another Bay of Pigs in-
vasion before it happened. She would be feted at the palace,
serenaded by a brass orchestra, seduced by El Líder himself on
a red velvet divan.

Celia brings the binoculars to rest in her lap and rubs her eyes
with stiffened fingers. Her wattled chin trembles. Her eyes smart
from the sweetness of the gardenia tree and the salt of the sea.
In an hour or two, the fishermen will return, nets empty. The
yanquis, rumors go, have ringed the island with nuclear poison,
hoping to starve the people and incite a counterrevolution. They

will drop germ bombs to wither the sugarcane fields, blacken the rivers, blind horses and pigs. Celia studies the coconut palms lining the beach. Could they be blinking signals to an invisible enemy?

A radio announcer barks fresh conjectures about a possible attack and plays a special recorded message from El Líder: "Eleven years ago tonight, *compañeros,* you defended our country against American aggressors. Now each and every one of you must guard our future again. Without your support, *compañeros,* without your sacrifices, there can be no revolution."

Celia reaches into her straw handbag for more red lipstick, then darkens the mole on her left cheek with a black eyebrow pencil. Her sticky graying hair is tied in a chignon at her neck. Celia played the piano once and still exercises her hands, unconsciously stretching them two notes beyond an octave. She wears leather pumps with her bright housedress.

Her grandson appears in the doorway, his pajama top twisted off his shoulders, his eyes vacant with sleep. Celia carries Ivanito past the sofa draped with a faded mantilla, past the water-bleached walnut piano, past the dining-room table pockmarked with ancient history. Only seven chairs remain of the set. Her husband smashed one on the back of Hugo Villaverde, their former son-in-law, and could not repair it for all the splinters. She nestles her grandson beneath a frayed blanket on her bed and kisses his eyes closed.

Celia returns to her post and adjusts the binoculars. The sides of her breasts ache under her arms. There are three fishing boats in the distance—the *Niña,* the *Pinta,* and the *Santa María.* She remembers the singsong way she used to recite their names. Celia moves the binoculars in an arc from left to right, the way she was trained, and then straight across the horizon.

At the far end of the sky, where daylight begins, a dense radiance like a shooting star breaks forth. It weakens as it advances, as its outline takes shape in the ether. Her husband emerges from the light and comes toward her, taller than the palms, walking on water in his white summer suit and Panama hat. He is in no hurry. Celia half expects him to pull pink tea roses from behind his back as he used to when he returned from his trips to distant provinces. Or to offer her a giant eggbeater wrapped in brown paper, she doesn't know why. But he comes empty-handed.

He stops at the ocean's edge, smiles almost shyly, as if he fears disturbing her, and stretches out a colossal hand. His blue eyes are like lasers in the night. The beams bounce off his fingernails, five hard blue shields. They scan the beach, illuminating shells and sleeping gulls, then focus on her. The porch turns blue, ultraviolet. Her hands, too, are blue. Celia squints through the light, which dulls her eyesight and blurs the palms on the shore.

Her husband moves his mouth carefully but she cannot read his immense lips. His jaw churns and swells with each word, faster, until Celia feels the warm breeze of his breath on her face. Then he disappears.

Celia runs to the beach in her good leather pumps. There is a trace of tobacco in the air. "Jorge, I couldn't hear you. I couldn't hear you." She paces the shore, her arms crossed over her breasts. Her shoes leave delicate exclamation points in the wet sand.

Celia fingers the sheet of onion parchment in her pocket, reads the words again, one by one, like a blind woman. Jorge's letter arrived that morning, as if his prescience extended even to the irregular postal service between the United States and Cuba. Celia is astonished by the words, by the disquieting ardor of her husband's last letters. They seemed written by a younger, more passionate Jorge, a man she never knew well. But his hand-writing, an ornate script he learned in another century, revealed his decay. When he wrote this last missive, Jorge must have known he would die before she received it.

A long time ago, it seems to her, Jorge boarded the plane for New York, sick and shrunken in an ancient wheelchair. "Butchers and veterinarians!" he shouted as they pushed him up the plank. "That's what Cuba is now!" *Her* Jorge did not resemble the huge, buoyant man on the ocean, the gentleman with silent words she could not understand.

Celia grieves for her husband, not for his death, not yet, but for his mixed-up allegiances.

For many years before the revolution, Jorge had traveled five weeks out of six, selling electric brooms and portable fans for an American firm. He'd wanted to be a model Cuban, to prove to his gringo boss that they were cut from the same cloth. Jorge wore his suit on the hottest days of the year, even in remote villages where the people thought he was crazy. He put on his boater with its wide black band before a mirror, to keep the angle shy of jaunty.

Celia cannot decide which is worse, separation or death. Separation is familiar, too familiar, but Celia is uncertain she can reconcile it with permanence. Who could have predicted her life? What unknown covenants led her ultimately to this beach and this hour and this solitude?

She considers the vagaries of sports, the happenstance of El Líder, a star pitcher in his youth, narrowly missing a baseball career in America. His wicked curveball attracted the major-league scouts, and the Washington Senators were interested in signing him but changed their minds. Frustrated, El Líder went home, rested his pitching arm, and started a revolution in the mountains.

Because of this, Celia thinks, her husband will be buried in stiff, foreign earth. Because of this, their children and their grandchildren are nomads.

Pilar, her first grandchild, writes to her from Brooklyn in a Spanish that is no longer hers. She speaks the hard-edged lexicon of bygone tourists itchy to throw dice on green felt or asphalt. Pilar's eyes, Celia fears, are no longer used to the compacted light of the tropics, where a morning hour can fill a month of days in the north, which receives only careless sheddings from the sun. She imagines her granddaughter pale, gliding through paleness, malnourished and cold without the food of scarlets and greens.

Celia knows that Pilar wears overalls like a farmhand and paints canvases with knots and whorls of red that resemble nothing at all. She knows that Pilar keeps a diary in the lining of her winter coat, hidden from her mother's scouring eyes. In it, Pilar records everything. This pleases Celia. She closes her eyes and speaks to her granddaughter, imagines her words as slivers of light piercing the murky night.

The rain begins again, softly this time. The finned palms record each drop. Celia is ankle deep in the rising tide. The water is curiously warm, too warm for spring. She reaches down and removes her pumps, crimped and puckered now like her own skin, chalked and misshapen from the saltwater. She wades deeper into the ocean. It pulls on her housedress like weights on her hem. Her hands float on the surface of the sea, still clutching her shoes, as if they could lead her to a new place.

She remembers something a *santera* told her nearly forty years ago, when she had decided to die: "Miss Celia, there's a wet landscape in your palm." And it was true. She had lived all these years by the sea until she knew its every definition of blue.

Celia turns toward the shore. The light is unbearably bright on the porch. The wicker swing hangs from two rusted chains. The stripes on the cushions have dulled to gray as if the color made no difference at all. It seems to Celia that another woman entirely sat for years on those weathered cushions, drawn by the pull of the tides. She remembers the painful transitions to spring, the sea grapes and the rains, her skin a cicatrix.

She and Jorge moved to their house in the spring of 1937. Her husband bought her an upright walnut piano and set it by an arched window with a view of the sea. He stocked it with her music workbooks and sheaves of invigorating Rachmaninoff, Tchaikovsky, and a selection of Chopin. "Keep her away from Debussy," she overheard the doctors warn him. They feared that the Frenchman's restless style might compel her to rashness, but Celia hid her music to *La Soirée dans Grenade* and played it incessantly while Jorge traveled.

Celia hears the music now, pressing from beneath the waves. The water laps at her throat. She arches her spine until she floats on her back, straining to hear the notes of the Alhambra at midnight. She is waiting in a flowered shawl by the fountain for her lover, her Spanish lover, the lover before Jorge, and her hair is twisted with high combs. They retreat to the mossy riverbank and make love under the watchful poplars. The air is fragrant with jasmine and myrtle and citrus.

A cool wind stirs Celia from her dream. She stretches her legs but she cannot touch the sandy bottom. Her arms are heavy, sodden as porous wood after a storm. She has lost her shoes. A sudden wave engulfs her, and for a moment Celia is tempted to relax and drop. Instead, she swims clumsily, steadily toward shore, sunk low like an overladen boat. Celia concentrates on the palms tossing their headdresses in the sky. Their messages jump from tree to tree with stolen electricity. No one but me, she thinks, is guarding the coast tonight.

Celia peels Jorge's letter from her housedress pocket and

holds it in the air to dry. She walks back to the porch and waits
for the fishermen, for daylight.

Felicia del Pino

Felicia del Pino, her head a spiky anarchy of miniature pink roll-
ers, pounds the horn of her 1952 De Soto as she pulls up to the
little house by the sea. It is 7:43 A.M. and she has made the
seventeen-mile journey from Havana to Santa Teresa del Mar
in thirty-four minutes. Felicia screams for her mother, throws
herself onto the backseat and shoulders open the car's only working door. Then she flies past the rows of gangly bird of paradise, past the pawpaw tree with ripening fruit, and loses a sandal
taking the three front steps in an inelegant leap.

"I know already," Celia says, rocking gently in her wicker
swing on the porch. Felicia collapses on her mother's lap, sending the swing lurching crazily, and wails to the heavens.

"He was here last night." Celia grips the wicker armrests as
if the entire swing would fly off of its own accord.

"Who?" Felicia demands.

"Your father, he came to say good-bye."

Felicia abruptly stops her lament and stands up. Her pale yellow stretch shorts slide into the crease of her fleshy buttocks.

"You mean he was in the neighborhood and didn't even stop
by?" She is pacing now, pushing a fist into her palm.

"Felicia, it was not a social visit."

"But he's been in New York four years! The least he could
have done was say good-bye to me and the children!"

"What did your sister say?" Celia asks, ignoring her daughter's outburst.

"The nuns called her at the bakery this morning. They said

Papi rose to heaven on tongues of fire. Lourdes was very upset. She's convinced it's a resurrection."

Ivanito stretches his arms around his mother's plump thighs. Felicia, her face softening, looks down at her son. "Your grandfather died today, Ivanito. I know you don't remember him but he loved you very much."

"What happened to Abuela?" Ivanito asks.

Felicia turns to her mother as if seeing her for the first time. Seaweed clings to her skull like a lethal plant. She is barefoot and her skin, encrusted with sand, is tinged a faint blue. Her legs are cold and hard as marble.

"I went for a swim," Celia says irritably.

"With your clothes on?" Felicia tugs on her mother's damp sleeve.

"Yes, Felicia, with my clothes on." The edge in Celia's voice would end any conversation save with her daughter. "Now, listen to me. I want you to send a telegram to your brother."

Celia hasn't spoken to her son since the Soviet tanks stormed Prague four years ago. She cried when she heard his voice and the sounds of the falling city behind him. What was he doing so far from the warm seas swimming with gentle manatees? Javier writes that he has a Czech wife now and a baby girl. Celia wonders how she will speak to this granddaughter, show her how to catch crickets and avoid the beak of the tortoise.

"What should I say?" Felicia asks her mother.

"Tell him his father died."

*   *   *

Felicia climbs into the front seat of her car, crosses her arms over the steering wheel, and stares out the windshield. The heat rises from the green hood, reminding her of the ocean the day before it wiped the beach clean of homes, God's bits of wood. It was 1944. Felicia was only six, her brother wasn't even born yet, but she remembers that day with precision. The sea's languid retreat into the horizon and the terrible silence of its absence. The way the she-crabs scurried after their young. The stranded dolphin towed out to sea by the Muñoz brothers, and the majestic shells, thousands of them, with intricate mauve chambers, arranged on a cemetery of wet sand. Felicia set aside pails of them but selected only one, a mother-of-pearl shell, a baroque Spanish fan with which later to taunt her suitors.

Her mother hurriedly wrapped gold-rimmed goblets with newspaper and packed them into a scuffed leather suitcase, all the while listening to the warnings on the radio. "I told you not to bring shells into this house," she reprimanded when Felicia held up her prize. "They bring bad luck."

Felicia's father was away on business in Oriente province when the tidal wave hit. He was always away on business. This time, he had promised to bring his wife a Jamaican maid from the east coast of the island so that she could spend her days resting on the porch, as the doctors ordered, and find solace in the patterns of the sea. Felicia's father didn't return with a maid but he brought back a signed baseball for her sister, Lourdes, that made her jump in place with excitement. Felicia didn't recognize the name.

The sea took more than seventy wooden homes from their stretch of coast. The del Pinos' house survived because it was sturdily built of brick and cement. When they returned, it was like an undersea cave, blanched by the ocean. Dried algae stuck to the walls and the sand formed a strange topography on the floors. Felicia laughed when she remembered how her mother had warned her not to bring shells home. After the tidal wave, the house was full of them.

"Girl, you're going to fry in there!" Herminia Delgado raps on Felicia's car window. She is carrying a basket with an unplucked chicken, four lemons, and a brittle garlic clove. "I'm making a fricassee later. Why don't you come over? Or are you too busy with your naughty daydreams again?"

Felicia, her face and forearms blotchy with heat, looks up at her best friend.

"My father died last night and I have to be at work in an hour. They're going to transfer me back to the butcher's if I'm late again. They're looking for an excuse since I singed Graciela Moreira's hair. They dumped her on me. Nobody likes to do her hair because it's so fine it tears like toilet paper. I've told her a million times she shouldn't get a permanent but does she listen?"

"Did Lourdes call?"

"The nuns told her it was like a Holy Ascension except Papi was dressed to go dancing. Then he shows up at my mother's house and nearly scares her half to death. I think she dove in the ocean after him."

Felicia turns away.

"He didn't even say good-bye." The last time Felicia saw her father, he had smashed a chair over her ex-husband Hugo's back. "If you leave with that sonofabitch, don't ever come back!" her father had shouted as they fled.

"Maybe his spirit is still floating free. You must make your peace with him before he's gone for good. I'll call La Madrina. We'll have an emergency session tonight."

"I don't know, Herminia." Felicia believes in the gods' benevolent powers, she just can't stand the blood.

"Listen, girl, there's always new hope for the dead. You must cleanse your soul of this or it will trail you all your days. It may even harm your children. Just a small offering to Santa Bárbara," Herminia coaxes. "Be there at ten and I'll take care of the rest."

"Well, okay. But please, tell her no goats this time."

That night, Felicia guides her car along a rutted road in the countryside a few miles from Santa Teresa del Mar. Her headlights have not worked since 1967 but she shines an oversized flashlight up the dirt pathway, startling two guinea hens and a dwarf monkey in a bamboo cage. The beam of light moves through the yard to the giant ceiba, thick as six lesser trees. Several identical red handkerchiefs are tied together around the trunk, midway up. The head of a freshly slaughtered rooster juts from one knot. Its beak hangs open, giving the bird a look of surprised indignation.

Herminia motions to her from a side door of the run-down house. She is wearing a cream-yellow blouse with a collar the luster of the absent moon. Her plump black arms stir the darkness. "Hurry up! La Madrina is ready!"

Felicia slides to the backseat of her car and opens the door with a scrape. Ferns and chicken feathers graze her ankles as she tiptoes in backless sandals toward her friend.

"*Por Dios,* we've been waiting for you for over an hour! What took you so long?" Herminia grabs Felicia's arm and pulls her to the door. "Let's go in before you make the gods angry."

She steers Felicia down an airless passageway lit on one side with red votive candles set on wooden tables coated with hardened wax. At the end of the corridor, long strands of shells hang in an arched doorway, the mollusks separated by odd-shaped bits of polished onyx.

"*Bienvenida, hija,*" La Madrina beckons in a voice hoarse with a vocation to the unfortunate. "We have been expecting you."

She gestures with upturned palms in an arc around her. Her face is an almond sheen of sweat under her white cotton turban, and her lace blouson, settled off her shoulders, reveals duplicate moles, big and black as beetles, at the base of her throat. Layers of gauze skirts, delicate as membranes, brush her feet, which are bare on the cold cement floor. The low-ceilinged sea-green room wavers with the flames and incense of a hundred candles.

Against the back wall, an ebony statue of Santa Bárbara, the Black Queen, presides. Apples and bananas sit in offering at her feet. Fragrant oblations crowd the shrines of the other saints and

gods: toasted corn, pennies, and an aromatic cigar for Saint Lazarus, protector of paralytics; coconut and bitter kola for Obatalá,
King of the White Cloth; roasted yams, palm wine, and a small
sack of salt for Oggún, patron of metals.

In the front of the room, Elleguá, god of the crossroads, in-
habits the clay eggs in nine rustic bowls of varying sizes. The
eggs have cowrie-shell eyes and mouths, and soak in an elixir
of herbs and holy water. Four mulattas, wearing gingham skirts
and aprons, kneel before the shrines, praying. One man, a pure
blue-black Yoruban, stands mute in the center of the room, a
starched cotton fez on his head.

"Herminia has told us of your dystopia." La Madrina is fond
of melodious words, although she doesn't always know what
they mean. She places a hand heavily ringed with ivory and be-
zoar stones on Felicia's shoulder and motions toward the *santero*.
"He has traveled many hours from the south, from the man-
groves, to be with us, to cleanse you of your infelicities. He will
bring you and your father peace, a peace you never knew while
he lived on this earth."

"Elleguá wants a goat," the *santero* says, his lips barely
moving.

"Oh no, not another goat!" Felicia cries and turns to her friend
accusingly. "You promised!"

"You have no choice," Herminia implores. "You can't dictate
to the gods, Felicia. Elleguá needs fresh blood to do the job
right."

"We will open the future to you, *hija*, you will see," La
Madrina assures her. "We have a friendly contact with the complicated surfaces of the globe."

La Madrina gathers the believers around Felicia. They wrap
her in garlands of beads and stroke her face and eyelids with
branches of rosemary. The *santero* returns with the goat, its
mouth and ears tied with string. Felicia takes a mouthful of
shredded coconut and spits it on the goat's face, kissing its ears

as it whines quietly. She rubs her breasts against its muzzle. "*Kosí ikú, kosí arun, kosí araye,*" the women sing.

The *santero* leads the goat over the offerings and quickly pierces its neck with a butcher knife, directing the stream of blood onto the clay eggs. The goat quivers, then is still. The *santero* shakes a box of salt on its head, then pours honey over the offering.

Felicia, reeling from the sweet scent of the blood and the candles and the women, faints on La Madrina's saint-room floor, which is still warm with sacrifice.

Going South

The continents strain to unloose themselves, to drift reckless and heavy in the seas. Explosions tear and scar the land, spitting out black oaks and coal mines, street lamps and scorpions. Men lose the power of speech. The clocks stop. Lourdes Puente awakens.

It is 4:00 A.M. She turns to her husband sleeping beside her. His reddish hair is flecked with gray and his nearsighted eyes disappear under weary, fleshy lids. She has exhausted poor Rufino again.

Lourdes puts on a size 26 white uniform with wide hip pockets and flat, rubber-soled shoes. She has six identical outfits in the closet, and two more pair of shoes. Lourdes is pleased with her uniform's implicit authority, with the severity of her unadorned face and blunt, round nose. The muscles in her right eye have been weak since she was a child, and every so often the eye drifts to one side, giving her a vaguely cyclopean air. It doesn't diminish her 20/20 vision, only skews it a bit. Lourdes is convinced it enables her to see things that others don't.

Lourdes pins a short braid against her head, twists on a hair-

17

net, and leaves a note for her daughter on the kitchen table. She wants Pilar at the bakery after school. Lourdes fired the Pakistani yesterday and she'll be alone behind the counter today if she doesn't get help. "No excuses this time!!" she scrawls in her sharply slanted script.

The street lamps shed their distorted lights. It is not yet daybreak, and ordinary noises do not startle Lourdes. A squirrel scratching up in an oak tree. A car engine stalling down the block. Between the brownstones and warehouses, the East River is visible, slow and metallic as the sky.

Lourdes enjoys walking in the dark unseen. She imagines her footprints sinking invisibly through the streets and the sidewalks, below the condensed archaeology of the city to underground plains of rich alluvial clay. She suspects the earth sheds its skin in layers, squandered of green.

The early-morning refuge of the bakery delights Lourdes. She is comforted by the order of the round loaves, the texture of grain and powdered sugar, the sustaining aromas of vanilla and almond. Lourdes bought the bakery five years ago from a French-Austrian Jew who had migrated to Brooklyn after the war. Before that, she'd been working as a file clerk at a nearby hospital, classifying the records of patients who had died. Now she wanted to work with bread. What sorrow could there be in that?

The refrigerated cakes come in flimsy cardboard boxes steaming with dry ice. There are Grand Marnier cakes and napoleons with striped icing and chantilly cream. Lourdes unpacks three Sacher tortes and a Saint Honoré studded with profiteroles, Linzer bars with raspberry jam, éclairs, and marzipan cookies in neon pink. In the summer, there'll be fresh peach strudel and blueberry tarts. In the fall, pumpkin pies and frosted cupcakes with toothpick turkeys.

Lourdes lines the display cases with paper doilies and organizes the croissants and coffee rings. She places the day-old pastries in the back of the rows, the easier to reach them. She scrapes the trays of raisins and honey and pops the sugary morsels into her mouth.

Lourdes saves the pecan sticky buns for last. She unloads a tray of them from the delivery cart, reserving two to eat later. As she sets the first pot of coffee to brew, Sister Federica of the Sisters of Charity Hospital calls.

"Your father is a saint," she whispers fiercely. The elfin nun from Santo Domingo is crazy about saints, often identifying the holy ones long before the Vatican even contemplates their canonization. "The mother superior would never believe me. It's a nest of lapsed bats here. But I wanted you to know the truth."

"What happened?" Lourdes asks, stripping the sticky buns of pecans and nervously chewing them one by one.

"I saw it with my own eyes, may his soul find sanctuary."

"My God!" Lourdes crosses herself rapidly.

"I was making my early rounds when I saw a blue light coming from your father's room. I thought he might have left the television on." Sister Federica pauses for a long moment, then resumes with an air more befitting a divine vision. "When I went in, he was fully dressed, standing there erect and healthy, except that his head and hands glowed as if lit from within. It was a nimbus of holiness, I am certain. You know I am an expert in matters of religious enigmas."

"And then?"

"He said, 'Sister Federica, I wish to thank you for your many kindnesses during these last days. But now another interval awaits me.' Just like that. Well, I fell to my knees and began a rosary to La Inmaculada. My hands are still trembling. He put on his hat, passed through the window, and headed south, leaving a trail of phosphorus along the East River."

"Did he say where he was going?"

"No."

"God bless you, Sister. I'll light you a candle."

Lourdes tries for nearly an hour to telephone her mother in Santa Teresa del Mar, but the operator tells her that the rains have knocked out the phone lines on the northwest coast of Cuba. Outside, customers tap on the glass door with keys and coins. She finally dials her sister Felicia's number in Havana.

The rest of the morning, Lourdes tends hurriedly to her customers, mixing up orders and giving the wrong change. Her worst mistake is decorating a christening cake in bold red script with the words "In sympathy." Lourdes telephones her husband at noon but nobody is home. The customers keep coming. Where is Pilar? Lourdes vows to punish her daughter. No painting for a month. That will teach her, she thinks. Then Lourdes calls Rufino again. Still no answer.

The flow of customers slows in the afternoon, and for the first time since Sister Federica called, Lourdes sits down with a watery cup of coffee and her sticky buns to figure things out. She remembers how after her father arrived in New York her appetite for sex and baked goods increased dramatically. The more she took her father to the hospital for cobalt treatments, the more she reached for the pecan sticky buns, and for Rufino.

The flesh amassed rapidly on her hips and buttocks, muting the angles of her bones. It collected on her thighs, fusing them above the knees. It hung from her arms like hammocks. She dreamt continually of bread, of grainy ryes and pumpernickels, whole wheat and challah in woven straw baskets. They multiplied prodigiously, hung abundantly from the trees, crowded the skies until they were redolent of yeast.

Lourdes had gained 118 pounds.

When she was a skinny child, strangers bought Lourdes treats on the beach or on the main street of town, believing she was malnourished and motherless. As a teenager, Lourdes would drink three or four milk shakes with dinner. Even on the day before her wedding, the seamstresses took in her bodice, begging her to eat and fill out her gown.

Now the extra weight did not alter her rhythmical gait, but men's eyes no longer pursued her curves. It was not a question of control. Lourdes did not battle her cravings; rather, she submitted to them like a somnambulist to a dream. She summoned her husband from his workshop by pulling vigorously on a ship's bell he had rigged up for this purpose, unpinned her hair, and led him by the wrist to their bedroom.

Lourdes's agility astounded Rufino. The heavier she got, the more supple her body became. Her legs looped and rotated like an acrobat's, her neck swiveled with extra ball bearings. And her mouth. Lourdes's mouth and tongue were like the mouths and tongues of a dozen experienced women.

Rufino's body ached from the exertions. His joints swelled like an arthritic's. He begged his wife for a few nights' peace but Lourdes's peals only became more urgent, her glossy black eyes more importunate. Lourdes was reaching through Rufino for something he could not give her, she wasn't sure what.

Lourdes closes her shop early and walks to the Sisters of Charity Hospital fourteen blocks away. Sister Federica escorts her down the dingy hallway. Lourdes lifts her dead father's gnarled hands, his papery, spotted wrists. She notices the way his fingers are twisted above the first joints, stiffened haphazardly like branches. His stomach is shaved and tracked with stitches, and his skin is so transparent that even the most delicate veins are visible. The vast white bed obscures him.

Her father had been a fastidious man, impeccable, close-shaven, with razor-sharp creases pressed into his trousers. He took pride in never walking barefoot, even in his own home, and shuffled around in highly polished leather slippers to protect himself from *microbios*. The very word lit a fire in his eyes. "They

are the enemy!" he used to bellow. "Culprits of tropical squa-
lor!"

For her father, conquering the *microbios* required unflagging
vigilance. It meant keeping the refrigerator so cold that
Lourdes's teeth ached from drinking Coca-Cola or biting into
pieces of leftover pork. "Food spoils quickly in our climate!" he
insisted, turning the dial to near freezing. It meant hearing his
loud complaints about her mother's culinary ambushes: chicken
bloody at the bone, undercooked vegetables, unpeeled fruit
served with room-temperature cream cheese.

The way her father washed his manicured hands was a minor
miracle in itself. To Lourdes, he looked solemn, like a doctor
preparing for surgery. He taught her and Felicia and their
younger brother, Javier, how to scrape under their nails with
miniature scrubbers, how to let the hot water run over their
hands for a slow, thirty-second count, how to dry between their
fingers with towels boiled in bleach so the germs could not breed
in the damp crevices.

In the hospital, her father despaired at incompetences and
breakdowns in procedures, at the rough, professional hands that
prodded him. Once a nurse inserted a suppository to loosen his
bowels and did not return, although he cramped his finger ringing the buzzer, until after he had soiled his pajamas. Lourdes
knew then her father would die. She handed her remaining savings to the nuns and requested a private room with a television
and the best nurse in the hospital.

Her father's last weeks were happy ones under the care of
Sister Federica, whose devotion to a bewildering array of saints
did not lessen her duty to cleanliness. Sister Federica doted on
her father and gave him the smoothest shaves he'd ever had.
Twice a day, she lathered his face with a stiff bristle brush and
with a straight razor expertly scraped the dent in his chin and
the narrow space between his nose and his upper lip. Then she
snipped his unruly nostril hairs and dusted his neck with talcum.

Lourdes knew that the little nun, with her puckish face and faint mustache, reminded her father of his barber in Havana, of the smell of his tonics and pomades, of the cracked red leather and steel levers of his enameled chairs.

Her father died with a clean shave. That, at least, would have made him happy.

When Pilar doesn't return home by nine o'clock, Lourdes calls the police station and begins defrosting a two-and-a-half-pound stash of pecan sticky buns. At ten o'clock, she telephones the fire department and preheats the oven. By midnight, she's alerted three hospitals and six radio stations and finished the last of the sticky buns.

Rufino cannot comfort her. Her father is dead. Their daughter is missing. "And where were you this afternoon?" Lourdes suddenly shouts at her husband, but she doesn't wait for an answer. Instead she tears through a shopping bag of photographs looking for a snapshot of her daughter, but all she finds is a wallet-sized school picture of Pilar in third grade. Pilar's hair is straight and black and parted neatly on the side. She's wearing a maroon plaid jumper, a white blouse with a Peter Pan collar and a matching snap-on tie. This girl looks nothing like her daughter.

Lourdes can no longer envision Pilar, only floating parts of her. An amber eye, a delicate wrist with a silver-and-turquoise bracelet, eyebrows arched and thick as if inviting danger. Lourdes imagines these pieces, broken and bruised in unspeakable places, on piers and in alleyways, drifting down the river to the sea.

She combs her daughter's room for the Jimi Hendrix poster she made her take down and tacks it back on the wall. Then Lourdes scoops up an armful of Pilar's grubby overalls and her paint-spattered flannel shirts and lies beneath them on her daughter's bed. She inhales the turpentine, the smell of defiance that is Pilar.

*

Her daughter was born eleven days after El Líder rode in triumph to Havana. Pilar slipped out like a tadpole, dark, hairless, and eager for light.

Lourdes had difficulty keeping nursemaids for Pilar. Few lasted more than a week or two. One girl left with a broken leg after slipping on a bar of soap Pilar dropped while the nanny was bathing her in the sink. Another woman, an elderly mulatta, claimed that her hair was falling out from the menacing stares the baby gave her. Lourdes fired her after she found Pilar in her bassinet smeared with chicken blood and covered with bay leaves.

"The child is bewitched," the frightened nanny explained. "I was trying to cleanse her spirit."

At dawn, Lourdes crosses the Brooklyn Bridge. The sun is low in the sky and she searches the silvery river for clues. A tugboat sounds mournfully, pulling its cargo of oil drums. The air smells of tar and clinging winter. Through the grid of steel cables, the skyscrapers divide into manageable fragments. To the north, more bridges are superimposed like a poker player's cards. To the east lie the flatlands of Brooklyn and an expressway to Queens.

Lourdes turns south. Everything, it seems, is going south. The smoke from the leaning chimneys in New Jersey. A reverse formation of sparrows. The pockmarked ships headed for Panama. The torpid river itself.

Lourdes imagines her father, too, heading south, returning home to their beach, which is mined with sad memories. She tries to picture her first winter in Cuba. It was 1936 and her mother was in an asylum. Lourdes and her father traversed the island in his automobile, big and black as a Sunday-night church. From the car window, Lourdes saw the island's wounded landscapes, its helices of palms. Fat men pressed their faces, snaked with purple veins, against her cheeks. They gave her cankered oranges, tasteless lollipops. Her mother's doleful rhythm followed them everywhere.

Pilar Puente

I'm trying on French-style garters and push-up brassières in the dressing room of Abraham & Straus when I think I hear his voice. I stick my head out and see them. My father looks like a kid, laughing and animated and whispering in this woman's ear. The woman is huge and blond and puffy like a 1950s beauty queen gone to seed. She has a cloud of bleached hair and high-muscled calves as if she's been walking in those heels since birth. "Shit!" I think. "Shit! I can't believe this!" I get dressed and follow them, hiding behind racks of hats and on-sale sweaters. At the candy counter, my father holds a toffee crunch above her flicking, disgusting tongue. She's a head taller than he is so it's not easy. It makes me sick to my stomach.

They walk down Fulton Street arm in arm, pretending to window-shop. It's just a run-down stretch of outdated stores with merchandise that's been there since the Bay of Pigs. I guess my father figures that nobody he knows will see him in this neighborhood. The beauty queen leans into him outside a stereo place that's blasting, incredibly, "Stop in the Name of Love." I see that flycatcher tongue of hers go into his mouth. Then my father holds her waxy, bloated face in his hands, as if it were a small sun.

That's it. My mind's made up. I'm going back to Cuba. I'm fed up with everything around here. I take all my money out of the bank, $120, money I earned slaving away at my mother's bakery, and buy a one-way bus ticket to Miami. I figure if I can

just get there, I'll be able to make my way to Cuba, maybe rent
a boat or get a fisherman to take me. I imagine Abuela Celia's
surprise as I sneak up behind her. She'll be sitting in her wicker
swing overlooking the sea and she'll smell of salt and violet
water. There'll be gulls and crabs along the shore. She'll stroke
my cheek with her cool hands, sing quietly in my ear.

I was only two years old when I left Cuba but I remember everything that's happened to me since I was a baby, even word-for-
word conversations. I was sitting in my grandmother's lap, playing with her drop pearl earrings, when my mother told her we
were leaving the country. Abuela Celia called her a traitor to the
revolution. Mom tried to pull me away but I clung to Abuela
and screamed at the top of my lungs. My grandfather came running and said, "Celia, let the girl go. She belongs with Lourdes."
That was the last time I saw her.

My mother says that Abuela Celia's had plenty of chances to
leave Cuba but that she's stubborn and got her head turned
around by El Líder. Mom says "Communist" the way some people says "cancer," low and fierce. She reads the newspapers page
by page for leftist conspiracies, jams her finger against imagined
evidence and says, "See. What did I tell you?" Last year when
El Líder jailed a famous Cuban poet, she sneered at "those leftist
intellectual hypocrites" for trying to free him. "They created
those prisons, so now they should rot in them!" she shouted,
not making much sense at all. "They're dangerous subversives,
red to the bone!" Mom's views are strictly black-and-white. It's
how she survives.

My mother reads my diary, tracks it down under the mattress,
or to the lining of my winter coat. She says it's her responsibility
to know my private thoughts, that I'll understand when I have
my own kids. That's how she knows about me in the tub. I like
to lie on my back and let the shower rain down on me full force.

If I move my hips to just the right position, it feels great, like little explosions on a string. Now, whenever I'm in the bathroom, my mother knocks on the door like President Nixon's here and needs to use the john. Meanwhile, I hear her jumping my father night after night until he begs her to leave him alone. You never would have guessed it by looking at her.

When Mom first found out about me in the tub, she beat me in the face and pulled my hair out in big clumps. She called me a *desgraciada* and ground her knuckles into my temples. Then she forced me to work in her bakery every day after school for twenty-five cents an hour. She leaves me nasty notes on the kitchen table reminding me to show up, or else. She thinks working with her will teach me responsibility, clear my head of filthy thoughts. Like I'll get pure pushing her donuts around. It's not like it's done wonders for her, either. She's as fat as a Macy's Thanksgiving Day float from all the pecan sticky buns she eats. I'm convinced they're doing something to her brain.

The bus ride down isn't too bad. After New Jersey, it's a straight shot down I-95. I'm sitting next to this skinny woman who got on in Richmond. Her name is Minnie French but she's weirdly old-looking for a young person. Maybe it's her name or the three shopping bags of food she's got under her seat. Fried chicken, potato salad, ham sandwiches, chocolate cupcakes, even a jumbo can of peaches in heavy syrup. Minnie takes dainty bites of everything, chewing it fast like a squirrel. She offers me a chicken thigh but I'm not hungry. Minnie tells me she was born in Toledo, Ohio, the last of thirteen children, and that her mother died giving birth to her. The family split up and Minnie was raised by a grandmother who can quote the Bible chapter and verse and drives a beat-up Cadillac with a CB radio in it. Minnie says her grandma likes talking to other born-again motorists on her way to Chicago to visit relatives.

I tell her how back in Cuba the nannies used to think I was

possessed. They rubbed me with blood and leaves when my mother wasn't looking and rattled beads over my forehead. They called me *brujita,* little witch. I stared at them, tried to make them go away. I remember thinking, Okay, I'll start with their hair, make it fall out strand by strand. They always left wearing kerchiefs to cover their bald patches.

I don't really want to talk about my father but I end up telling Minnie how he used to take me horseback riding on our ranch, strapping me in his saddle with a leather seat belt he designed just for me. Dad's family owned casinos in Cuba, and had one of the largest ranches on the island. There were beef cattle and dairy cows, horses, pigs, goats, and lambs. Dad fed them molasses to fatten them, and gave the chickens corn and sorghum until they laid vermilion eggs, rich with vitamins. He took me on an overnight inspection once. We camped out under a sapodilla tree and listened to the pygmy owls with their old women's voices. My father knew I understood more than I could say. He told me stories about Cuba after Columbus came. He said that the Spaniards wiped out more Indians with smallpox than with muskets.

"Why don't we read about this in history books?" I ask Minnie. "It's always one damn battle after another. We only know about Charlemagne and Napoléon because they *fought* their way into posterity." Minnie just shakes her head and looks out the window. She's starting to fall asleep. Her head is lolling about on her shoulders and her mouth is half open.

If it were up to me, I'd record other things. Like the time there was a freak hailstorm in the Congo and the women took it as a sign that they should rule. Or the life stories of prostitutes in Bombay. Why don't I know anything about them? Who chooses what we should know or what's important? I know I have to decide these things for myself. Most of what I've learned that's important I've learned on my own, or from my grandmother.

Abuela Celia and I write to each other sometimes, but mostly

I hear her speaking to me at night just before I fall asleep. She tells me stories about her life and what the sea was like that day. She seems to know everything that's happened to me and tells me not to mind my mother too much. Abuela Celia says she wants to see me again. She tells me she loves me.

My grandmother is the one who encouraged me to go to painting classes at Mitzi Kellner's. She's a lady down the block who used to hang out in Greenwich Village with the beatniks. Her house stinks of turpentine and urine from all her cats. She gave an art class Friday afternoons for the neighborhood kids. We started off doing blind contour drawings of our hands, then of lettuce leaves, gourds, anything wrinkly. Mitzi told us not to worry about copying objects exactly, that it was the strength of our lines that counted.

My paintings have been getting more and more abstract lately, violent-looking with clotted swirls of red. Mom thinks they're morbid. Last year, she refused to let me accept the scholarship I won to art school in Manhattan. She said that artists are a bad element, a profligate bunch who shoot heroin. "I won't allow it, Rufino!" she cried with her usual drama. "She'll have to kill me first!" Not that the thought hadn't crossed my mind. But Dad, in his unobtrusive way, finally persuaded her to let me go.

After I started art school last fall, Dad fixed up a studio for me in the back of the warehouse where we live. He bought the warehouse from the city for a hundred dollars when I was in third grade. It had lots of great junk in it until Mom made him move it out. There were a vintage subway turnstile and an antique telephone, the shell of a Bluebird radio, even the nose fin of a locomotive. Where my mother saw junk, Dad saw the clean lines of the machine age.

Dad tells me the place was built in the 1920s as temporary housing for out-of-town public-school teachers. Then it was a dormitory for soldiers during World War II, and later the Transit Authority used it for storage.

A cinder-block wall divides the warehouse in two. Mom wanted a real home up front, so Dad built a couple of bedrooms and a kitchen with a double sink. Mom bought love seats and lace doilies and hung up a tacky watercolor landscape she had brought with her from Cuba. She installed window boxes with geraniums.

My father likes to sift through street castoffs and industrial junk heaps for treasures. Like a proud tomcat showing off the spoils of his hunt, he leaves what he finds for my mother in the kitchen. Mostly she doesn't appreciate it. Dad likes raising things, too. It's in his blood from his days on the farm. Last summer he left a lone bee in a jar on the kitchen counter for my mother.

"What does this mean?" Mom asked suspiciously.

"Apiculture, Lourdes. I've got a nest out back. We're going to grow our own honey, maybe supply all of Brooklyn."

The bees lasted exactly one week. Mom wrapped herself in beach towels and released them all one afternoon when Dad and I were at the movies. They stung her arms and face so badly she could hardly open her eyes. Now she never goes to the back of the warehouse, which is better for us.

Dad has his workshop next to mine and tinkers with his projects there. His latest idea is a voice-command typewriter he says will do away with secretaries.

To get hold of us, Mom rings a huge bell that Dad found in the abandoned shipyard next door. When she's upset, she pulls on the damn thing like the hunchback of Notre Dame.

Our house is on a cement plot near the East River. At night, especially in the summer when the sound carries, I hear the low whistles of the ships as they leave New York harbor. They travel south past the Wall Street skyscrapers, past Ellis Island and the Statue of Liberty, past Bayonne, New Jersey, and the Bay Ridge

Channel and under the Verrazano Bridge. Then they make a left at Coney Island and head out to the Atlantic. When I hear those whistles, I want to go with them.

When Minnie wakes up, she says she knows she shouldn't be telling me this, that I'm too young to hear it, but I swear I'm thirteen and that seems to satisfy her. She's seventeen and a half. Minnie says she's going down to Florida to see a doctor her boyfriend knows and get herself an abortion. She doesn't have any children and she doesn't want any either, she tells me. Her voice is flat and even and I hold her hand until she falls asleep again.

I think about how the New Guinea islanders didn't connect sex with pregnancy. They believed that children float on logs in the heavens until the spirits of pregnant women claim them. I'm not too tired so I stay up reading the neon signs off the highway. The missing letters make for weird messages. There's a Shell station missing the "S."

-hell

Open 24 Hours

My favorite, though, is one, I swear it, in North Carolina that says Cock----s, with an electric martini minus the olive.

No matter how hard I try, though, I keep seeing the bloated face of that aging beauty queen bouncing off the lights into my father's outstretched hands. I guess my parents don't see all that much of each other anymore except when Mom rings for Dad. He always looks real worried, too. Dad used to help Mom in the bakery but she lost patience with him. As handy as he is for some things, he couldn't get the hang of the pastry business, at least not the way my mother runs it.

These days, Mom goes through her employees like those damn pecan sticky buns she eats. Nobody ever lasts more than a day or two. She hires the real down-and-outs, immigrants from Russia or Pakistan, people who don't speak any English, figuring she can get them cheap. Then she screams at them half the day because they don't understand what she's saying. Mom thinks they're all out to steal from her so she rifles through their coats and shopping bags when they're working. Like what are they going to steal? A butter cookie? A French bread? She told me to check someone's purse once and I said no fucking way. She believes she's doing them a favor by giving them a job and breaking them in to American life. Hell, if she's the welcome wagon, they'd better hitch a ride with someone else.

I remember when we first came to New York. We lived in a hotel in Manhattan for five months while my parents waited for the revolution to fail or for the Americans to intervene in Cuba. My mother used to take me for walks in Central Park. Once, an agent from the Art Linkletter show stopped us at the Children's Zoo and asked my mother if I could be on the show. But I didn't speak English yet so he passed.

Mom used to dress me in a little maroon woolen coat with a black velveteen collar and cuffs. The air was different from Cuba's. It had a cold, smoked smell that chilled my lungs. The skies looked newly washed, streaked with light. And the trees were different, too. They looked on fire. I'd run through great heaps of leaves just to hear them rustle like the palm trees during hurricanes in Cuba. But then I'd feel sad looking up at the bare branches and thinking about Abuela Celia. I wonder how my life would have been if I'd stayed with her.

I saw my grandfather, Abuela Celia's husband, when he came to New York to get treated for his stomach cancer. They took him off the plane in a wheelchair. Abuelo Jorge's face was dry and brittle like old parchment. He slept in my bed, which my mother fixed up with a new nubby beige bedspread, and I slept on a cot next to him. Mom bought him a black-and-white television and Abuelo watched the fights and the Spanish *novelas* on

Channel 47. No matter how much my mother bathed him, he always smelled of burnt eggs and oranges.

My grandfather was so weak that he'd usually fall asleep by eight o'clock. I'd take his teeth out for him and put them in a glass of water fizzing with denture tablets. He'd whistle softly through his gums all night. Sometimes he'd have nightmares and box the air with his fists. "Come here, you good-for-nothing Spaniard!" he'd shout. "Come and fight like a man!" But then he'd settle down, muttering a few curses.

When Mom first started taking him for cobalt treatments I imagined sharp blue beams aimed at his stomach. A strange color for healing, I thought. Nothing we eat is blue, not *blue* blue like my grandfather's eyes, so why didn't the doctors change the color of those damn beams to green? We eat green, it's healthy. If only they had changed those lights to green, I thought, a nice jade green, he'd have gotten better.

My grandfather told me once that I reminded him of Abuela Celia. I took that as a compliment. He used to write her letters every day, when he still had the strength, long letters in an old-fashioned script with flourishes and curlicues. You wouldn't expect him to have such fine handwriting. They were romantic letters, too. He read one out loud to me. He called Abuela Celia his "dove in the desert." Now he can't write to her much. And he's too proud to ask any of us to do it for him. Abuela Celia writes back to him every once in a while, but her letters are full of facts, about this meeting or that, nothing more. They make my grandfather sad.

Minnie rides as far as Jacksonville. I'm curious so I look out the window to see who's come to pick her up. But by the time the bus pulls away she's still waiting.

The scenery gets so dull in Florida that I finally fall asleep. I remember one dream. It's midnight and there are people around me praying on the beach. I'm wearing a white dress and turban and I can hear the ocean nearby, only I can't see it. I'm sitting on a chair, a kind of throne, with antlers fastened to the back. The people lift me up high and walk with me in a slow procession toward the sea. They're chanting in a language I don't understand. I don't feel scared, though. I can see the stars and the moon and the black sky revolving overhead. I can see my grandmother's face.

The House on Palmas Street

T he late-afternoon downpour sends the students' mothers scurrying under the coral tree in the yard of the Nikolai Lenin Elementary School. A lizard vibrates in the crook of the tree's thickest branch. Celia stands alone in the rain in her leather pumps and jade housedress waiting for her twin granddaughters to return from their camping trip to the Isle of Pines. It seems to her that she has spent her entire life waiting for others, for something or other to happen. Waiting for her lover to return from Spain. Waiting for the summer rains to end. Waiting for her husband to leave on his business trips so she could play Debussy on the piano.

The waiting began in 1934, the spring before she married Jorge del Pino, when she was still Celia Almeida. She was selling American photographic equipment at El Encanto, Havana's most prestigious department store, when Gustavo Sierra de Armas strode up to her display case and asked to see Kodak's smallest camera. He was a married Spanish lawyer from Granada and said that he wanted to document the murders in Spain

35

through a peephole in his overcoat. When the war came, no one could refute his evidence.

Gustavo returned to Celia's counter again and again. He brought her butterfly jasmine, the symbol of patriotism and purity, and told her that Cuba, too, would one day be free of bloodsuckers. Gustavo sang to her beauty mark, the *lunar* by her mouth. He bought her drop pearl earrings.

> *Ese lunar que tienes, cielito lindo,*
> *junto a la boca . . .*
> *No se lo des a nadie, cielito lindo,*
> *que a mí me toca.*

When Gustavo left her to return to Spain, Celia was inconsolable. The spring rains made her edgy, the greenery hurt her eyes. She saw mourning doves peck at carrion on her doorstep and visited the *botánicas* for untried potions.

"I want a long, easy solace," she told the *gitanas*.

She bought tiger root from Jamaica to scrape, a cluster of indigo, translucent crimson seeds, and lastly, a tiny burlap pouch of herbs. She boiled teas and honeycombs, steamed open her pores, adjusted the shutters, and drank.

Celia took to her bed by early summer and stayed there for the next eight months. That she was shrinking there was no doubt. Celia had been a tall woman, a head taller than most men, with a full bosom and slender, muscled legs. Soon she was a fragile pile of opaque bones, with yellowed nails and no monthly blood. Her great-aunt Alicia wrapped Celia's thinning hair with colorful bandannas, making her appearance all the more startling.

The doctors could find nothing wrong with Celia. They examined her through monocles and magnifying glasses, with metal instruments that embossed her chest and forearms, thighs and forehead with a blue geometry. With pencil-thin flashlights they peered into her eyes, which hung like lanterns in her sleepless face. They prescribed vitamins and sugar pills and pills to make her sleep, but Celia diminished, ever more pallid, in her bed.

Neighbors suggested their own remedies: arnica compresses, packed mud from a holy well, ground elephant tusk from the Niger to mix in her daily broth. They dug up the front yard for buried maledictions but found nothing. The best cooks on Palmas Street offered Celia coconut custard, *guayaba* and cheese tortes, bread pudding, and pineapple cakes. Vilma Castillo lit a baked Alaska that set the kitchen aflame and required many buckets of water to extinguish. After the fire, few people came to visit Celia. "She is determined to die," they concluded.

Desperate, her great-aunt called a *santera* from Regla, who draped Celia with beaded necklaces and tossed shells to divine the will of the gods.

"Miss Celia, I see a wet landscape in your palm," the little *santera* said, then turned to Tía Alicia. "She will survive the hard flames."

Celia wrote her first letter to Gustavo Sierra de Armas upon the insistence of Jorge del Pino, who came courting during her housebound exile. Jorge was fourteen years older than she and wore round steel glasses that shrank his blue eyes. Celia had known him since she was a child, when her mother had sent her from the countryside to live with her great-aunt in Havana.

"Write to that fool," Jorge insisted. "If he doesn't answer, you will marry me."

November 11, 1934

Mi querido Gustavo,
    A fish swims in my lung. Without you,
what is there to celebrate?

I am yours always,
Celia

For twenty-five years, Celia wrote her Spanish lover a letter on the eleventh day of each month, then stored it in a satin-covered chest beneath her bed. Celia has removed her drop pearl earrings only nine times, to clean them. No one ever remembers her without them.

*   *   *

Celia's twin granddaughters recount how on their camping trip they fed midget bananas to a speckled horse and examined horned earthworms peculiar to the island. Celia knows that Luz and Milagro are always alone with one another, speaking in symbols only they understand. Luz, older by twelve minutes, usually speaks for the two of them. The sisters are double stones of a single fruit, darker than their mother, with rounder features and their father's inky eyes. They have identical birthmarks, diminutive caramel crescents over their left eyelids, and their braids hang in duplicate ropes down their backs.

The three of them hitch a ride to the house on Palmas Street. Their driver, a balding man with gently serrated teeth, shakes Celia's hand with fingers the texture of cork. She correctly surmises that he is a plumber. Celia has prided herself on guessing occupations since her days at El Encanto, when she could precisely gauge how much a customer had to spend on a camera. Her biggest sales went to Americans from Pennsylvania. What did they take so many pictures of up there?

The driver turns left on Palmas Street with its matched rows of closely set two-story houses, all painted a flamboyant yellow. Last fall, the line at the hardware store snaked around the block for the surplus paint, left over from a hospital project on the other side of Havana. Felicia bought the maximum amount allowed, eight gallons, and spent two Sundays painting the house with borrowed brushes and ladders.

"After all," she said, "you could die waiting for the right shade of blue."

The air is damp from the afternoon rains. Celia gathers her granddaughters close. "Your grandfather died last week," she tells them, then kisses each one on the cheek. She takes Luz and Milagro by the hand and walks up the front steps of the house on Palmas Street.

"My girls! My girls!" Felicia waves at them frantically from the second-story bedroom window, lost behind the tamarind tree heavy with sparrows and tawny pods. Her face is spotted and enlivened with heat. She is wearing her American-made flannel nightgown with the pale blue roses. It is buttoned to the top of her throat. "I made coconut ice cream!"

Store-bought ice cream is cheap, but for Felicia, making ice cream from scratch is part of the ritual that began after her husband left in 1966. Felicia's delusions commence suddenly, frequently after heavy rains. She rarely deviates from her original pattern, her hymn of particulars.

Felicia coaxes her young son to join her. Celia and her granddaughters enter the house on Palmas Street, to find Ivanito, his dimpled hands clasped, singing the lyrics to a melodramatic love song.

> *Quieres regresar, pero es imposible*
> *Ya mi corazón se encuentra rebelde*
> *Vuélvete otra vez*
> *Que no te amaré jamás*

*   *   *

That night, Celia lies awake in the bare dining room of the yellow house on Palmas Street, the house that once belonged to her mother-in-law and where Felicia now lives. Sleep is an impossibility in this room, in this bed with memories that plague her for days. This house, Celia thinks, has brought only misfortune.

She remembers when she returned from her honeymoon in Soroa with a white orchid in her hair, one that Jorge had clipped from the terraced gardens high above the sulfur baths. Her mother-in-law, who had a fleshy-tipped nose and a pendulous, manly face, snatched the flower from Celia's ear and crushed it in her hand.

"I will have no harlotry in my house," Berta Arango del Pino snapped, staring hard at the darkened mole by Celia's mouth.

Then she turned to her only son.

"I'll fry you a red snapper, *mi corazón,* just the way you like it."

Jorge's business trips stretched unendurably. During the first months of their marriage, he called Celia every night, his gentle voice assuaging her. But soon his calls came less frequently, and his voice lost its comforting tone.

When he was home, they made love tensely and soundlessly while his mother slept. Their marriage bed was a narrow cot that was hidden in the dining-room closet during the day. Afterward, they would dress themselves in their nightclothes and fall asleep in each other's arms. At dawn, Berta Arango del Pino would enter with a short knock, open the shutters, and announce breakfast.

Celia wanted to tell Jorge how his mother and his sister, Ofelia, scorned her, how they ate together in the evenings without inviting her. "Did you see the shirt she sewed for our Jorge today?" she heard Ofelia scoff. "She must think he's growing a third arm." They left her scraps to eat, worse than what they fed the dogs in the street.

One day, while the two of them went to buy embroidery threads, Celia decided to cook them a savory flank-steak stew.

She set the dining-room table with the good linen and silver-ware, collected fruit from the tamarind tree, and squeezed and strained a pitcherful of juice. Hopeful and nervous, she waited for their return. Ofelia got to the kitchen first.

"What do you think you're doing?" she said, opening and closing the lid of the pot like a cymbal.

Berta Arango del Pino followed on her thick-ankled legs. She took two dishrags and carried the pot impassively through the living room, down the front steps and across the yard, then poured the steaming casserole into the gutter.

Jorge's mother and his sister played dominoes in the dining room until late, delaying Celia's sleep, her only solace. Celia knew that Ofelia joined her mother at her dressing table, where they sat on their bony behinds and rubbed whitening cream into their dark, freckled faces. Berta Arango del Pino left the paste on overnight to remove any evidence of her mulatto blood. She had a taste for absinthe, too, and exuded a faint licorice smell. In the mornings, her cheeks and forehead burned from the bleach and the potent liqueur.

On Saturdays, she and Ofelia went to the beauty parlor and returned with identical helmets of girlish curls, which they protected fiercely with hairpins and kerchiefs. Ofelia still hoped for suitors although her mother had long since driven off the few men that dared come around, nervously clutching flowers or mints. She wore her decorous dresses to morning mass, and around her neck displayed the short single strand of pearls she had received on her fifteenth birthday.

Ofelia was afraid of the attention men once paid her but seemed more fearful now of her invisibility. In quiet moments she must have asked: Who am I whitening my skin for? Who notices the tortoiseshell combs in my hair? Would anyone care if the seams on my stockings were crooked? Or if I didn't wear any at all?

*

Celia awoke one morning and knew she was pregnant. She felt as if she had swallowed a bell. The rigid edges of her wedding ring sliced into her tumid finger. Days passed but her husband did not call. She took Ofelia aside and told her in confidence, but Ofelia absently touched her own milkless breasts and ran with the news to her mother.

"The indecency!" Berta Arango del Pino protested. "How many more mouths can my poor son feed?"

Ofelia took to appropriating Celia's dresses and shoes. "You won't be needing this anymore," she said, clutching a cream linen suit, which hung better on the wire hanger than on her desiccated frame. "After the baby, none of this will fit you anyway." She stole Celia's leather pumps when her feet got too swollen to wear them and tore the backs open with her calcarated heels.

Celia wished for a boy, a son who could make his way in the world. If she had a son, she would leave Jorge and sail to Spain, to Granada. She would dance flamenco, her skirts whipping a thousand crimson lights. Her hands would be hummingbirds of hard black sounds, her feet supple against the floorboards of the night. She would drink whiskey with tourists, embroider histories flagrant with peril, stride through the darkness with nothing but a tambourine and too many carnations. One night, Gustavo Sierra de Armas would enter her club, walk onstage, and kiss her deeply to violent guitars.

If she had a girl, Celia decided, she would stay. She would not abandon a daughter to this life, but train her to read the columns of blood and numbers in men's eyes, to understand the morphology of survival. Her daughter, too, would outlast the hard flames.

Jorge named their daughter Lourdes for the miracle-working shrine of France. In the final dialogue with her husband, before he took her to the asylum, Celia talked about how the baby had no shadow, how the earth in its hunger had consumed it. She held their child by one leg, handed her to Jorge, and said, "I will not remember her name."

*   *   *

After her sleepless night in the house on Palmas Street, Celia wanders to the ceiba tree in the corner of the Plaza de las Armas. Fruit and coins are strewn by its trunk and the ground around the tree bulges with buried offerings. Celia knows that good charms and bad are hidden in the stirred earth near its sacred roots. Tía Alicia told her once that the ceiba is a saint, female and maternal. She asks the tree permission before crossing its shadow, then circles it three times and makes a wish for Felicia.

Celia rests in the interior patio of the plaza, where royal palms dwarf a marble statue of Christopher Columbus. Inside the museum there's a bronze weathervane of Doña Inés de Bobadilla, Cuba's first woman governor, holding the Cross of Calatrava. She became governor of the island after her husband, Hernando de Soto, left to conquer Florida. Doña Inés, it is said, was frequently seen staring out to sea, searching the horizon for her husband. But de Soto died on the banks of the Mississippi River without ever seeing his wife again.

Celia passes by the Hotel Inglaterra, drab and peeling from neglect. Celia imagines her dead husband staring up at the shuttered windows, carrying a late-model electric broom. He studies the ornate balconies like a burglar, gazes through the blue panes of stained glass until he spots her with the Spaniard, naked and sharing a cigarette. She imagines him swinging the broom round and round in a quickening circle, scattering pigeons and beggars, swinging so hard that the air breaks in a low whistle, swinging and swinging, then releasing the broom until it flies high above him, crashing through the window and shattering her past.

*

Celia hitchhikes to the Plaza de la Revolución, where El Líder, wearing his customary fatigues, is making a speech. Workers pack the square, cheering his words that echo and collide in midair. Celia makes a decision. Ten years or twenty, whatever she has left, she will devote to El Líder, give herself to his revolution. Now that Jorge is dead, she will volunteer for every project— vaccination campaigns, tutoring, the microbrigades.

In the back of the plaza, flatbed trucks are accepting volunteers for the fields. "There is no need to worry," El Líder assures them. "Work for the revolution today and tomorrow will take care of itself." Celia pulls on a hand stretched before her, its nails blunt and hard as hooves. A bottle of rum passes from mouth to mouth. Celia smooths her housedress then lifts the bottle. The liquor burns in her chest like a hot cloud.

For the next two weeks, Celia consigns her body to the sugarcane. From the trucks, the acres of cane are green and inviting. But deep in the fields the brownish stalks rise from the earth to more than twice her height, occluding her vision. There are rats everywhere, hollowing the sweetest stalks, and insects too numerous to swat. Celia learns to cut the cane straight across at the base, strip its leaves with her machete, then chop it in even pieces for the gatherers. Despite her age or because of it, Celia advances steadily through the fields, hardening her muscles with every step, every swing. She rips her hands on the tough, woody stalks. The sun browns her skin. Around her, the sugarcane hums.

One day, a worker slashes a volunteer with a machete. Celia stares as the blood mingles with the sweat of his victim's chest. "Amateurs!" the *machetero* shouts so everyone can hear. "Sunday peasants! Go to hell, all of you!" Several men grab the worker from behind and take him from the fields. Oblivious of the tumult, a Creole woman spits out a curse. Celia does not know to whom.

Celia imagines the cane she cuts being ground in the *centrales,* and its thick sap collected in vats. The furnaces will transform it to moist, amber crystals. She pictures three-hundred-pound sacks of refined white sugar deep in the hulls of ships. People in Mexico and Russia and Poland will spoon out her sugar for coffee, or to bake in their birthday cakes. And Cuba will grow prosperous. Not the false prosperity of previous years, but a prosperity that those with her on these hot, still mornings can share. Next season the cane will regenerate, a vegetal mystery, and she will return to cut it again. In another seven years, the fields will be burned and replanted.

In the evenings, the stink of sugarcane coats Celia's nostrils and throat, sweetening her meat and rice and the cigarettes she smokes. She soaks her feet in balms of herb water, plays cards past midnight, eats oranges under a full moon. She examines her hands daily with pride.

One dream recurs. A young girl in her Sunday dress and patent shoes selects shells along the shore, filling her limitless pockets. The sea retreats to the horizon, underlining the sky in a dark band of blue. Voices call out to the girl but she does not listen. Then the seas rush over her and she floats underwater with wide-open eyes. The ocean is clear as noon in winter. Bee hummingbirds swim alongside pheasants and cows. A mango sapling grows at her side. The fruits swell and burst crimson and the tree shrivels and dies.

When Celia returns from the fields, she finds her daughter's condition has declined. Felicia's skin appears enameled in pinks like the wallpaper of Old Havana inns. The blue roses of her flannel nightgown adhere to her damp filth. Celia washes her daughter's hair over the kitchen sink then untangles it with a broken comb. She cannot persuade Felicia to take off her nightgown, to allow light in the tenebrous house.

"They stole my hair and sold it to the gypsies," Felicia complains. "The sun burns our imperfections."

"What are you talking about?" Celia asks impatiently.

"Light infiltrates. It's never safe."

"Please, *hija,* give me your gown to wash."

Felicia runs upstairs to her bed and lies with her hands tightly clasped under her breasts.

The twins complain that they've had nothing but ice cream to eat for days, that their mother dances with Ivanito and warns them of the dangers of daylight. Luz accuses Ivanito of repeating their mother's pretentious phrases, of saying things like "The moon glares with a vivid indifference."

"Come here, *chiquitico,*" Celia coaxes, lifting her grandson to her lap. "I'm sorry I left you. I thought your mother would get better in a day or two."

Milagro touches a blister on her grandmother's palm. Celia displays her hands, marred by cuts and callouses. Her granddaughters explore the scarred terrain.

"Pack your bathing suits; we're going to Santa Teresa del Mar."

"I won't go!" Ivanito cries, and runs to bury himself in his mother's bed.

"Just for a few days. Your mother must rest," Celia calls after him. Suddenly she remembers her great-aunt's hands floating on a white surf of keys, overlapping like gulls in the air. Celia used to play duets with her Tía Alicia, side by side on the piano bench. Neighbors would stop and listen to the music, and occasionally invite themselves in for a cup of tea.

"You can't steal him," Felicia warns her mother, rocking Ivanito beneath the sheets.

Celia leads the twins away from the house on Palmas Street. The girls do not speak but their thoughts tumble together like gems in the polishing, reaching their hard conclusions. Celia fears their recollections—the smashed chairs that left splinters in their feet, the obscenities that hung like electric insects in the air.

Their father, Hugo Villaverde, had returned on several occasions. Once, to bring silk scarves and apologies from China. Another time, to blind Felicia for a week with a blow to her eyes. Yet another, to sire Ivanito and leave his syphilis behind.

Despite this, Luz and Milagro insisted on keeping their father's name. Even after he left for good. Even after Felicia reverted to using her maiden name. The girls, Celia realized, would never be del Pinos.

Celia sits in the front seat of the bus with her granddaughters. As they leave Havana, a brisk rain falls, rattling the tin bus. Celia cannot mourn for her husband, she doesn't know why. She loved him, that she learned once, but the grief still won't come. What separates her from sorrow, she wonders. Felicia's delusions? The fortnight in the sugarcane fields? The swelter of the afternoon rains? Had she simply grown too accustomed to Jorge's absence?

Already it seems a long time since her husband walked on water in his white summer suit and Panama hat. Much longer still since he'd boarded the plane for New York.

The rain stops as abruptly as it began. By the time Celia and the twins arrive in Santa Teresa del Mar, the sun is as certain as if the day had just begun.

Celia examines the withered contents of her refrigerator: three carrots, half a green pepper, a handful of spongy potatoes. She sends the twins to the bodega with an empty can and the last of her monthly coupons. She wants the fattest chicken they can find, a sack of rice, two onions, six brown eggs, and a refill of lard.

Memory cannot be confined, Celia realizes, looking out the kitchen window to the sea. It's slate gray, the color of undeveloped film. Capturing images suddenly seems to her an act of cruelty. It was an atrocity to sell cameras at El Encanto department store, to imprison emotions on squares of glossy paper.

When her granddaughters return, Celia presses her thumb against the rotting onions, indenting them. She picks the pebbles from the rice and rinses it in the sink. Tufts of feathers sprout from the chicken's skull, and its feet secrete a sticky liquid. Celia sterilizes the bird over a flame and watches the puckered skin blacken and curl. She remembers her husband's fastidiousness, his war against germs. How he drove her crazy with his complaints!

What was it he read to her once? About how, long ago, the New World was attached to Europe and Africa? Yes, and the continents pulled away slowly, painfully after millions of years. The Americas are still inching westward and will eventually collide with Japan. Celia wonders whether Cuba will be left behind, alone in the Caribbean sea with its faulted and folded mountains, its conquests, its memories.

She finishes chopping the onions and stirs them in a frying pan with a teaspoon of lard. They turn a golden yellow, translucent and sweet.

Celia's Letters: 1935–1940

March 11, 1935

Mi querido Gustavo,

In two weeks I will marry Jorge del Pino. He's a good man and says he loves me. We walk along the beach and he shields me with a parasol. I've told him about you, about our meetings in the Hotel Inglaterra. He tells me to forget you.

I think of our afternoons in those measured shafts of light, that spent light, and I wish I could live underwater. Maybe then my skin would absorb the sea's consoling silence. I'm a prisoner on this island, Gustavo, and I cannot sleep.

Yours forever,
Celia

April 11, 1935

Querido Gustavo,

I'm writing to you from my honeymoon. We're in Soroa. It hasn't rained a single day since we've been here. Jorge makes loves to me as if he were afraid I might shatter. He kisses my eyes and ears, sealing them from you. He brushes

49

my forehead with moist petals to wipe away memory. His kindnesses make me cry.

I am still yours,
Celia

January 11, 1936

Gustavo,
    I am pregnant.

Celia

August 11, 1936

Querido Gustavo,
    A fat wax grows inside me. It's looting my veins. I rock like a buoy in the harbor. There's no relief from the heat. I rinse my dresses and put them on wet to cool off. I hope to die of pneumonia.
    They poison my food and milk but still I swell. The baby lives on venom. Jorge has been away in Oriente for two months. He's afraid to come home.
    If it's a boy, I'll leave him. I'll sail to Spain, to Granada, to your kiss, Gustavo.

I love you,
Celia

September 11, 1936

Gustavo,
    The baby is porous. She has no shadow. The earth in its hunger has consumed it. She reads my thoughts, Gustavo. They are transparent.

December 11, 1936

G.,
    J. has betrayed me. They've hung gold stars in the hall-ways. There's a northern tree with metallic leaves that spin

in the sun. Malaria feeds the hungry clocks, the feverish hands spin and stop. They flay my skin and hang it to dry. I see it whipping on the line. The food is inedible. They digest their own faces here. How's the weather there? Send me olives stuffed with anchovies. Thank you.

C.

January 11, 1937

Mi amor,

The pills they watch me swallow make my thoughts stick like cotton. I lie to the doctors. I tell them my father raped me, that I eat rusted sunsets, scald children in my womb. They burn my skull with procedures. They tell me I'm improving.

Jorge visits me on Sundays. I tell him to line up the electric brooms and turn them all on at once. He doesn't laugh. He sits with me on a wrought-iron bench. Nature is at right angles here. No bougainvillea. No heliconia. No flowering cactus burning myths in the desert. He holds my hands and speaks of Lourdes. Others surround us in the sun. Their words are muted as the winds they allow through the netting. It's a sweet-scented rot.

I've made a friend here, Felicia Gutiérrez. She killed her husband. Doused him with gasoline. Lit a match. She is unrepentant. We're planning to escape.

Tu Celia

February 11, 1937

Querido Gustavo,

They killed Felicia. She burned in her bed. They say it was a cigarette but none of the guards will admit to giving her one. Four men carried her ashes and bones. She trailed a white liquid that I could not read. The director wiped it up himself. No one else would.

I leave tomorrow. Jorge tells me we'll live by the sea. I must pack. My clothes smell of mud.

Celia

November 11, 1938

Mi Gustavo,

I've named my new baby Felicia. Jorge says I'm dooming her. She's beautiful and fat with green eyes that fix on me disarmingly. I'll be a good mother this time. Felicia loves the sea. Her skin is translucent, much like the fish that feed along the reefs. I read her poetry on the porch swing.

Lourdes is two and a half years old. She walks to the beach on her skinny brown legs. Strangers buy her ice cream and she tells them that I'm dead. Jorge calls her every night when he travels. "When are you coming home, Papi? When are you coming home?" she asks him. On the day he returns, even if he's not expected until midnight, she wears her frilly party dress and waits for him by the front door.

Love,
Celia

February 11, 1939

Mi querido Gustavo,

I get up while it's still dark to see the fishermen push their boats into the sea. I think of everyone who might be awake with me—insomniacs, thieves, anarchists, women with children who drowned in their baths. They're my companions. I watch the sun rise, burning its collection of memories, and I draw strength for another day. At dusk I grieve, thinking the earth is dying. I sleep a little.

Yours always,
Celia

July 11, 1940

Querido Gustavo,

Last week, Jorge took us on a Sunday drive through Pinar del Río province. The sight of mountains left me breathless. My vision is so accustomed to a shifting horizon, to the metamorphoses of ocean and clouds, that to see such a mass of rock, immovable against the sky, was astonishing. Nature had seemed more flexible. We drove past fields of sugarcane, rice, pineapples, and tobacco. Acres of coffee trees stretched in all directions.

We stopped in the capital for lunch. It reminds me of Havana when I was a girl. Hibiscus grew everywhere, as if painted by legions of artists. The pace was slow and there were rambling houses with columned verandas. I thought of Tía Alicia, her hair braided like mine with a blue ribbon, sitting at the piano playing Schumann's *Kinderszenen,* her peacock brooch at her throat.

There were always children in the house who took lessons for a few months or a year or two, and shifted uneasily on the piano bench. They relaxed in her presence, brought her crayon drawings or flowers they had picked from their mothers' gardens. Tía Alicia would take the canaries from their cage and let the children feed them seeds or grains of rice they'd saved from their lunch.

I remember Tía Alicia's coconut cakes, the layers inflated with air. Her hands were always scented with the violet water she combed into my hair. She took me for long walks through the city's parks and along its boulevards, revealing intriguing histories. She's the most romantic person I've ever known.

Lourdes and Felicia were quiet most of the day, staring out the window. Felicia usually follows Lourdes around, imitating her sister until Lourdes gets exasperated. But today the two of them hardly said a word, I don't know why.

Jorge coaxed me to try a *guayabita del pinar,* a local drink, and I surprised myself by finishing four. The girls shared a plate of pork chops.

Much love,
Celia

September 11, 1940

Querido Gustavo,

I'm sorry I didn't write to you last month but Jorge was in a terrible accident and I had to rush to Holguín with the girls. He crashed his car into a milk truck and broke both arms, his right leg, and four ribs. He was in the hospital for over a month and has splinters of glass in his spine that the doctors can't remove. Jorge is home now and moves around on crutches but he won't be able to go back to work for a while. Lourdes refuses to leave his side. I've set up a child's cot for her next to his bed. Felicia cries and wants to play with them but they ignore her.

Jorge is a good man, Gustavo. It surprised me how my heart jumped when I heard he'd been hurt. I cried when I saw him bandaged in white, his arms taut in midair like a sea gull. His eyes apologized for having disturbed me. Can you imagine? I discovered I loved him at that moment. Not a passion like ours, Gustavo, but love just the same. I think he understands this and is at peace.

I'd forgotten the poverty of the countryside. From the trains, everything is visible: the bare feet, the crooked backs, the bad teeth. At one station there was a little girl, about six, who wore only a dirty rag that didn't cover her private parts. She stretched out her hands as the passengers left the train, and in the bustle I saw a man stick his finger in her. I cried out and he hurried away. I called to the girl and lowered our basket of food through the window. She ran off like a limping mongrel, dragging it beside her.

Yours,
Celia

A Grove of Lemons

Pilar Puente

It's hot as hell when I finally get off that bus. The sun is burning my scalp, so I duck into a luncheonette. Everything looks antiquated, like the five-and-dime counters in New York. They're the best places to get a BLT, so that's what I order here, with an orange soda.

If I call my father's parents, forget it. I'll be on the next plane to New York. Abuela Zaida, my grandmother, would crow for days about how Mom can't control me, how I'm running wild like the American kids with no respect for their elders. Those two hate each other from way back. Something happened between them before I was born.

There's one cousin down here who's not too bad. His nickname is Blanquito because he's so white he has to wear a hat and T-shirt even when he's swimming. I got to know him at Abuelo Guillermo's eightieth birthday party two years ago in Miami. I figure if I can get hold of him, he'll hide me for a day or two, then take me to Key West, where I'll get a boat to Cuba. Maybe he'll even come with me.

It's Saturday so I'll have to go looking for him at home. The only problem is that the entire Puente tribe practically lives at his house. Blanquito's parents have one of these ranch-style jobs in Coral Gables with a pool in the back. The rest of the family lives in apartments, so on weekends my uncles gather there to watch football and eat themselves sick.

I look up the number in the phone book. Blanquito's mother answers so I hang up. I'd recognize her breathy voice anywhere. She's always on the verge of collapsing from one imaginary illness or another. Last I heard, she thinks she has lumbago. That's nothing compared to some of the other diseases she says she's suffered from—tetanus, malaria, sprue, typhus. You name it, she's had it. Her diseases are usually tropical and debilitating, but only occasionally deadly.

I stop in a church not far from their house. I swore I'd never set foot in anything remotely Catholic again but it feels good to get out of the sun. It's dim and cool, and blue and red dots float in front of my eyes like after somebody snaps a flash picture. I remember how the nuns got upset when I called the Spanish inquisitors Nazis. My mother pleaded with the nuns to take me back. Catholics are always dying to forgive somebody, so if you say you're sorry, you're usually home free. But this time, they said, I'd gone too far.

Our neighborhood was mostly Jewish then and my mother was always saying, "They killed Christ! They pushed in the crown of thorns!" I felt sorry for the Jews getting thrown out of Egypt and having to drag themselves across the desert to find a home. Even though I've been living in Brooklyn all my life, it doesn't feel like home to me. I'm not sure Cuba is, but I want to find out. If I could only see Abuela Celia again, I'd know where I belonged.

The last time I got kicked out of Martyrs and Saints, the school nurse recommended a psychiatrist whose name was Dr. Vincent Price. "Tell me about your urge to mutilate the human form," he asked me. He looked like the real Vincent Price, too, with the same widow's peak and goatee. Mom must have told him about my paintings. But what could I say? That my mother is driving me crazy? That I miss my grandmother and wish I'd never left Cuba? That I want to be a famous artist someday? That a paintbrush is better than a gun so why doesn't everybody just leave me alone? Painting is its own language, I wanted to tell him. Translations just confuse it, dilute it, like words going from Spanish to English. I envy my mother her Spanish curses sometimes. They make my English collapse in a heap.

Dr. Price told Mom that we should start some mother-and-daughter activities, that I was starved for a female primate, or something like that, so she enrolled us in a flamenco class in a studio over Carnegie Hall. Our teacher, Mercedes García, was a bosomy woman with jackhammer feet who taught us how to drop our heels in time to her claps and castanets. Our first lesson was all stamping, first as a group then individually across the floor. What a thunder we made! Mercedes singled me out—"A proud chest, yes! See how she carries herself? *Perfecto! Así, así!*" Mom watched me closely. I could read in her face that we wouldn't return.

The light refracts through the stained-glass windows into long fans of blue. Why do they always have to ruin places like this with religion? I think about the king-sized crucifix nailed to the front of my old principal's desk. Christ's wounds were painted in Day-Glo colors—the gash on his side where the nuns told us the last of his bodily fluids poured out; the beads of blood staining his forehead; the wounds where his hands and feet hung from spikes. The nuns knew from grief all right. I still remember how in third grade Sister Mary Joseph told Francine Zenowitz that her baby brother was going to limbo because her parents didn't baptize him before he died. Francine cried like a baby herself, with her face all screwed up. That day I stopped praying (before I stopped praying altogether) for the souls in purgatory and devoted all my Hail Marys to the kids in limbo, even though I knew it probably wouldn't do them any good.

I still don't know what I'm supposed to do next. All I could think of the whole way down to Florida was getting here. Now that I'm here, and sitting in a church of all places, I haven't got a clue. My mind whirs this way and that, weighing the alternatives, then grinds to a halt under the strain.

The shops along the Miracle Mile look incredibly old-fashioned. It's like all the mannequins have been modeled after astronauts' wives. Who could ever have thought a beehive was attractive? I imagine these men sitting in fashion control centers around the world thinking of new ways to torture women, new ways to make them wince twenty years from now when they look at old photographs of themselves. I had a friend in grammar school whose mother wore hot pants and white vinyl go-go boots just like Nancy Sinatra. I mean, who was she trying to impress?

It's getting late. The sky looks like a big bruise of purples and oranges. It's funny how when the land is so flat, and the buildings so low, the sky seems to take over everything, announcing itself in a way you can't ignore. In New York, the sky gets too much competition.

All the streets in Coral Gables have Spanish names—Segovia, Ponce de Leon, Alhambra—as if they'd been expecting all the Cubans who would eventually live here. I read somewhere that the area started off as just another Florida land scheme. Now it's one of the ritzy neighborhoods of Miami, with huge Spanish colonial houses and avenues of shade trees. I suppose if enough people believe in the hype, anything is possible.

There are lights on in every room of my cousin's house, and several of my uncles' junky cars are in the driveway. I make my way along the south wall of the house, past a clump of banana trees, still green with miniature fruit. I hear voices coming from the kitchen. It's Abuela Zaida and Blanquito's mother, Rosario. Abuela is complaining that there was too much salt in the *ropa vieja,* that high blood pressure runs in the family, and that Rosario should be careful not to aggravate their condition. Abuela Zaida always speaks in the collective "we," meaning her and her husband and her eight sons. All the daughters-in-law are never "we" but "you."

I look over the edge of the windowsill. Abuela Zaida is wearing her hair in lacquered coils, like huge schnecken over each ear. She grows her nails so long that she scratches you even while she strokes your face and says nice things. Mom tells me that Abuela Zaida had all her sons out of wedlock in Costa Rica then convinced my grandfather he should marry her and move to Cuba. Now she's the most fakely pious person I know. She calls any woman who even wears lipstick a whore.

Through the living-room curtains, I see five of my uncles lined up on two sofas and a La-Z-Boy, grumbling over the news. They're arguing over whether Angela Davis, who's on trial in California for murder, kidnapping, and conspiracy, is one of El Líder's agents or a direct emissary from Moscow.

"She'll never be acquitted," Tío Arturo says in Spanish. "Mark my words."

"Forget it, *hombre,* they've bought that jury lock, stock, and barrel," Tío Osvaldo shoots back.

No sign of Blanquito. I go around by the pool, which is drained and covered with plastic sheeting. There's a half-inflated rubber alligator reclining on a lounge chair looking like it could use a drink. I check out the small window on the other side of the pool. My grandfather is asleep on his back, his enormous stomach piled two feet in the air. For someone who's always coughing and spitting and clearing his throat, Abuelo Guillermo sleeps soundly, with smooth, even breaths.

When he's conscious, my grandfather is a blustery *caballero* who insists that even his wife call him "Don Guillermo." He's from Cádiz and stowed away to the Caribbean when he was twelve, then made it big in the casino business after World War I. My parents lived in his country villa when I was born. On the weekends, they gave big parties for their college friends. Everyone danced under Chinese lanterns and went for late-night dips in the oval swimming pool.

I remember one day, when I was about a year and a half, I escaped from my carriage through the broken drop latch and tumbled past the front lawn toward a dirt tractor road. I plopped myself down in my polka-dotted sunsuit and picked off the fattest ants to eat. César, a Doberman pinscher guard dog that had a soft spot for me, started barking and tugging at my diapers, trying to drag me off the road. Everyone ran from the house, thinking the dog was attacking me, and my goddamn grandfather took out his pistol and killed poor César with a shot between his eyes.

The air is suddenly very still, and a moment later the rain roars down. I press my back against the side of the house, trying to protect myself under the eaves but it's no use. The ground turns to mud and my sneakers are soaked in no time. There's a jacaranda tree in full bloom and its flowers come loose in waves of lavender. The rain eases up but it's a full fifteen minutes before it stops completely. My watch quits at exactly 7:17 and 42 seconds. I'm staring at it when it stops.

I get discouraged. I look in through the rest of the windows without even trying to hide. Two of my aunts are conferring in the bathroom but I can't hear what they're saying. Still no Blanquito. I'm tired and feel faintly ridiculous. Like what am I? A fugitive from my mother's bakery? I go back around to the pool. The plastic covering is concave with the weight of the rain, and the alligator has slumped to the ground. I take its place on the lounge chair and adjust the metal bracing until I'm lying flat on my back. The clouds speed through the darkening skies, probably headed for Cuba. It'll rain there, too, in another hour or so.

For a minute I can't remember where I am. All I see is my mother's face when she finds out I've run away. She can look like the dogs guarding hell, except she sounds more like a terrier or a Chihuahua. "You can't compare yourself to me!" she yaps no matter what I complain about. "I work fourteen hours a day so you can be educated!" So who's comparing?

I might be afraid of her if it weren't for those talks I have with Abuela Celia late at night. She tells me that my mother is sad inside and that her anger is more frustration at what she can't change. I guess I'm one of those things she can't change. Still, Mom can get pretty violent. In her hands, bedroom slippers are lethal weapons.

Back in Cuba, everybody used to treat Mom with respect. Their backs would straighten and they'd put on attentive faces like their lives depended on the bolt of fabric she chose. These days, all the neighborhood merchants hate her. "Where are the knobs, kid?" they ask me when her volume goes up. I don't think Mom's ever bought something and not returned it. Somebody somewhere must be keeping track of this. One day, she'll walk into a department store and there'll be camera lights and a big brass band and Bob Barker will announce, "Congratulations, Mrs. Puente! This marks the thousandth time you've come in here to complain!"

I wake up feeling the wet bands of the lounge chair against my cheek. My head seems insulated with felt, like a soundproof room. Everything is muted, far away.

"Come in, *mi cielo*, you'll die of pneumonia!" It's Tía Rosario. She reaches down and tries to lift me, but she's too weak. Her shoulders feel like chicken bones stitched together. I'm afraid they'll snap in two.

The morning is bleaching the edges of the sky. Shit. It's back
to Brooklyn for me. Back to the bakery. Back to my fucking
crazy mother.

"What time is it?" I ask Tía feebly.

"Three minutes after six," she answers without looking at her
watch, as if she tallied each second in her head.

Three minutes after six and counting, I think.

Lourdes Puente

"Lourdes, I'm back," Jorge del Pino greets his daughter forty
days after she buried him with his Panama hat, his cigars, and
a bouquet of violets in a cemetery on the border of Brooklyn
and Queens.

His words are warm and close as a breath. Lourdes turns,
expecting to find her father at her shoulder but she sees only the
dusk settling on the tops of the oak trees, the pink tinge of sliding
darkness.

"Don't be afraid, *mi hija*. Just keep walking and I'll explain,"
Jorge del Pino tells his daughter.

The sunset flares behind a row of brownstones, linking them
as if by a flaming ribbon. Lourdes massages her eyes and begins
walking with legs that feel held by splints.

"I'm glad to see you, Lourdes. Thank you for everything, *hija,*
the hat, the cigars. You buried me like an Egyptian king, with
all my valuables!" Jorge del Pino laughs.

Lourdes perceives the faint scent of her father's cigar. She has
taken to smoking the same brand herself late at night when she
totals the day's receipts at the kitchen table.

"Where are you, Papi?"

The street is vacant, as if a force has absorbed all living things.
Even the trees seem more shadow than substance.

"Nearby," her father says, serious now.

"Can you return?"

"From time to time."

"How will I know?"

"Listen for me at twilight."

Lourdes arrives home with a presentiment of disaster. Is her mind betraying her, cultivating delusion like a hothouse orchid? Lourdes opens the refrigerator, finds nothing to her liking. Everything tastes the same to her these days.

Outside, the spring rains resume ill-temperedly. The drops enter through the kitchen window at impossible angles. A church bell rings, shaking down the leaves of the maple tree. What if she has exhausted reality? Lourdes abhors ambiguity.

She pulls on the shipyard bell that rings in Rufino's workshop. Her husband will assure her, Lourdes thinks. He operates on a material plane. His projects conduct electricity, engage motion with toothed wheels, react in concert with universal laws of physics.

Rufino appears, dusted with blue chalk. His fingernails, too, are blue, an indigo blue.

"He's back," Lourdes whispers hoarsely, peering under the love seats. "He spoke to me tonight when I was walking home from the bakery. I heard Papi's voice. I smelled his cigar. The street was empty, I swear it." Lourdes stops. Her chest rises and falls with every breath. Then she leans toward her husband, narrowing her eyes. "Things are wrong, Rufino, very wrong."

Her husband stares back at her, blinking rapidly as if he'd just awakened. "You're tired, *mi cielo*," Rufino says evenly, coaxing Lourdes to the sofa. He rubs her insteps with a cool lotion called Pretty Feet. She feels the rolling pressure of his thumbs against her arches, the soothing grip of his hands on her swollen ankles.

*

The next day, Lourdes works extraconscientiously, determined to prove to herself that her business acumen, at least, is intact. She sails back and forth behind the bakery counter, explaining the ingredients in her cakes and pies to her clients. "We use only real butter," she says in her accented English. "Not margarine, like the place down the block."

After her customers make their selections, Lourdes leans toward them. "Any special occasions coming up?" she whispers, as if she were selling hot watches from a raincoat. If they answer yes—and it's always a musical yes to Lourdes's ears—she launches into her advance-order sales pitch.

By two o'clock, when the trainee reports for work, Lourdes has cash deposits on seven birthday cakes (including one peanut-butter-and-banana-flavored layer cake topped with a marzipan Elvis); a sixty-serving sheet cake for the closing recital of the Bishop Lowney High School marching band; a two-tiered fiftieth-anniversary cake "For Tillie and Ira, Two Golden Oldies"; and a double-chocolate butter cream decorated with a wide high heel for the retirement of Frankie Zaccaglini of Frankie's EEE Shoe Company.

Lourdes's self-confidence is restored.

"See this," she announces to her new employee, Maribel Navarro, riffling her orders like a blackjack dealer. "This is what I want from you." Then she hands Maribel a bottle of Windex and a roll of paper towels and orders her to clean every last inch of the counter.

Lourdes spends the afternoon training Maribel, a pretty Puerto Rican woman in her late twenties with a pixie cut and stylishly long nails. "You're going to have to trim those if you want to work here," Lourdes snaps. "Unsanitary. The health department will give us a citation."

Maribel is pleasant with the customers and gives the correct change, but she doesn't show much initiative.

"Don't let them get away so easily," Lourdes coaches her. "You can always sell them something else. Some dinner rolls, a coffee ring for tomorrow's breakfast."

Nobody works like an owner, Lourdes thinks, as she places fresh doilies under the chiffon pies. She pulls out a tray of Florentine cookies and shows Maribel how to arrange them on overlapping strips of wax paper so they look more appealing.

"The Florentines are seven ninety-five a pound, two dollars more than the other cookies, so weigh them separately." Lourdes pulls a sheet of tissue paper from a metal dispenser and places it on the scale with a cookie. "See. This Florentine alone weighs forty-three cents. I can't afford to throw that kind of money away."

Business picks up after five o'clock with the after-work crowd stopping by for desserts. Maribel works efficiently, tying the boxes of pastries firmly with string just as she was taught. This pleases Lourdes. By now, she has almost dispelled the effect of her father's visitation yesterday. Could she have imagined the entire incident?

Suddenly Lourdes's wandering eye, like a wary spy, fixes on the quarters sliding across the counter to Maribel. It observes Maribel packing the two cinnamon crullers in a white paper bag, folding the top over neatly, and thanking the customer. It watches as she turns to the register and rings up fifty cents. Then, just as the eye is about to relax its scrutiny, it spots Maribel slipping the coins into her pocket.

Lourdes continues waiting on her customer, an elderly woman sizing up a mocha petit four. When she's done, Lourdes strides to the register, pulls out nine singles and a roll of pennies for the afternoon's work, and hands it to Maribel.

"Get out," Lourdes says.

Maribel removes her apron, folds it into a compact square on the counter, and leaves without saying a word.

*

An hour later, Lourdes walks home from the bakery as if picking her way through a mine field. The Navarro woman has shattered Lourdes's fragile peace of mind. Breezes from the sluggish river seem to inscribe her skin with metal tips. She crawls to an edge inside herself, longs to be insensate, a slab of brick. Lourdes thinks she detects the scent of her father's cigar, but when she turns there's only a businessman hailing a taxi, his hand waving a cigarette. Behind him, a linden tree drops a cluster of seeds.

When Lourdes was a child in Cuba, she used to wait anxiously for her father to return from his trips selling small fans and electric brooms in distant provinces. He would call her every evening from Camagüey or Sagua la Grande and she would cry, "When are you coming home, Papi? When are you coming home?" Lourdes would welcome her father in her party dress and search his suitcase for rag dolls and oranges.

On Sunday afternoons, after high mass, they went to baseball games and ate roasted peanuts from brown paper cones. The sun darkened Lourdes's skin to the shade of the villagers on the bleachers, and the mix of her father's cologne and the warm, acrid smells of the ballpark made her giddy. These are her happiest memories.

Years later, when her father was in New York, baseball became their obsession. During the Mets' championship season, Lourdes and her father discussed each game like generals plotting a battle, assessing the merits of Tom Seaver, Ed Kranepool, and Jerry Koosman. They glued transistors to their ears all summer, even during Jorge del Pino's brief hospital stays, and cheered when the Mets caught fire and the Cubs finally folded.

On October 16, 1969, Lourdes, her father, doctors, nurses, orderlies, patients, nuns, and a priest who arrived to administer last rites to a dying man crowded the television room of the Sisters of Charity Hospital for the fifth game of the World Series. When Cleon Jones camped under the final fly ball against the

Orioles, all hell broke loose. Patients, bare-assed in their hospital gowns, streaked down the corridors chanting, "WE'RE NUMBER ONE!" Someone popped a bottle of champagne and tears streamed down the faces of the nuns, who'd prayed fervently for such a miracle.

At Shea Stadium, the crowd tore onto the field, ripping up home plate, pulling up fat clods of turf and raising them high over their heads. They set off orange flares and firecrackers and chalked the outfield fence with victory slogans. Across the river in Manhattan, on Wall Street and Park Avenue, Delancey Street and Broadway, people danced under showers of computer cards and ticker tape. Lourdes and her father laughed and embraced for a long, long time.

*   *   *

When she had first left Cuba, Lourdes hadn't known how long they'd be away. She was to meet Rufino in Miami, where the rest of his family had fled. In her confusion, she packed riding crops and her wedding veil, a watercolor landscape, and a paper sack of birdseed.

Pilar ran away in the Miami airport, her crinoline dress swinging like a tiny bell through the crowd. Lourdes heard her daughter's name announced over the loudspeaker. She couldn't speak when she found Pilar, sitting on the lap of a pilot and licking a lime lollipop. She couldn't find the words to thank the uniformed American who escorted them to their gate.

After several days, they left Miami in a secondhand Chevrolet. Lourdes couldn't stand Rufino's family, the endless brooding over their lost wealth, the competition for dishwasher jobs.

"I want to go where it's cold," Lourdes told her husband. They began to drive. "Colder," she said as they passed the low salt marshes of Georgia, as if the word were a whip driving them north. "Colder," she said through the withered fields of a Carolina winter. "Colder," she said again in Washington, D.C., despite the cherry-blossom promises, despite the white stone monuments hoarding winter light. "This is cold enough," she finally said when they reached New York.

Only two months earlier, Lourdes had been pregnant with her second child back in Cuba. She'd been galloping through a field of dry grasses when her horse reared suddenly, throwing her to the ground. The horse fled, leaving her alone. Lourdes felt a density between her breasts harden to a sharp, round pain. The blood bleached from her fingernails.

A large rodent appeared from behind an aroma tree and began nibbling the toes of her boots. Lourdes threw a rock at it, killing it instantly. She stumbled for nearly an hour until she reached their dairy farm. A worker lent her his horse and she rode at a breakneck pace back to the villa.

Two young soldiers were pointing their rifles at Rufino. His hands circled nervously in the air. She jumped from her horse and stood like a shield before her husband.

"Get the hell out of here!" she shouted with such ferocity that the soldiers lowered their guns and backed toward their Jeep.

Lourdes felt the clot dislodge and liquefy beneath her breasts, float through her belly, and slide down her thighs. There was a pool of dark blood at her feet.

Rufino was in Havana ordering a cow-milking machine when the soldiers returned. They handed Lourdes an official sheet of paper declaring the Puentes' estate the property of the revolutionary government. She tore the deed in half and angrily dismissed the soldiers, but one of them grabbed her by the arm.

"You're not going to start that again, are you, *compañera?*" the tall one said.

Lourdes heard the accent of Oriente province and turned to

look at him. His hair, tamed with brilliantine, grew dense and low on his forehead.

"Get out of my house!" Lourdes yelled at the men, more fiercely than she had the week before.

But instead of leaving, the tall one increased the pressure on her arm just above the elbow.

Lourdes felt his calloused palm, the metal of his ring clapping her temple. She twisted free from his grip and charged him so abruptly that he fell back against the vestibule wall. Lourdes tried to run past him but the other soldier blocked her way. Her head reverberated with the clapping palm.

"So the woman of the house is a fighter?" the tall soldier taunted. He pressed his face close to Lourdes's, pinning her arms behind her back.

Lourdes did not close her eyes but looked directly into his. They were unremarkable except for the whites, which were tinged with the filmy blue of the blind. His lips were too full for a man. As he tried to press them to Lourdes's mouth she snapped her head back and spat in his face.

He smiled slowly and Lourdes saw a stained band along his front teeth, like the watermarks on a pier. His gums were a soft pink, delicate as the petals of a rose.

The other soldier held Lourdes down as his partner took a knife from his holster. Carefully, he sliced Lourdes's riding pants off to her knees and tied them over her mouth. He cut through her blouse without dislodging a single button and slit her bra and panties in two. Then he placed the knife flat across her belly and raped her.

Lourdes could not see but she smelled vividly as if her senses had concentrated on this alone.

She smelled the soldier's coarse soap, the salt of his perspiring back. She smelled his milky clots and the decay of his teeth and the citrus brilliantine in his hair, as if a grove of lemons lay hid-

den there. She smelled his face on his wedding day, his tears
when his son drowned at the park. She smelled his rotting leg
in Africa, where it would be blown off his body on a moonless
savanna night. She smelled him when he was old and unbathed
and the flies blackened his eyes.

When he finished, the soldier lifted the knife and began to
scratch at Lourdes's belly with great concentration. A primeval
scraping. Crimson hieroglyphics.

The pain brought a flood of color back to Lourdes's eyes. She
saw the blood seep from her skin like rainwater from a sodden
earth.

Not until later, after the tall soldier had battered her with his
rifle and left with his lumpy, quiet friend, after she had scoured
her skin and hair with detergents meant for the walls and the
tile floors, after stanching the blood with cotton and gauze and
wiping the steam from the bathroom mirror, did Lourdes try to
read what he had carved. But it was illegible.

*   *   *

Seven days after her father's visitation, Lourdes looks out her
bakery window. The twilight falls in broad violet sheets. In the
corner store, the butcher closes out his register. Bare fluorescent
tubes and a rack of ribs hang from the ceiling, obscuring his
profile. The florist rattles shut his gate next door, securing it with
a fist-sized lock. Across the street, the liquor store is open, a
magnet to the wiry man in the sagging tan suit cajoling people
for spare change.

Lourdes recognizes a passerby, a heavyset woman with a
veiled pillbox hat who praised her Boston cream pies. She is
dragging by the hand a little boy in short pants and knee socks.
His feet barely touch the ground.

On her way home, Lourdes passes a row of Arab shops, recent additions to the neighborhood. Baskets of figs and pista-

chios and coarse yellow grains are displayed under their awnings. Lourdes buys a round box of sticky dates and considers the centuries of fratricide converging on this street corner in Brooklyn. She ponders the transmigrations from the southern latitudes, the millions moving north. What happens to their languages? The warm burial grounds they leave behind? What of their passions lying stiff and untranslated in their breasts?

Lourdes considers herself lucky. Immigration has redefined her, and she is grateful. Unlike her husband, she welcomes her adopted language, its possibilities for reinvention. Lourdes relishes winter most of all—the cold scraping sounds on sidewalks and windshields, the ritual of scarves and gloves, hats and zip-in coat linings. Its layers protect her. She wants no part of Cuba, no part of its wretched carnival floats creaking with lies, no part of Cuba at all, which Lourdes claims never possessed her.

Four blocks from her home, Lourdes smells her father's cigar behind a catalpa tree.

"*Mi hija,* have you forgotten me?" Jorge del Pino chides gently.

Lourdes feels her legs as if from a distance. She pictures them slipping from their sockets and moving before her in a steady gait, still wearing their rubber-soled shoes, their white-ribbed stockings. Cautiously, she follows them.

"You didn't expect to hear from me again?"

"I wasn't even sure I heard you the first time," Lourdes says tentatively.

"You thought you'd imagined it?"

"I thought I heard your voice because I wanted to, because I missed you. When I was little I used to think I heard you opening the front door late at night. I'd run out but you were never there."

"I'm here now, Lourdes."

There's a ship leaving the harbor, its whistle resigned as an abbot in prayer, fracturing the dusk.

Lourdes recalls the plane ride to Miami last month to pick up Pilar. The airport was congested and they circled the city for nearly an hour before landing. Lourdes could smell the air before she breathed it, the air of her mother's ocean nearby. She imagined herself alone and shriveled in her mother's womb, envisioned the first days in her mother's unyielding arms. Her mother's fingers were stiff and splayed as spoons, her milk a tasteless gray. Her mother stared at her with eyes collapsed of expectation. If it's true that babies learn love from their mothers' voices, then this is what Lourdes heard: "I will not remember her name."

"Papi, I don't know what to do anymore." Lourdes begins to cry. "No matter what I do, Pilar hates me."

"Pilar doesn't hate you, *hija*. She just hasn't learned to love you yet."

The Fire Between Them

Felicia del Pino doesn't know what brings on her delusions. She knows only that suddenly she can hear things very vividly. The scratching of a beetle on the porch. The shifting of the floorboards in the night. She can hear everything in this world and others, every sneeze and creak and breath in the heavens or the harbor or the gardenia tree down the block. They call to her all at once, grasping here and there for parts of her, hatching blue flames in her brain. Only the Beny Moré records, played loud and warped as they are, lessen the din.

The colors, too, escape their objects. The red floats above the carnations on her windowsill. The blues rise from the chipped tiles in the kitchen. Even the greens, her favorite shades of greens, flee the trees and assault her with luminosity. Nothing is solid until she touches it. She blames the sun for this, for the false shadows it casts in her house, and she tightens the shutters against enemy rays. When she dares look outside, the people are paintings, outlined in black, their faces crushed and squarish. They threaten her with their white shining eyes. She hears them talking but cannot understand what they say. She never knows the time.

Felicia's mind floods with thoughts, thoughts from the past, from the future, other people's thoughts. Things come back as symbols, bits of conversation, a snatch of an old church hymn. Every idea seems to her connected to thousands of others by a tangle of pulsing nerves. She jumps from one to another like a nervous circus horse. It is worse when she closes her eyes.

Felicia remembers how when she was in grammar school the paraphernalia of faith had proved more intriguing than its over-wrought lessons. After mass, long after the priest's words stopped echoing against the cement walls, she remained in church, inspecting the pews for forgotten veils or rosary beads. She collected prayer cards and missals engraved with gold initials and filled glass jars with holy water, which she later used to baptize Ilda Limón's chickens. Once she pried loose a crucifix with an ivory Jesus from a Station of the Cross and blessed her baby brother, Javier, with three mild raps to his forehead.

During high mass, her sister and father recited the Lord's Prayer with loud precision and clung forever to the last syllables of the hymns.

"Alleluiaaaaaaaaaaaaaaaaaaaaaa!" they sang, releasing the "a" only when those around them began to stare.

Felicia knew that her mother, who stayed at home reading her books and rocking on the porch swing, had an instinctive distrust of the ecclesiastical. She suspected her mother of being an atheist and only hoped she wouldn't burn in hell for eternity as Lourdes and the nuns said.

Although Celia was not a believer, she was wary of powers she didn't understand. She locked her children in the house on December 4, the feast day of Changó, god of fire and lightning, and warned them that they'd be kidnapped and sacrificed to the black people's god if they wandered the streets alone. For good measure, she forbade Felicia to visit her best friend, Herminia, whose father everyone denounced as a witch doctor.

Lourdes took advantage of their confinement to tell Felicia how the shriveled tin peddler, who rattled by with his trolley at noon, abducted children to caves with flapping bats that nested in human hair. At night, he'd scoop out their eyes with a wooden spoon and drink their blood like milk. Lourdes insisted that the tin man had left the eyes of a dozen sacrificed children under Felicia's bed as an omen. Felicia, her eyes closed tight, cautiously patted the floor until she touched the peeled grapes her sister had left for her there, and screamed to holy hell.

As the summer of coconuts wears on, Felicia hears Saint Sebastian speaking to her inside her head. She can't stop his words, which come in rhymes sometimes or jumbled together like twisted yarn. He doesn't let her think. He reminds her how much she used to love him, how much she has disappointed him over the years.

Felicia first became fascinated with Saint Sebastian before her confirmation. She marveled over how he'd been shot through with arrows and left for dead, how he'd survived his murder only to be beaten to death by the Roman Emperor's soldiers and buried in the catacombs. Sebastian's double death appealed to Felicia. She studied his image, his hands tied above his head, his eyes rolled heavenward, arrows protruding from his chest and sides, and felt a great sympathy for him. But the nuns refused to let Felicia choose Sebastian as her confirmation name.

"Why don't you pick María like your sister?" the nuns had suggested. Their faces were pink, puffy squares cut off at the brows, their pores enlarged from the pressure of their tightly bound habits. "That way Our Blessed Virgin Mother will always look after you."

In the end, Felicia refused to be confirmed at all and Jorge del Pino blamed his daughter's later troubles on that fact.

*

Felicia thinks of her father, of his death and resurrection, and finds it hard to concentrate. Judgment Day is at hand and she isn't ready, not ready at all. So she plays the Beny Moré records over and over and teaches her son to dance, teaches him every dance there is to learn. He is only five years old but he can mambo and cha-cha, do the *danzón* and the *guaracha* with the facility of a gigolo. "Dance, Ivanito, dance!" Felicia shouts, exultant, laughing and applauding his silken moves. Everything makes sense when they dance. Felicia feels as though she were in love again, at the center of the universe, privy to its secrets and inner workings. She has no doubts.

But when the music stops, she sees her husband's hands, big-knuckled with long, square-tipped fingers, inordinately large even for his frame. The nail of his right thumb is missing and the stump that remains is blanched and corrugated. He is long-boned and loose-jointed, over six feet, with the angular face of a cacique and a handsome nose somewhat swollen at the base.

The day she met him, he sat alone in the back booth of El Ternero Dorado restaurant staring at her. She approached him, nervously wiping the backs of her hands on her canvas apron.

"We have a sea bass special today," she stammered. "Grilled, nice and fresh."

"Have you eaten?" he asked, placing a heavy hand on her wrist. That was all it took.

Felicia removed her apron as if commanded by Saint Sebastian himself and followed Hugo Villaverde out the door.

Her future husband walked with a slow, loping gait like the giraffes Felicia had seen at the zoo, so much so that she half expected him to stretch out his neck and nibble at the laurel trees along the Paseo del Prado. She imagined his thick lips moving like warm, softened rubber.

Hugo bought Felicia a paper cone of fritters and a box of chocolates with a bright red bow. He spoke of his childhood in Holguín, where his father, a descendant of slaves, had worked in the nickel mines. Hugo joined the merchant marines at sixteen and on his first trip went to Dakar, where the markets were filled with monstrous fruits grown in soils of uncommon minerals.

"Not like these," he said, indicating a fruit vendor's display of withered melons.

Felicia told him how she'd left high school and answered an ad for international escorts in the newspaper. The office was located on the second floor of a building between a notary public and Dr. Zatarain's venereal clinic. A prim woman with bobbed hair and a throaty French accent asked Felicia to remove her shoes and knee socks, then made a note in a calfskin ledger.

"If a girl does not take care of her feet, there is no point in going further," Madame Thibaut said.

She asked Felicia to unbutton her blouse. Felicia's nipples tightened as she did so. She knew her breasts were admired by the boys in Santa Teresa del Mar. Finally, Madame Thibaut insisted that Felicia remove her skirt and panties.

"Walk," the Frenchwoman ordered.

Felicia felt her ample, dimpled behind quake seductively as she moved.

"Your buttocks are too large for Europe," Madame Thibaut told her. "But for here they will do."

Felicia had only one job for the Bon Temps International Escort Agency, with an obese, freckled rancher from Oklahoma, who wore mismatched snakeskin boots. For a small sum, Madame Thibaut loaned Felicia high heels and a silver-sequined gown sleek as a fish. Merle Grady took Felicia to a casino and rubbed her hips eagerly every time he won. He called her Lady Luck and blew gusts of whiskey breath into her ear. When she refused to return with him to his hotel room, Grady tore at her cleavage and demanded a refund. Felicia watched as the glittering scales of her rented dress clicked and scattered on the marble floor.

*

Felicia went with Hugo Villaverde to the Hotel Inglaterra, an
ornate wedding cake of an edifice opposite the Parque Central.
The inn's reputation was eclipsed by more modern establish-
ments with roulette wheels and long-legged dancing girls, but
it continued to attract honeymooners from the provinces, who
admired its worn charm and elaborate iron grillwork.

Hugo and Felicia stripped in their room, dissolving easily into
one another, and made love against the whitewashed walls.
Hugo bit Felicia's breasts and left purplish bands of bruises on
her upper thighs. He knelt before her in the tub and massaged
black Spanish soap between her legs. He entered her repeatedly
from behind.

Felicia learned what pleased him. She tied his arms above his
head with their underclothing and slapped him sharply when he
asked.

"You're my bitch," Hugo said, groaning.

In the morning he left, promising to return in the summer.

When they met again late in hurricane season, Felicia was seven
months pregnant and working as a cashier in a butcher shop.
She sat on a stool behind the counter ringing up newspaper-
wrapped packets and rubbing her lower back. Her cheeks were
threaded with a web of fine veins.

Bleeding carcasses hung on hooks the length of her arm.
Chickens dangled in the window, bumping her shoulder. A
hog's head sat on the back shelf like a trophy. Felicia watched
the thickset butchers cleave and carve the flesh like sculptors,
could scarcely tell them apart, in fact, from the marbled slabs of
beef at their elbows. Her customers, too, began to look like their
purchases: Compañera Sordo with her bristly jowls and upturned nose, Compañero Llorente with his pink eyes and jerking
chin.

"I'm red meat," Felicia repeated to herself. She felt bloated, grotesque.

Hugo married Felicia at city hall the week of the Cuban missile crisis. Herminia brought a bottle of champagne from Spain but no one remembered to open it. Jorge del Pino refused to attend.

After the ceremony, Felicia and Hugo moved into the house on Palmas Street, which had been empty since Berta Arango del Pino's only daughter, Ofelia, died of tuberculosis. Hugo settled into the sofa and stared straight ahead, saying nothing. Felicia finally approached him.

"If you want, I can tie you up the way you like," she offered.

Hugo pressed his fist under Felicia's chin until he choked off her breath, until she could see the walls of the living room behind her.

"If you come near me, I'll kill you. Do you understand?"

Hugo slept on the sofa and left for sea the next day. His twin daughters were born without him on Christmas Eve.

*   *   *

Toward the end of the summer, Felicia's condition worsens, as if a heavy curtain is drawn over her brain. Her own voice is mute to her, far away, and the chandelier wavers in the fetid air. She smokes stale cigarettes her husband left behind years ago, smokes them down to the butts until her son snatches them from her burning fingers. Ivanito's lips are moving, Felicia can see that. She sees his teeth and his eyes, his cheeks and his jet-black hair swelling and shrinking like an accordion. What is he saying? Each word is a code she must decipher, a foreign language, a streak of gunshot. She cannot hear and see him simultaneously. She closes her eyes.

Felicia remembers the moment she decided to murder her

husband. It was 1966, a hot August day, and she was pregnant with Ivanito. The nausea had persisted for weeks. Her sex, too, was infected with syphilis and the diseases Hugo brought back from Morocco and other women. That afternoon, as she was frying plantains in a heavy skillet, the nausea suddenly stopped.

It gave her a clarity she could not ignore.

Felicia dropped a rag into the skillet and watched it go limp with oil. She removed it with a pair of tongs and carried it dripping into the living room. The oil sizzled onto the floorboards.

She lit a match and approached her husband, asleep on the couch. His head was thrown back against a pillow, his mouth open, his throat exposed and still. She noticed that his lids barely covered his blank, rolled-up eyes.

Felicia carefully brought the blue flame to the tip of the rag. She smelled the quick sulfur and the plantains frying in the kitchen. She watched until the delicate flames consumed the rag, watched until the blaze was hot and floating in the air. Hugo awoke and saw his wife standing over him like a goddess with a fiery ball in her hand.

"You will never return here," Felicia said and released the flames onto his face.

She laughs when she recalls her husband's screams, the way he bolted out the door, his head a flaming torch. She plays this over and over in her mind, from one angle and then another, in bits and pieces like a torn photograph. The fire ate the flesh on Hugo's face and hands, and the stench remained on Palmas Street for many months.

Felicia feels herself getting younger in her sleep, so young in fact that she fears she will die, be driven beyond the womb to oblivion. She grieves in her dreams for lost children, for the prostitutes in India, for the women raped in Havana last night. Their faces stare at her, plaintive, uncomplaining. What do they want with her? Felicia is afraid to sleep.

Her mother visits her with packets of food, greasy meats that slide on wax paper. She refuses to eat them, considers them poison. Her mother tries to talk to her, but Felicia hides in her bed. Her son will not leave her, that much she knows. She opens her mouth but her thoughts erase themselves before she can speak. Something is wrong with her tongue. It forms broken trails of words, words sealed and resistant as stones. She summons one stone and clings to it, a drowning woman, then summons another and another until she cries, "Mami, I grieve in my dreams."

Ivanito Villaverde

The day after his grandfather dies, Ivanito asks his mother if he can go to the Hungarian circus in Havana. He's seen billboards with fire-eating clowns and a pretty woman in a feathered headdress. A boy told him there were albino elephants from Siam. But Ivanito never found out if it was true.

His mother's days begin with the ritual of a Beny Moré song called "Rebel Heart." The record is warped and scratched from the heat and so much playing, and the words bend as if they're underwater. But Ivanito and his mother sing them that way after a while. Felicia has a strong, unbroken voice that begins deep inside her throat. She encourages Ivanito to sing with her and he does, at the top of his lungs. He knows the song by heart.

Ivanito watches his mother put on her flannel nightgown then wrap herself in a frayed Chinese tunic embroidered with chrysanthemums, a onetime gift from his father. His sisters still have the silk scarves Papá brought back from China. They keep them hidden in the back of their dresser drawer. Ivanito found a photograph of his father hidden in the same drawer. He is standing on the Paseo Prado with Havana harbor in the background. His beret is pushed low on his forehead, and his mouth is stretched wide, with big square teeth like a horse. Ivanito knows his father is a merchant marine and sails around the world. Luz and Milagro tell him that Papá still loves them, but Ivanito cannot be sure it is true.

His mother claims that he almost died because of Papá, from a venereal disease that infected him when he was born. In the hospital, she pinned a tiny onyx badge on his diaper to guard against the evil eye. She and her friend Herminia burned votive candles in the nursery until the doctor threatened to throw them both out of the hospital. He said they were killing the oxygen.

There's a bin full of coconuts at the bodega. Felicia trades in her remaining food coupons for every last one, and the grocer throws in a chocolate bar for Ivanito. Then they go door to door, hunting for more coconuts. Ivanito follows his mother as she wanders farther and farther from Palmas Street in her tunic and scuffed pink slippers. Felicia's hair springs from her head like electric wires, and she swings her arms in great arcs, as if her chaos had a rhythm.

They play a game with colors as they walk. "Let's speak in green," his mother says, and they talk about everything that makes them feel green. They do the same with blues and reds and yellows. Ivanito asks her, "If the grass were black, would the world be different?" But Felicia doesn't answer.

His mother collects coconuts from strangers, promising haircuts and manicures in exchange. Others are not so kind. They shout insults at her from their windows and balconies, hiding behind the boughs of acacia trees.

"They're afraid to call me a whore to my face," his mother says disdainfully.

A gaunt mulatta tells Ivanito he smells of death. This scares him but his mother tells him not to worry, that the lady is probably crazy. On the way back, his bag rips and the coconuts scatter in the street like billiard balls. Cars brake and screech but his mother doesn't notice the commotion. Instead, she scolds the coconuts one by one as if they were errant children.

At home, his mother removes her tunic and slippers. She takes a hammer and rusty chisel and shatters each coconut, scraping the blinding white, perfumed flesh from the shells. Ivanito helps her blend the coconut with egg yolks, vanilla, condensed milk, sugar, cornstarch, and salt, and holds the empty tin vegetable-oil containers while she fills them with the mixture. Together they arrange them in the freezer. With the leftover egg whites, she fashions star-shaped meringues, which she serves with the ice cream day after day, for breakfast, lunch, and dinner. His mother believes the coconuts will purify them, that the sweet white milk will heal them.

Felicia's spirits soar as the coconut ice cream diminishes. She makes pronouncements that Ivanito doesn't understand, stays up all night hearing prophecies in her head, forgives her father and ex-husband long lists of past trespasses. She dances for days to her Beny Moré records, her hands in position for an impossibly lanky partner, to "Rebel Heart," her slippers scraping the floor, to "Treat Me As I Am," a buoyant *guaracha*. There's a Brazilian samba she stamps to in bare feet, waving her arms until she is flushed and exuberant with the rhythm of the drums. When she presses Ivanito to her chest, he can feel her heart jumping like it wants to come out of its cage.

When his sisters return from their camping trip, Ivanito can tell by their faces that something is wrong.

"We've seen Mamá this way before," Milagro whispers.

"What way?" Ivanito asks, but she hushes him.

After Abuela Celia leaves, their mother rips the telephone from the wall and locks them all in the house. Ivanito continues to eat the ice cream his mother serves them but Luz and Milagro dump it in the sink. Undeterred, Felicia stubbornly refills their bowls.

The twins tell Ivanito stories of what happened before he was born. They say their father ran from the house with his head and hands on fire. That Mamá sat on the living-room floor laughing and banging on the walls with metal tongs. That the police came and took her away. That the kitchen curtains burned from the plantains she left frying on the stove.

That night Ivanito stands by his sisters' bedroom window transfixed by the branches of the tamarind tree, so black against the sky. He repeats something he heard his mother say: "The moon glares with a vivid indifference."

His sisters bristle. They tell him that he'll end up crazy like Mamá, that he's starting to show her symptoms. Luz says that families are essentially political and that he'll have to choose sides.

Ivanito senses even then that something has come between them. He will never speak his sisters' language, account for his movements like a cow with a dull bell. He is convinced, although he couldn't say why, that they're united against him, against his happiness with Mamá.

In his room, the wallpaper comes alive in the moonlight. Ivanito imagines the vines and tendrils, taut and violent as a killing rope, snaking along the floor to his bed, wrapping him in place, tighter and tighter, choking off his breath while his sisters sleep.

*   *   *

As the summer of coconuts wears on, Felicia's obsessions grow like something botanical, dense and violent. She insists that the sun will damage her son's lungs.

"We inhabit the eye of the swamp, Ivanito," she warns, tightening the shutters against malevolent rays. "We are breathing the final village."

Celia comes to their house with packets of food and encourages her grandson to eat, but Ivanito rarely touches the croquettes or the pork tamales she brings. He doesn't want to betray his mother.

On the last day of August, his grandmother packs his clothes: his bathing trunks with the elastic band broken at the waist, his buckled sandals, the round straw hat he's taken to wearing indoors. His mother promises that they'll go to the beach tomorrow. Tomorrow, after they rest. But they don't rest.

The minute Abuela Celia leaves, his mother becomes very animated. She mops and scours the kitchen floor until her hands are crinkly. She presses the bed sheets as if expecting a lover and sweeps the veranda clean of the summer's dust. She throws open the shutters with finality.

Ivanito goes with her to the bodega. This time, they buy a whole chicken, two pounds of rice, onions, green peppers, and all the sweet plantains in the store. His mother cooks an *arroz con pollo* and leaves the plantains warming in the oven for their dinner.

Down the street, a gardenia tree is lush with blossoms. Ivanito steadies the ladder as his mother clips an armful of flowers. He watches as she floats the white gardenias in her bath and rubs her thighs and breasts with walnut oil. She sets her hair and brushes it until the luster returns. Then she slips on a peach satin negligee, another token from his father, and examines her face in the dressing-table mirror. It's the only mirror left in the house. The others were broken during her marriage.

"Mirrors are for misery, nothing more," his mother says calmly. "They record decay."

Ivanito notices the two deep creases that begin at her nostrils and end in hooks below her lips. If she doesn't grin wide, the tooth she chipped on a rice stone is hardly noticeable. Lines criss-cross at the corners of her eyes. They're green, Ivanito thinks, like discovery.

He touches his mother's arm. It's soft and newborn pale after the summer retreat from the sun. Her hands, too, are soft. Ivanito watches as his mother powders her face like a geisha and rubs rouge high on her cheeks. She paints in arched eyebrows, then outlines her lips a bright orange. Ivanito thinks her face looks nailed on, like a mask on a wall.

After she finishes, his mother bathes him with the remaining gardenias. She combs his hair and kisses his eyes and forehead, the small of his back, and the tips of each finger. She shakes talcum powder on him until he looks like a pastry. This makes Ivanito afraid. Then she lays his clothes out on the bed. His short pants and jacket, his knee socks and his only pair of lace-up shoes. She dresses him carefully as if he might break, then holds him up before the mirror.

"Imagination, like memory, can transform lies to truths," Felicia whispers in her son's ear. Nobody else teaches him that.

Ivanito helps his mother set the table for two. They use his great-grandmother's silverware, her lead-crystal goblets, and her china, with its pageantry of gold leaves. His mother lights the stub of a candle and places it in the chandelier that can accommodate twenty-three more. Ivanito counts the empty holders.

His mother serves him huge portions of chicken and rice, fill-ing his plate twice. Ivanito eats three of the warm plantains in brown-sugar syrup and drinks mango juice chilled with ice. His mother speaks continuously. "You must imagine winter, Ivanito," she tells him. "Winter and its white extinguishings."

Ivanito tries to imagine winter. He's heard of snow and thinks of lacy ice falling from the sky. He covers everything and every-one he knows with this ice. Ice on the house on Palmas Street,

ice on the tamarind tree, ice coating the ships on the dock and
the sparrows in midflight. Ice on the roads and the fields, and
the beach where his grandmother lives. Ice collapsing her wicker
swing, his sisters at her feet. His father would float in a sea of
white ice, his grandfather atop the white palms.

His mother crushes pink tablets on the last of their ice cream.
Hard, bittersweet shards.

"This will give us strength, Ivanito."

Felicia carries her son upstairs and gently places him on the
fresh sheets. She adjusts the shutters, lies down next to him, and
fans her satin gown over them both.

"Close your eyes, *mi hijo*. Be very still."

Then she crosses her hands over her breasts and they sleep.

Celia del Pino

More and more, Celia thinks, Ivanito looks like his father. He
is tall for his age, with large, premature teeth, and arms that hang
too long at his sides. He is only five years old but there is something already adolescent about him. Celia fears how this resem-
blance is affecting Felicia. What can be going through her head
in that shuttered house, dancing in the dark with her only son?

The last time Celia saw Hugo Villaverde, Felicia was pregnant with Ivanito. Hugo's hair was combed back in neat furrows
and he wore a pressed *guayabera* open at the neck. Celia tried to
dissuade them from entering her house. Jorge had threatened to
kill his son-in-law if he dared show his face in Santa Teresa del
Mar. But Celia could see that Hugo was in a mood to test his
limits. He pushed his way past her, took a bottle of orange soda
from the rusted refrigerator, sat with one hand flat against the
dining-room table, and waited.

Jorge emerged from the bedroom in his slippers and under-shirt. He had been napping but no trace of sleep lingered in his face. The heat of his breath clouded his round glasses. Without a word, he lifted a dining-room chair and swung it in a wide arc against the back of his son-in-law. The fragments exploded across the room as if a gigantic tree had been sloppily felled. Hugo stood up slowly, turned to Jorge, and grinned with his big horse teeth. Then he punched him full in the face. Jorge slid to the ground, his face lacquered with blood.

"If you leave with that sonofabitch, don't ever come back!" Jorge shouted at Felicia, his mouth pinched white with rage. But Felicia followed Hugo out the door. Celia wiped the blood from Jorge's despondent blue eyes with a wet cloth.

By the end of the summer, Felicia is dancing infrequently and her pronouncements are few. Sometimes nothing will rouse her from her bed, from a somnolence that coats the very air she breathes. Celia washes her daughter's hair and tries to remove the grimy flowered nightgown, which Felicia insists protects her from the sun. Then she bathes Ivanito and dries his hair, know-ing that she'll find him unwashed and uncombed again.

Celia frequently stops by the ceiba tree in the Plaza de las Armas on her way home from Palmas Street. She places an or-ange and a few coins by its trunk, and says a short prayer for her daughter. Now and then she runs into Herminia Delgado carrying baskets filled with crusty roots and ratoons and fresh, healing spices for Felicia. Aniseed for hysteria. Sarsaparilla for the nerves and any remaining traces of syphilis. River fern and *espartillo* to ward off further evil. Herminia never mentions the ceiba tree, but Celia recognizes the distinct cluster of its leaves among her many herbs.

Celia is uneasy about all these potions and spells. Herminia is the daughter of a *santería* priest, and Celia fears that both good and evil may be borne in the same seed. Although Celia dabbles

in *santería*'s harmless superstitions, she cannot bring herself to
trust the clandestine rites of the African magic.

*   *   *

The day Felicia tries to kill herself is like many others that summer. At two o'clock, Celia walks from her little brick-and-cement house to the highway and hitches a ride to Havana. She
carries, as usual, packets of warm, salted food for her grandson,
a nail file, and a new bar of soap. A bearded textile worker in a
tumbledown Dodge leaves her at Felicia's door.

Celia tells Felicia that her job is still waiting for her at the
beauty shop, but that she'll have to start from the bottom again,
sweeping hair clippings and doing shampoos. Then she packs
her grandson's clothing and threatens to take him to Santa
Teresa del Mar. Felicia remains quiet. She has no energy left for
defiance.

Celia strokes her daughter's hair, murmuring a worn lullaby,
a poem she set to music once. Felicia remembers the tune,
mouths the words as she cries. Then she promises to go to the
beach the following day with Ivanito. Celia leaves, confident that
the intolerable season is over.

Outside the sun is too bright. Sounds Celia cannot distinguish
blare thickly in the air. Faces and buildings seem enlarged, exposing their scars.

Celia passes by a theater in Old Havana and recognizes two
of her half brothers standing by the entrance. She identifies them
by their high cheekbones and their small, even teeth. The afternoon sun sharpens their profiles, her father's profile. She stares
at them, twin ghosts, and nervously pats her throat. A fluttering
like a steady motor whirs in her breast.

The taller one wears trousers patched with careless stitches.
He pushes up his hat and offers his brother a wheel of pineapple

to eat. Celia notices their ungainly hands, *campesino* hands, stained with tobacco. She decides not to speak to them.

Celia takes the bus home, so she can think. All summer, it seems to her, since she returned from the sugarcane fields, she has lived in her memories. Sometimes she'll glimpse the hour on a dusty Canada Dry clock, or look at the sun low in the sky, and realize she cannot account for her time. Where do the hours go? Her past, she fears, is eclipsing her present.

Her half brothers remind Celia of when she was a baby, and a confusion of brothers and sisters surrounded her. She barely recalls their faces, only the fringe of their dense hair leaning into her carton crib. Most days, Celia lay under a fan palm beside the *bohío,* its thatched roof steaming after the morning rains. She remembers this infant landscape, the waving haze of fronds through the torn netting that someone fastened to her face to keep out the flies.

Celia's father had maintained two families, each with nine children. His second family lived less than a mile away but they might as well have been across the world. They never acknowledged one another, not even in the village church, with its six splintering pews.

When Celia's parents divorced, they dispersed their children among relatives throughout the island. Celia's destination was Havana, with her Great-Aunt Alicia, known for her cooking and her iconoclasm. Celia was alone only this once: when she was four, and her mother put her on the daybreak train bound for the capital.

Solitude, Celia realizes now, exists for us not to remember but to forget.

On the long train ride from the countryside, Celia lost her mother's face, the lies that had complicated her mouth. The life Celia was leaving seemed no longer significant. For hours she watched the rapid sequence of textures that flapped like streamers outside her window: vast *latifundios,* provinces of royal palms, black mountains encircled with clouds. Each station along the way rippled with activity, with curiosities. How could she have slept?

Then the bells rang at noon to welcome her, singing from all corners of the city. Tía Alicia appeared in a petticoated dress, carrying a parasol against the mild winter sun. Celia noticed the tiny ivory buttons down her aunt's spine, marveled at their uselessness. She and her aunt picked their way across the cobblestones, avoiding the horses with their brisk clippity clops and the boxy black cars with chauffeurs in patent-brimmed caps. Celia walked uncertainly, twisting her ankles on the hard, uneven surfaces, and for a brief moment she itched to go barefoot, to feel the padding of fresh earth beneath her feet.

But Celia soon grew to love Havana, its crooked streets and the balconies like elegant chariots in the air. Oh, and the noise! So much delightful noise! The horse-drawn milk carts at dawn. The broom vendor with his mops and dusters and stiff bristle brushes. The newspaper boys with the latest edition of *El Mundo* or *Diario de la Marina*. Tía Alicia took her to museums and the symphony and the ancient ceiba tree. Celia ran around it three times for every wish, until the tree repeated itself like a flashing deck of cards.

Her aunt did not attend church and derided those who did. Once she took Celia to the foot of the hill crowned with the Church of Saint Lazarus. A procession of suppliants climbed the knoll on bare, bloodied knees to show their devotion or purge their grief or beg forgiveness in the slow tearing of flesh and bone. They wrung rosaries and veils between their fingers, clutched their chests, ripped their hair. Their prayers rose from the pavement like the din of insects on summer evenings.

On Saturdays Celia and her aunt would go to the picture show. The organ player, a plump man who scrambled to keep up with the action on-screen, appeared relieved when the love scenes came. He'd play a minor chord or two with his left hand

and, with a flourish of his right, wipe his perspiring face with an enormous white handkerchief. Tía Alicia considered the American films naive and overly optimistic but too much fun to resist. She named her two canaries Clara and Lillian after Clara Bow and Lillian Gish. When Clara laid eggs, however, Tía Alicia changed Lillian's name to Douglas, after Douglas Fairbanks. Their babies were Charlie, Mary, and Gloria.

There is an electric power outage in Santa Teresa del Mar. Celia walks along the peaceful, darkened streets and smells the frying meat from open windows, observes the candle flames blinking shadows on the kitchen walls. She would have preferred to live by candlelight, she suddenly decides.

The twins surprise her with an omelet-and-rice dinner. They kiss her with dry lips, slip off her pumps, and boil pots of water for her bath. They do not ask about their mother or brother.

Celia settles in her wicker swing to watch the ocean, jumping with silver light. Is it flying fish or dolphins or some undiscovered pulse? The sky is alive with lightning, feeding on the earth's heat. How many seasons has she searched its horizon for signs? Many more seasons than she has lived, it seems to her, many more.

> *El campo*
> *de olivos*
> *se abre y se cierra*
> *como un abanico.*
> *Sobre el olivar*
> *hay un cielo hundido*
> *y una lluvia oscura*
> *de luceros fríos.*

Celia is partial to the poetry of Federico García Lorca. She heard him give a reading more than forty years ago at the Principal de la Comedia Theater. It was the last of his five lectures in Havana and Celia listened, entranced, to his sonorous voice as he played the sad songs of the gypsies. Lorca explained that the *cante jondo* was a primitive flamenco from his native Andalusia, a region enriched by Moorish invaders, and that the songs had inspired his own gypsy ballad poems.

During his presentation, a torrential rainstorm fell and the black sounds of the *duende* shivered in the air with mystery and anguish and death. Death was alluring, seductive, and Celia longed to die in the thrill of it over and over again.

That night Celia sleeps restlessly. Voices call to her in ragged words stitched together from many languages, like dissonant scraps of quilt. The syllables float overhead, drifting into an icy blur of white. Celia awakes to an ominous pattern of moonlight on her sheets. She shouts for her granddaughters.

"Run to Herminia's house! Tell her she must drive us to Havana right away!"

Celia's hands flutter like disoriented birds. They cannot settle to button her jade housedress. She runs on stiff legs past the sofa draped with the faded mantilla, past the water-bleached walnut piano, past the dining-room set missing a chair, and waits in front of the house.

"*Mi hija, mi hija, mi hija,*" she repeats as if her words alone could save Felicia.

The night is stenciled with stars but Celia does not notice. In a corner of the sky, a desolate quarter moon hangs. Celia smells the ocean from the highway, smells it all the way to Havana.

Celia's Letters: 1942–1949

December 11, 1942

Querido Gustavo,

The Civil War came and went and now there are dictatorships in both our countries. Half the world is at war, worse than it's ever been before. Death alone is reliable.

I still love you, Gustavo, but it's a habitual love, a wound in the knee that predicts rain. Memory is a skilled seducer. I write to you because I must. I don't even know if you're alive and whom you love now.

I asked myself once, "What is the nature of obsession?" But I no longer question it. I accept it the way I accept my husband and my daughters and my life on the wicker swing, my life of ordinary seductions. I've begun teaching myself French.

Tu Celia

November 11, 1944

Mi amor,

Have you read about the tidal wave that hit Cuba? Hundreds of people lost their homes, everything they owned.

A widower in our village, Nestor Prendes, drowned because he refused to leave his house. He said he wanted to join his wife, that it was his right to die. Nestor fought his children off with a cane when they tried to lift him from his chair, and he cried with such a pitiful hoarseness that they finally left him in peace.

Our house is still drying out after being underwater for so long. The only thing I'm really worried about is the piano. Jorge bought it for me when we first moved here. The rich walnut is now a chalky white. I press the keys but there's only the sound of wet felt. When we fix the piano, I know what I'll play first. Debussy, of course.

Love,
Celia

April 11, 1945

Querido Gustavo,

The days rain tyranny. I survey my interior as a general does a map, dispassionately, calculating the odds. I remember our spring walks through Havana. The destitute were everywhere, spread out on the benches in the Parque Central, asleep on yesterday's newspapers. Remember the young woman with the dangling wooden leg and the single oxford? The beggar families from the countryside looking for work in the iron-fenced mansions of Vedado? The smart couples in their convertible roadsters driving by without a second glance? I remember how all the men wore boaters in those days. Even the poorest of the poor had them— soiled, ripped, brimless, covering their faces as they slept in the park, but boaters just the same.

Why is it that most people aspire to little more than comfort?

Celia

May 11, 1945

Gustavo,

The familiar is insistent and deadly. I study the waves and keep time on my wicker swing. If I was born to live on an island, then I'm grateful for one thing: that the tides rearrange the borders. At least I have the illusion of change, of possibility. To be locked within boundaries plotted by priests and politicians would be the only thing more intolerable.

Don't you see how they're carving up the world, Gustavo? How they're stealing our geography? Our fates? The arbitrary is no longer in our hands. To survive is an act of hope.

Celia

July 11, 1946

Querido Gustavo,

My son was born with a caul. Jorge tells me there's been only one boy born to each generation of del Pinos and each had a caul. He tells me it's a sign of good luck, that the del Pino men have never died by drowning. I've called him Javier, after my father. He'll look like him, too, I can see that already. Papá had a broad face and cheekbones you could rest coins on. His lips were plush cushions and his teeth were like a woman's, small and even. He was a tall man, muscular, with hands that hung like hams at his sides. Those hands knew intimately every woman in our village.

I saw his face in my Tía Alicia's. That's why I remember him so clearly. She told me he was killed when I was thirteen, by cuckolds with machetes in a grove of banana trees. I didn't mourn for him until Tía Alicia died, just before I married, and she left me her treasured peacock brooch.

Of my mother I remember next to nothing, only hard eyes that seemed to float like relics in her forehead, and her voice, so queer and feathery. When she put me on the day-break train to Havana, I called to her from the window but she didn't turn around. I watched her back in a striped blue dress round a corner. The train was delayed a quarter of an hour. On the way to Havana, I forgot her. Only the birth of my son makes me remember.

Love,
Celia

October 11, 1946

Gustavo,

Jorge says my smile frightens him, so I look in the mirror and try on old smiles. My girlfriends and I used to paint our mouths like American starlets, ruby red and heart-shaped. We bobbed our hair and wore cloche hats at co-quettish angles and tried to sound like Gloria Swanson.

We used to go to Cinelandia every Friday after work. I remember seeing *Mujeres de Fuego* with Bette Davis, Ann Dvorak, and Joan Blondell. There were three of them—just like there were three of us—and one of them had to die. We used to joke about which one of us would go first. Then I'd look at the women in the food lines across the street, thin women with shawls too warm for the weather, and be ashamed of my thoughts.

After you left me I took to my bed, Gustavo. I stayed there for months playing back every minute of our time together, watching it like I watched the movies, trying to make sense of the days we buried squandering love. Jorge saved me, but for what I don't know.

Tu Celia

February 11, 1949

Mi querido Gustavo,

I've been reading the plays of Molière and wondering what separates suffering from imagination. Do you know?

My love,
Celia

IMAGINING WINTER

The Meaning of Shells

(1974)

Felicia del Pino cannot remember why she is marching in the Sierra Maestra this hot October afternoon. The camouflage helmet feels like a metal ring around her head, and the rifle, slung over her left shoulder, keeps bumping up against it, making the space behind her eyes reverberate with pain. The cheap Russian boots pinch her feet as she trudges, the last of a single file of would-be guerrillas, up the intolerably fragrant mountainside. "Let's talk in green," her son would have told her, trying to distract her from her misery.

"*Vámonos, vámonos!*" a petite mulatta roars ten yards ahead of Felicia. Lieutenant Xiomara Rojas has an undershot jaw, and her jumble of yellowish teeth is visible when she shouts. "El Líder never slowed down in these mountains! For him it was a matter of life and death, not a Sunday outing! Keep moving!"

Felicia looks down at the trail of moist trampled grasses. Her face is flushed and sweaty, and she can't tell whether the salt in her eyes is from perspiration or involuntary tears. Lieutenant

Rojas is from these parts, Felicia thinks, that's why she doesn't sweat. Nobody from Santiago de Cuba ever sweated. It's a known fact.

"Compañera del Pino, you must keep up the rear! It's the most vulnerable position after the leader!" Lieutenant Rojas bellows, not unkindly.

Felicia's calves feel like baseballs below her knees. The earth, muddy and pliable, sucks at her feet. Every tendon is straining, stretched taut like the muscles of cows at the butcher shop that had died in fear. Their meat was never as tender as the flesh of the animals that hadn't anticipated death. Felicia fumbles for her canteen. She twists off the cap, attached by a chain to its neck. Her hands are a stranger's, swollen and coarse, her fingernails dirty.

"Fatherland or death!" Lieutenant Rojas shouts, as Felicia tips the water toward her mouth.

"Fatherland or death!" the guerrillas echo, all except Felicia, who wonders whether all this shouting wouldn't alert the enemy in a real war.

At the makeshift camp, the guerrillas set up their tents and open cans of pinto beans and pressed meat the color of dung. It's their fifth day of this food and it's given some of the soldiers diarrhea, others constipation, and all of them gas. Only Lieutenant Rojas seems unaffected and eats with enthusiasm. Felicia looks around at the others in her mostly middle-aged brigade. Everyone is there for the same reason, whether they admit it or not. They are a unit of malcontents, a troop of social misfits. It is Lieutenant Rojas's mission to reshape them into revolutionaries.

Felicia is there because she nearly killed herself and her son. She doesn't remember this but everyone has told her it is so. "Why did you do it?" her mother asked her sadly, stretching her hands on the starched white bed. "Why did you do it?" the psychiatrist with the severe pageboy questioned her, as if Felicia were a willful child. "Why, Felicia?" her best friend, Herminia, beseeched her, all the while rubbing Felicia's forehead with herbs behind the nurse's back.

But each time Felicia reached for the memory, a white light burned in its place.

The doctors deemed Felicia an "unfit mother," and accused her of irreparably damaging her son that summer on Palmas Street. Nobody knows if Ivanito understands what happened to him. The boy never speaks of it. But the doctors, her mother, even her coworkers at the beauty parlor finally persuaded Felicia to send Ivanito to boarding school. To toughen him up, to catch up with boys his own age, to integrate him. That was the word everyone used. Integrate.

"Don't you love me anymore?" Ivanito called to her from the bus window with eyes that strafed her with grief.

Felicia visits her son the first Sunday of each month at his school in the potato fields outside San Antonio de los Baños. They say little in the hours allotted them. The emotion of their reunions exhausts them so that they often nap together under a tree, or in Ivanito's narrow bunk bed. They speak mainly with their eyes and with their hands, which never stop touching.

Everyone tells Felicia that she must find meaning in her life outside of her son, that she should give the revolution another try, become a New Socialist Woman. After all, as her mother points out, the only thing Felicia ever did for the revolution was pull a few dandelions during the weed-eradication campaign in 1962, and then only reluctantly. Her lack of commitment is a source of great rancor between them.

Felicia tries to shake off her doubts, but all she sees is a country living on slogans and agitation, a people always on the brink of war. She scorns the militant words blaring on billboards everywhere. WE SHALL OVERCOME . . . AS IN VIETNAM . . . CHANGE DEFEAT INTO VICTORY . . . Even the lowly weed pullers had boasted a belligerent name: The Mechanized Offensive Brigade. Young teachers are Fighters for Learning. Students working in the fields are the Juvenile Column of the Centenary. Literacy volunteers are The Fatherland or Death Brigade. It goes on and on, numbing her, undermining her willingness to fight for the future, hers or anybody else's. If only her son could be with her.

Felicia pulls a rusted nail file and a small plastic bottle of hand cream from her knapsack, and gets to work. She pushes back her cuticles with the rounded edge of the file, then expertly picks and scrapes under her nails until they are spotless. With short, brisk strokes she evens the broken nail on her left thumb. Then she squirts the pink lotion onto the backs of her hands, massages it in with a circular motion, and rubs her palms together until her hands are soft and slightly greasy again.

The other members of the troop, except for Lieutenant Rojas, who is listening to a crackling radio in her tent, watch Felicia attentively, as if witnessing an intricate ritual they'll be required to duplicate, like the dismantling and reassembling of their rifles. When Felicia finishes, they turn away, clumping together in twos or threes to talk.

"It was my daughter who turned me in for insisting we say grace at the dinner table," Silvia Lores complains. "That's what they teach her at school, to betray her parents. Now I'm considered an 'antisocial.'"

"It could be worse," a genial man named Paco consoles her. "My neighbor's son was sent off to the marble quarries on the Isle of Pines because he listened to American jazz and wore his hair too long. Now I'm not in favor of long hair, mind you, but hard labor? In that sun?"

"They send the seminarians there, too. They say the church is reactionary," Silvia Lores says.

"The leaders forget what they looked like themselves fifteen years ago," the only young man in the group pronounces. "Today, they'd be thrown in a Social Disgrace Unit with drug addicts and *maricones*. Look at me. They say I'm rebellious, but it was rebels who made the revolution!"

"Calm down, *chico*, calm down. She might hear you," Paco cautions, gesturing toward Lieutenant Rojas's tent.

"Chances are, one of us is a spy anyway," the young man says contemptuously. "It's impossible to hide here."

Felicia listens to the conversation as she rolls a cigarette of strong black tobacco. She took up smoking again in the psychiatric hospital. It gave her something to do with her hands. Now she longs for the satisfying burning it produces deep in her lungs.

The others in her troop tried to draw her out during their first days in the mountains, but Felicia refused to say anything. She doesn't know these people and has no reason to trust them. Perhaps they think *she* is the spy.

Felicia volunteers again for night duty. In the dark, in the moonless jungle, the fissures are not so visible, the hypocrisies and lies less disturbing. Her eyes, she decides, could get accustomed to this darkness. Perhaps she should have lived in the night all along, with the owls and bats and other nocturnal creatures. Herminia told her once of the gods that rule the night, but Felicia cannot remember their names. It was to these gods that the slaves had prayed to preserve a shred of their souls. It had strengthened them for the indignities of their days.

Celia, too, once prayed in the night, rocking in her wicker swing until dawn. Sometimes, when Felicia was a child and couldn't sleep, she'd join her mother on the porch. They'd sit together for hours listening to the rhythm of the sea and the poems her mother recited as if in a dream.

> *Por las ramas del laurel*
> *vi dos palomas oscuras.*

La una era el sol,
la otra la luna.

Felicia learned her florid language on those nights. She would borrow freely from the poems she'd heard, stringing words together like laundry on a line, connecting ideas and descriptions she couldn't have planned. The words sounded precisely right when she said them, though often people told her she didn't make any sense at all. Felicia misses those peaceful nights with her mother, when the sea had metered their intertwined thoughts. Now they fight constantly, especially about El Líder. How her mother worships him! She keeps a framed photograph of him by her bed, where her husband's picture used to be. But to Felicia, El Líder is just a common tyrant. No better, no worse than any other in the world.

In fact, Felicia can't help feeling that there is something unnatural in her mother's attraction to him, something sexual. She has heard of women offering themselves to El Líder, drawn by his power, by his unfathomable eyes, and it is said he has fathered many children on the island. But there is a coldness to El Líder, a bitterness she doesn't trust. They say his first wife, his one great love, betrayed him while he was imprisoned on the Isle of Pines, after his ill-fated attack on the Moncada barracks. She accepted money from the government, the government he was trying to overthrow. El Líder never forgave her, and they divorced. There's been another woman in his life since his days in these very mountains, but everyone knows she's only a companion—a mother, a sister, not a true lover. El Líder, it seems, saves his most ardent passions for the revolution.

Still, Felicia muses, what would he be like in bed? Would he remove his cap and boots? Leave his pistol on the table? Would guards wait outside the door, listening for the sharp pleasure that signaled his departure? What would his hands be like? His mouth, the hardness between his thighs? Would he churn inside her slowly as she liked? Trail his tongue along her belly and lick her *there?* Felicia slips her hand down the front of her army fatigue pants. She feels his tongue moving faster, his beard against her thighs. "We need you, Compañera del Pino," she hears him murmur sternly as she comes.

(1975)

It is the first Thursday in December. Nearly three hundred people squeeze into Santa Teresa del Mar's only movie theater, sharing seats, cigarettes, and soft drinks. The town has arrived for what promises to be a lively fight: Ester Ugarte, the postmaster's wife, has accused Loli Regalado of seducing her husband, a charge that Loli vehemently denies. On nights like these, nobody minds missing the theater's ordinary fare of grainy Cuban films.

Celia del Pino settles on a folding chair behind a card table facing the audience. It is her third year as a civilian judge. Celia is pleased. What she decides makes a difference in others' lives, and she feels part of a great historical unfolding. What would have been expected of her twenty years ago? To sway endlessly on her wicker swing, old before her time? To baby-sit her grandchildren and wait for death? She remembers the gloomy letters she used to write to Gustavo before the revolution, and thinks of how different the letters would be if she were writing today.

Since her husband's death, Celia has devoted herself completely to the revolution. When El Líder needed volunteers to build nurseries in Villa Clara province, Celia joined a microbrigade, setting tiles and operating a construction lift. When he launched a crusade against an outbreak of malaria, Celia inoculated schoolchildren. And every harvest, Celia cut the sugarcane that El Líder promised would bring prosperity. Three nights per month, too, Celia continues to protect her stretch of shore from foreign invaders. She still dresses up for these all-night vigils, putting on red lipstick and darkening the mole on her cheek, and imagines that El Líder is watching her, whispering in her ear with his warm cigar breath. She would gladly do anything he asked.

Celia has judged 193 cases since she was elected to the People's Court, from petty thievery and family disputes to more serious crimes of medical malpractice, arson, and counterrevolutionary activities. But she delights in judging juvenile cases most of all. Reform, not punishment, is her modus operandi, and Celia has succeeded in converting many young delinquents into productive revolutionaries. One girl, Magdalena Nogueras, who at sixteen was caught stealing a pig and a wrench from her neighbor, went on to become a principal actress with the National Theater Company of Cuba. Later, Celia would learn with sadness that the girl had defected while on tour in Oaxaca and was playing a psychotic housewife on a popular Mexican *novela.*

Celia signals the opening of tonight's case with four taps of her hammer, wobbly on its handle. It is her make-do gavel. She senses the audience is evenly split in its support of one woman or the other. Everyone, it seems, has a stake in the outcome.

Since the Family Code passed earlier this year, more and more people are turning to the courts with their problems. Women who claim their husbands are not doing their share of their housework or who want to put a stop to an extramarital affair bring the matter before a judge. Very few men, however, take their complaints to the People's Court for fear of appearing weak or, unthinkably, as cuckolds. Celia dislikes these cases. To her, such matters are private and should not be settled before a public hungry for entertainment. Besides, after all the negotiating, divorce is nearly always the solution. Perhaps if she had to choose again, she herself would have followed her Tía Alicia's example and never married at all.

"I was borrowing a cup of corn flour when her husband threw off his bathrobe and pushed himself on me." Loli Regalado is a curvaceous woman in her early thirties. Her dyed blond hair is pulled back in a high ponytail.

"That's not true!" Ester Ugarte shrieks. "She was seducing my Rogelio! She had on a tight dress that came up to here, with a neckline to there!" Ester indicates her navel both times.

"That wouldn't leave much of a dress, now would it, Compañera Ugarte?" Celia asks, and the audience erupts with laughter.

Loli then recounts how Ester rushed at her with an ironing board and chased her into the stairwell of their building, knocking her against the wall and holding her there like a prisoner.

"She called me a *puta,*" Loli complains angrily.

"I never called her a *puta!* Though God knows she deserves it!"

"Everyone knows your husband doesn't love you because you're so jealous," Loli taunts. "He puts the moves on every woman in the neighborhood."

"Liar!"

Celia pounds her hammer on the card table to quiet the spectators, who are hissing and hollering as if it were a boxing match. But Celia knows, as everyone does in Santa Teresa del Mar, that what Loli says is true. Rogelio Ugarte, like his father and his father before him, cannot keep his ungual hands to himself. It's a genetic trait, like his widow's peak and his slow brown eyes and the job he inherited at the post office. Celia remembers the rumors about Rogelio, how he sent off to Chicago for a carton of little rubber tips for his penis that made women crazy with pleasure. That was before the blockade. Celia always wondered how those tips stayed in place.

Several witnesses give their statements, but their information is so contradictory that it proves almost useless. Celia's arm tires from banging her hammer and her voice is hoarse from calling for order. Incredibly, she hears some *desgraciado* selling peanuts in the back of the theater. Before she can throw him out, another voice breaks through the commotion.

"Let's try that sonofabitch postmaster! *He's* the one that should be here!" Nélida Grau yells from the third row, and in an instant the spectators are on their feet, arguing in every direction.

By the time Celia restores a tenuous calm, she has come to a decision.

"Compañera Grau has a point," Celia begins, silencing a heckler, a cousin of Rogelio's, with a harsh look. "It seems to me, *compañeras,* that your problem is not with each other, but with Rogelio."

"What do you expect with someone like her coming around to tempt him? He's only human!" Ester protests.

"Ha!" Loli sneers. "He should be licking his stamps instead of his chops! Maybe then we'd get some mail around here!"

"I'm not going to pass judgment on someone who isn't here," Celia announces over a fresh round of bickering. "You!" She points a finger at Rogelio's cousin, Ambrosio Ugarte, who is surrounded by a circle of angry women. "Bring Rogelio here. You have five minutes."

The auditorium vibrates with discord. Every combination of argument is going full tilt. Husbands against wives. Married women against the single and divorced. The politicized against the apolitical. The fight between Loli Regalado and Ester Ugarte is an excuse for everyone to unleash frustrations at family members, neighbors, the system, their lives. Old wounds are reopened, new ones inflicted.

Celia looks out at the unrest that is Santa Teresa del Mar. She is disheartened. It seems to her that so much of Cuba's success will depend on what doesn't exist, or exists only rarely. A spirit of generosity. Commitments without strings. Are these so against human nature?

Suddenly, all eyes turn to the back door. Rogelio Ugarte has arrived. He stands in the doorway, hesitant to enter. His slow brown eyes search the audience for friends.

"Please come to the front, *compañero*," Celia orders.

There is none of Rogelio's easy manner, none of his usual bantering or joking. He looks like a forlorn puppet jerking woodenly down the aisle.

"Now we'll get to the bottom of this!" Ester crows, and pandemonium breaks out anew.

As Celia pounds the card table, the head of her hammer finally gives way and flies backward, tearing a hole the size of a fist in the movie screen. It is most effective in securing the audience's attention.

"Compañero Ugarte, you are responsible for causing a great deal of division among your neighbors," Celia resumes loudly. "It has become clear to the court that it is you—not your wife or Compañera Regalado—who must stand before us with an explanation. Now please answer truthfully. Did you or did you not attempt to seduce Compañera Regalado against her will on the afternoon of October twenty-third?"

"Yes."

"Yes what?"

"I did try to seduce her."

The audience cheers, each person for his or her own reasons. It's as if Rogelio's response has justified every polemic.

"Liar!" Ester screams, flushed and trembling. Then in a spectacular leap that no one thought her capable of, Ester knocks her husband to the ground, pulls at his hair, and bites his cheek. By the time her friends pry her away, Ester is crying uncontrollably.

Celia steps onto her metal folding chair and stands over the crowd until no sound can be heard except the steady wheezing of Ester's sobs.

"I have come to a decision," Celia says deliberately. "Rogelio Ugarte, I sentence you to one year of volunteer work at the state nursery in Santa Teresa del Mar."

"What?" Rogelio looks up from the floor, still dazed from his wife's attack.

"The nursery is short-staffed, and our *compañeras* need help changing diapers, warming milk, washing linen, and organizing the children's playtime. You will be the first man to ever work there, *compañero,* and I will be checking up to see that your behavior is one of a model Socialist man in all respects. This case is adjourned."

Celia's decision wins her both bravos and more full-throated squabbling.

"Why don't you send him to Africa?" Nélida Grau shouts, one hand on her hip, the other indicating the direction.

Loli Regalado, while pleased with her exoneration, complains that putting Rogelio with the *compañeras* at the state nursery is akin to dropping the fox off at the henhouse with a knife and fork.

Celia watches, dispirited, as her neighbors file out of the auditorium, already merrily expectant for next month's "love motel" case. In January, Hilario and Vivian Ortega, who live down the street from Celia, will defend themselves against charges that they have been illegally renting by the hour two rooms of their beachfront home. Celia fears that the citizens of Santa Teresa del Mar once again will consider the court as hardly more than occasion for a live soap opera.

Outside the theater, the peanut vendor continues to work the crowd. He offers Celia a packet, and she accepts it without reproaching him. Then she walks unhurriedly back to her brick-and-cement house by the sea, chewing the peanuts one by one.

*   *   *

Later that night, Celia rocks in her wicker swing and considers the star-inscribed sky, as if its haphazard arrangements might reveal something to her. But tonight it is as formal and unilluminating as a tiara.

Celia enters her kitchen and warms a little milk on the stove, then sweetens it with a few lumps of sugar. How is it possible that she can help her neighbors and be of no use at all to her children? Lourdes and Felicia and Javier are middle-aged now and desolate, deaf and blind to the world, to each other, to her. There is no solace among them, only a past infected with disillusion.

Her daughters cannot understand her commitment to El Líder. Lourdes sends her snapshots of pastries from her bakery in Brooklyn. Each glistening éclair is a grenade aimed at Celia's political beliefs, each strawberry shortcake proof—in butter, cream, and eggs—of Lourdes's success in America, and a reminder of the ongoing shortages in Cuba.

Felicia is no less exasperating. "We're *dying* of security!" she moans when Celia tries to point out the revolution's merits. No one is starving or denied medical care, no one sleeps in the streets, everyone works who wants to work. But her daughter prefers the luxury of uncertainty, of time unplanned, of waste.

If only Felicia could take an interest in the revolution, Celia believes, it would give her a higher purpose, a chance to participate in something larger than herself. After all, aren't they part of the greatest social experiment in modern history? But her daughter can only wallow in her own discomforts.

Nothing shakes Felicia's settled indifference. Not the two weeks she spent guerrilla training in the mountains. Not the day and a half she lasted cutting sugarcane. Felicia returned from the fields complaining of her wrenched back, her shredded hands, of the clumps of dust she'd swallowed. After that, she vowed to drink her coffee bitter. No more sugar.

Felicia's doctors recommended that she join a theater group, saying that many malcontents had finally made their peace with the revolution through acting. But Felicia showed no aptitude for the stage. Her daughter's talents, Celia realized ruefully, lay in her unsurpassed drama for the everyday. In the post office, in the plaza, or in the beauty shop where she worked, Felicia could have earned standing ovations and showers of red carnations.

Celia rummages through her nightstand drawer for her favorite photograph of her son. He is tall and pale as she is, with a mole on his left cheek identical to hers. Javier is wearing his Pioneers uniform, bright and new as the revolution, as his optimistic face. She cannot imagine him any older than he is in this picture.

Her son was almost thirteen when the revolution triumphed. Those first years were difficult, not because of the hardships or the rationing that Celia knew were necessary to redistribute the country's wealth, but because Celia and Javier had to mute their enthusiasm for El Líder. Her husband would not tolerate praise of the revolution in his home.

Javier never fought his father openly. His war was one of silent defiance, and he left for Czechoslovakia secretly in 1966, without saying good-bye to anyone.

Javier wrote her a long letter after his father died three years ago, and said he'd finally become a professor of biochemistry at the University of Prague, lecturing in Russian, German, and Czech. He didn't mention his wife, not even in passing, but he wrote that he spoke Spanish to his little girl so she'd be able to talk with her grandmother someday. This touched Celia, and she wrote a special note to Irinita encouraging her to keep up her Spanish and promising to teach her how to swim.

Over the years, her son had written her only sporadically, quick notes jotted down, it seemed to Celia, between his lectures. Rarely did he write anything of substance, as if only the most superficial news was suitable for her. What she learned most about Javier came from the family picture her daughter-in-law, Irina, dutifully sent every Christmas. Celia saw her son age in these photographs, watched his mouth acquire his father's obstinate expression. And yet there was something vulnerable in his eyes that heartened Celia, that reminded her of her little boy.

In bed, Celia adjusts her breasts so she can sleep comfortably on her stomach. Every morning she wakes up on her back, her arms and legs spread, the cover sheet on the floor. She cannot account for her inquietude. Her dreams seem to her mere sparks of color and electricity, cut off from the current of her life.

Celia closes her eyes. She doesn't like to admit to herself that, despite all her activities, she sometimes feels lonely. Not the loneliness of previous years, of a reluctant life by the sea, but a loneliness borne of the inability to share her joy. Celia remembers the afternoons on the porch when her infant granddaughter seemed to understand her very thoughts. For many years, Celia spoke to Pilar during the darkest part of the night, but then their connection suddenly died. Celia understands now that a cycle between them had ended, and a new one had not yet begun.

Luz Villaverde
(1976)

For a man with such large hands, my father fidgeted with delicate things—a loose thread on his jacket, a twirling match, the tiniest clasps. He had the touch of a young girl's nimble fingers. I watched him sew a minuscule button on my dress once and, later, unfasten a prostitute's black mask.

My father had been a handsome man. I have the picture to prove it. It was Mamá who destroyed him.

Now his nails are embedded with grime and his face and neck are the texture of cured hides. He owns one shirt, polka-dotted, which he wears rolled up to his elbows, and a greasy pair of trousers too long in the seat. The lines in his face look as if each one were put there by a distinct calamity rather than a slow accumulation of sorrow. His teeth are blackened and ground down with worry, and he eats only mashed foods like a baby. He keeps his wedding ring in a blue velvet box with tight springs. I remember how he used to slip the ring on and off his finger easily as if it were greased, and the things he did when it was off didn't count. My father was a man who could not turn down an adventure.

After Mamá set him on fire, we knew Papi wouldn't return. In fact, we didn't see him again for nine years. But I fantasized about how he'd come back to take Milagro and me away from Mamá and her coconuts. We kept the scarves he'd brought us back from China when we were two years old, silks with a graceful pattern of cranes. It didn't matter that we were too young to wear them, only that he thought we could. I imagined riding on the backs of those cranes, flying to wherever he was.

Milagro and I lied to our friends about him. "He's coming back for us," we'd say. "He's been delayed in Australia." But after a while we stopped. What was the use? By then everyone else's parents were divorced, too, so it didn't seem to matter as much.

Luckily, Milagro and I have each other. We're a double helix, tight and impervious. That's why Mamá can't penetrate us.

"Do you know the meaning of shells?" she asked Milagro once, all honey-voiced. "They're the jewels of the goddess of the sea. They bring good luck not bad, like everyone says. You're my little jewel, Milagro."

And then Mamá turned to me and said, "You, Luz, you're the

light in the night that guides our dreams. You guard what's most precious."

This was just like her. Pretty words. Meaningless words that didn't nourish us, that didn't comfort us, that kept us prisoners in her alphabet world.

My sister and I call our mother "not-Mamá." As in not-Mamá charred the chicken and is cursing in the kitchen. Not-Mamá is playing that record again, dancing by herself in the dark. Watch out, not-Mamá is feeling sorry for herself. She wants us to tell her we love her. When we don't, she looks right past us as if she could see another pair of girls just behind us, girls who will tell her what she wants to hear.

Ivanito thinks we're cruel to Mamá but he never saw what we saw, he never heard what we heard. We try to protect him but he doesn't want to be protected. He is her gullible rag doll.

Since the summer of coconuts, Milagro and I have had a pact to ignore Mamá, to stay as far away from her as possible. We're studying hard so when we grow up we can get good jobs and go wherever we please. Abuela Celia tells us that before the revolution smart girls like us usually didn't go to college. They got married and had children while they were still children themselves. I'm glad we don't have to worry about that. I'm going to be a veterinarian and operate on the biggest animals on the planet—elephants, rhinoceroses, giraffes, hippopotamuses. I'll probably have to go to Africa for that, but Milagro says she'll come with me. She wants to be a mycologist specializing in tropical fungi. She keeps fuzzy specimens in an aquarium at school. I tell her as long as it stays out of our room it's okay with me.

My sister is more sentimental than I am, so sometimes when she starts feeling sorry for Mamá I remind her of our ninth birthday party, when the entire fourth-grade class came to our house on Palmas Street. There were a frosted cake and homemade cone hats, and Mamá wore a satiny cape and sparkles on her face and

did magic tricks. She pulled rings from behind our ears and rubber spiders from a bowl floating with gardenias. A donkey piñata
with button eyes hung from the ceiling.

Mamá blindfolded me and handed me a broom. At first I
swung wildly, battering Manolo Colón, the smart, shy boy who
liked me. He almost ran home, but Mamá wiped his face with a
damp rag and gave him a piece from the best part of the cake.
Then she blindfolded me again and I whipped the air with the
broomstick until the piñata burst open, releasing long, gooey
tentacles of raw egg.

Eggs. Mamá had filled the piñata with eggs.

Everyone laughed and screamed and began smearing each
other with yolk, chasing each other up and down the house,
rocking its frame with their stamping feet.

"Come back soon!" Mamá yelled after them as they ran toward their parents, who were too stunned at the egg in their
children's hair and clothes to notice my mother shaking with
laughter.

Milagro and I went to our room without saying anything to
Ivanito or Mamá. We picked bits of shell from our hair, looked
at each other, and cried.

We got our first postcard from Papi last summer. Later, we
learned that he had sent us others but that Mamá burned them
the way she'd burned his face. It was a sunny day and the post-
man made a second trip to our house to deliver the postcard he'd
forgotten. Mamá was not at home.

The postcard was of a tobacco factory, row after row of
women bunching bronze leaves into cigars. The caption on the
back said "*Cuba . . . alegre como su sol.*" Papi wrote that he'd returned from his travels and was settled in a hotel on the wharf.
He said he very much wanted to see us and called us his "two
precious beans." He said he had never forgotten us.

Milagro and I took out our crane scarves and flew around our room, watching the birds flutter in the air behind us. We folded and refolded our clothes and waited for escape.

A few days later, Mamá was leaving for one of her overnight voodoo meetings. Milagro and I persuaded her to let us stay by ourselves in Havana instead of going to Abuela Celia's house. After she left, Milagro and I packed our clothes in a duffel bag and looped the crane scarves around our necks. We waited for a taxi by the plaza, and didn't look back.

The moon was already high in the sky, impatient for night to fall. It seemed to draw light from the waning sun. We drove up one alley and then another, bouncing on the cobblestones and the taxi's creaking springs. The waiting seemed longer than all the waiting before it. Would we be able to escape?

When we stopped, I looked up at the decayed hotel, I looked up at our future.

Milagro seemed to know where to go so I followed her through the wrought-iron archway and up the steep, curved stairs reeking with filth. The banister wobbled in place as we climbed one flight, then another.

"He's in there." Milagro pointed to a wooden door with no number. She strode up to it as if she were coming to collect the rent and knocked hard, twice.

Our father's face was hung with slack ugly folds that dragged down his eyes until the rims showed red, that dragged down the stump of his nose and his misshapen ears, dragged them down until his skull was taut and bare. And before we could scream or run away, Papi stretched out his arms, his once-beautiful hands, and called our names.

Milagro and I continued to see our father in secret whenever we could. If Mamá had found out, who knows what she would have done. Our father's room, formerly a servant's, had a single window that looked out over an alley where mongrels fought. At night, Papi said, he could hear the moans of the ships leaving Havana. It made him feel alone.

After Mamá burned him, Papi said a captain in the merchant marines took pity on him and doctored his papers so they'd say he was injured during an explosion on board. Papi's disability pension was meager so I don't know how he afforded the gifts he gave us—huge dolls with creamy skin and velvety bows, plastic purses with cartoons on them, colorful barrettes for our hair, which we hid from our mother. It's as if now that we'd grown, Papi wanted to turn back the clock. He wanted us smaller, younger, pocket-size. I think he may have bought the gifts long ago but wanted desperately for us still to like them, still to like him.

After a while, it wasn't difficult for us to look at our father's face. In his sagging eyes we found the language we'd been searching for, a language more eloquent than the cheap bead necklaces of words my mother offered.

We brought Papi mashed-up food and wiped clean the folds of his scarred flesh. I worked extra time in my school's lemon groves and earned coupons for a cassette radio. Milagro bought him an *Irakere* jazz tape that he played over and over again. He didn't say what he did when we weren't there, but I suspect he never left his room.

"I was the fastest runner in high school," he told us once. The past was as vivid to him as if he could live it over at will. He was his parents' only son, born years after they'd stopped praying for a baby, and he was pampered and fussed over like a first grandchild. "I won the hundred-yard dash even though I was much heavier than the other boys. I made it to the finish in thirteen seconds."

He told us, too, how he'd lasted only one morning in the nickel mines before joining the merchant marines. But when he returned from his first voyage to Africa, his parents had died.

One day, Papi asked to see Ivanito, I don't know why. Milagro and I warned him that Ivanito probably wouldn't come, that all he'd heard were lies and more lies about him. Maybe we were jealous. We wanted to keep Papi for ourselves.

But then we changed our minds. We wanted Ivanito to see what Mamá had done to our father, what she'd done to us.

There was a hurricane warning that day. The wind whipped up the garbage in the streets and the air was so wet that the buildings gleamed through it. Down by the harbor, the ocean was rough and high on the piers. No watermarks showed. The three of us ran with linked arms, clutching our jackets, and felt the first drops of rain as we reached Papi's hotel.

"I don't think he's home." Milagro looked at me strangely but neither of us knew why. Ivanito began jumping nervously in place, jumping brisk little jumps like he was trying to stay warm.

If it hadn't been for the rain that fell hard and sudden, we wouldn't have gone up those stairs. If we hadn't been afraid of the dogs fighting in the alley, we might have taken Ivanito away. If we hadn't seen the ships, big ones with curled Russian lettering, moored to the docks like Gullivers, we might have come back another day. But we didn't.

My father's door was slightly open and we heard a low grunting, like newborn pigs suckling their mother's teats. Ivanito pushed open the door and we saw my father, his face terrible and swollen and purple as his sex, open his mouth wide and shudder as his milk sputtered on the breasts of the masked naked woman below him.

We're back at boarding school now. We like it here. Milagro and I volunteer to feed the horses in the stables, and then we ride them through the woods and the lemon groves, the horses all buckteeth and happy.

Ivanito is at boarding school, too. His teachers say he's very intelligent but maladjusted, that he cries every night and disturbs the other boys' sleep. Ivanito feels guilty about visiting Papi. He fears that Mamá may find out and then he'll never be able to go home. But we tell him that nobody but us knows what happened, and swore him to lifelong secrecy. The three of us pricked our fingers and mingled our blood to make certain.

What my brother doesn't realize yet is that nothing Mamá does has anything to do with him, or with Abuela Celia, or with any of us.

Enough Attitude

(1975)

Lourdes Puente is walking her beat. It's a five-block square of Brooklyn with brownstones and linden trees, considered safe as neighborhoods go on this side of Atlantic Avenue. Lourdes is an auxiliary policewoman, the first in her precinct. She scored one hundred on her written test by answering "c" to the multiple-choice questions she wasn't sure of or didn't understand. Captain Cacciola congratulated her personally. He wanted to make sure she was tough enough on crime. Lourdes said she believed drug dealers should die in the electric chair. This pleased the captain, and she was sent on patrol Tuesday and Thursday nights between seven and ten.

Lourdes enjoys patrolling the streets in her thick-soled black shoes. These shoes, it seems to her, are a kind of equalizer. She can run in them if she has to, jump curbs, traverse the buckled, faulted sidewalks of Brooklyn without twisting an ankle. These shoes are power. If women wore shoes like these, she thinks, they wouldn't worry so much about more abstract equalities.

They would join the army reserve or the auxiliary police like her, and protect what was theirs. In Cuba nobody was prepared for the Communists and look what happened. Now her mother guards their beach with binoculars and a pistol against Yankees. If only Lourdes had had a gun when she needed it.

It's Thursday, just after nine. There's a full moon out. It hangs fat and waxy in the sky, creased with shadows.

"Every loony in New York comes out of the woodwork on nights like this," the regular beat cop had warned her.

But so far everything's been quiet. It's too cold for loiterers. Lourdes suddenly remembers how her daughter had ridiculed Armstrong's first words on the moon. "He had months to think up something and that's all he could say?" Pilar was only ten years old and already mocking everything. Lourdes slapped her for being disrespectful, but it made no difference to her daughter. Pilar was immune to threats. She placed no value on normal things so it was impossible to punish her. Even now, Pilar is not afraid of pain or of losing anything. It's this indifference that is most maddening.

The last of the Jews have moved out of the neighborhood. Only the Kellners are left. The others are on Long Island or in Westchester or Florida, depending on their ages and their bank accounts. Pilar thinks Lourdes is bigoted, but what does her daughter know of life? Equality is just another one of her abstractions. "I don't make up the statistics," she tells Pilar. "I don't color the faces down at the precinct." Black faces, Puerto Rican faces. Once in a while a stray Irish or Italian face looking scared. Lourdes prefers to confront reality—the brownstones converted to tenements in a matter of months, the garbage in the streets, the jaundice-eyed men staring vacantly from the stoops. Even Pilar couldn't denounce her for being a hypocrite.

Lourdes feels the solid ground beneath her solid black shoes as she walks. She breathes in the wintry air, which stings her lungs. It seems to her as if the air were made of crystal filaments, scraping and cleaning her inside. She decides she has no patience for dreamers, for people who live between black and white.

Lourdes slides her hand up and down her wooden nightstick. It's the only weapon the police department will issue her. That and handcuffs. Lourdes has used the stick only once in her two months of patrolling, to break up a fight between a Puerto Rican kid and three Italians down at the playground. Lourdes knows the Puerto Rican's mother. She's the one who worked at the bakery for an afternoon. Lourdes caught her pocketing fifty cents from the sale of two crullers, and threw her out. No wonder her son is a delinquent. He sells plastic bags of marijuana behind the liquor store.

Lourdes's son would have been about the same age as the Navarro boy. *Her* son would have been different. He wouldn't have talked back to her or taken drugs or drunk beer from paper bags like the other teenagers. *Her* son would have helped her in the bakery without complaint. He would have come to her for guidance, pressed her hand to his cheek, told her he loved her. Lourdes would have talked to her son the way Rufino talks to Pilar, for companionship. Lourdes suffers with this knowledge.

Down the street, the trees are imprisoned equidistantly in square plots of dirt. Everything else is concrete. Lourdes remembers reading somewhere about how Dutch elm disease wiped out the entire species on the East Coast except for a lone tree in Manhattan surrounded by concrete. Is this, she wonders, how we'll all survive?

It became clear to Lourdes shortly after she and Rufino moved to New York that he would never adapt. Something came unhinged in his brain that would make him incapable of working in a conventional way. There was a part of him that could never leave the *finca* or the comfort of its cycles, and this diminished him for any other life. He could not be transplanted. So Lourdes got a job. Cuban women of a certain age and a certain class consider working outside the home to be beneath them. But Lourdes never believed that.

While it was true that she had grown accustomed to the privileges that came with marrying into the Puente family, Lourdes never accepted the life designated for its women. Even now, stripped of their opulence, crowded into two-bedroom apartments in Hialeah and Little Havana, the Puente women clung to their rituals as they did their engraved silverware, succumbing to a cloying nostalgia. Doña Zaida, once a formidable matriarch who ruled her eight sons by a resolute jealousy, spent long afternoons watching *novelas* on television and perfuming her thickening wrists.

Lourdes knew she could never be this kind of woman. After her honeymoon, she got right to work on the Puente ranch. She reviewed the ledgers, fired the cheating accountant, and took over the books herself. She redecorated the musty, coffer-ceilinged mansion with watercolor landscapes, reupholstered the sofas with rustic fabrics, and discarded the cretonne drapes in favor of sliding glass doors that invited the morning light. Out went the ornate bric-a-brac, the austere furniture carved with the family crest. Lourdes refilled the mosaic-lined fountain with sweet water and built an aviary in the garden, stocking it with toucans and cockatoos, parrots, a macaw, and canaries that sang in high octaves. Sometimes at night, she could hear the cries of the quail doves and solitaires interspersed with the songs from the aviary.

When a disgruntled servant informed Doña Zaida about the changes in her country house, she descended on the ranch in a fury and restored the villa to its former state. Lourdes, who defiantly rebuilt the aviary and restocked it with birds, never spoke to her mother-in-law again.

*

Lourdes misses the birds she had in Cuba. She thinks of joining a bird-watching society, but who would take care of the bakery in her absence? Pilar is unreliable and Rufino can't tell a Danish from a donut. It's a shame, too, because all Lourdes ever sees in Brooklyn is dull little wrens or those filthy pigeons. Rufino has taken to raising pigeons in wire-mesh cages in their back-yard the way he saw Marlon Brando do in *On the Waterfront*. He prints messages on bits of paper, slips them through metal rings on the pigeons' legs, then kisses each bird on the head for good luck and lets it loose with a whoop. Lourdes doesn't know or care what her husband is writing, or to whom. By now, she accepts him the way she accepts the weather. What else can she do?

Rufino has stopped confiding in her. She hears secondhand snippets about his projects from Pilar, and knows he's trying to develop a super carburetor, one that will get two hundred miles to the gallon. Lourdes knows, too, that her husband is still brooding about artificial intelligence. She is not sure what this means although Rufino explained to her once that it would do for the brain what the telephone did for the human voice, take it farther and faster than it could go unassisted. Lourdes cannot understand why this is so difficult. She remembers seeing robots at the World's Fair ten years ago. She and Rufino and Pilar ate in a restaurant observatory shaped like a spaceship. The food was terrible. The view was of Queens.

These days, Lourdes recognizes her husband's face, his thinning reddish hair, and the crepey pouches under his eyes, but he is a stranger to her. She looks at him the way she might look at a photograph of her hands, unfamiliar upon close inspection.

Lourdes is herself only with her father. Even after his death, they understand each other perfectly, as they always have. Jorge del Pino doesn't accompany Lourdes on her beat because he doesn't want to interfere with her work. He is proud of his daughter, of her tough stance on law and order, identical to his own. It was he who encouraged Lourdes to join the auxiliary police so she'd be ready to fight the Communists when the time came. "Look how El Líder mobilizes the people to protect his causes," Jorge del Pino told his daughter. "He uses the techniques of the Fascists. Everyone is armed and ready for combat at a moment's notice. How will we ever win Cuba back if we ourselves are not prepared to fight?"

Pilar makes fun of Lourdes in her uniform, of the way she slaps the nightstick in her palm. "Who do you think you are, Kojak?" she says, laughing, and hands her mother a lollipop. This is just like her daughter, scornful and impudent. "I'm doing this to show you something, to teach you a lesson!" Lourdes screams, but Pilar ignores her.

Last Christmas, Pilar gave her a book of essays on Cuba called *A Revolutionary Society*. The cover showed cheerful, clean-cut children gathered in front of a portrait of Che Guevara. Lourdes was incensed.

"Will you read it?" Pilar asked her.

"I don't have to read it to know what's in it! Lies, poisonous Communist lies!" Che Guevara's face had set a violence quivering within her like a loose wire.

"Suit yourself," Pilar shot back.

Lourdes snatched the volume from under the Christmas tree, took it to the bathroom, filled the tub with scalding water, and dropped it in. Che Guevara's face blanched and swelled like the dead girl Lourdes had seen wash up once on the beach at Santa Teresa del Mar with a note pinned to her breast. Nobody ever came to claim her. Lourdes fished Pilar's book out of the tub with barbecue tongs and placed it on the porcelain platter she reserved for her roasted pork legs. Then she fastened a note to the cover with a safety pin. "Why don't you move to Russia if you think it's so great!" And she signed her name in full.

All this she left on Pilar's bed. But it did not provoke her daughter. The next day, the platter was back in the cupboard and *A Revolutionary Society* was drying on the clothesline.

Lourdes's walkie-talkie crackles as she works her way along the length of river that forms the western boundary of her territory. The night is so clear that the water reflects every stray angle of light. Without the disruptions of ships and noise, the river is a mirror. It reminds Lourdes of a photograph she saw once of the famous Hall of Mirrors in the Palace of Versailles with its endless ricocheting light.

At the edge of her vision, the darkness shifts. Her spine stiffens and her heart is audible deep inside her ears. She turns and squints but she cannot make out the figure, crouched and still, by the river. Lourdes grips her nightstick with one hand and pulls on her flashlight with the other. When she looks up again, the figure springs across the low fence and jumps into the river, shattering the light.

"Stop!" she shouts, running toward the spot as if chasing a part of herself. Lourdes turns her flashlight on the river, penetrating its rippled surface, then hoists herself over the fence. "Stop!" she shouts again at nothing at all. Lourdes pulls her walkie-talkie from its holster and screams too close to the speaker. She cannot remember what to say, the codes she had carefully memorized. A voice is talking to her now, calm and officious. "Tell us your location," it says, " . . . your location." But Lourdes jumps into the river instead. She hears the sirens wailing as the cold envelops her, numbing her face and her hands, her feet in their thick-soled shoes. The river smells of death.

Only one more fact is important. Lourdes lived and the Navarro boy died.

Pilar
(1976)

The family is hostile to the individual. This is what I'm thinking as Lou Reed says he has enough attitude to kill every person in New Jersey. I'm at a club in the Village with my boyfriend, Max. I figure I have enough attitude to kill a few people myself, only it never works on the right ones.

"I'm from Brooklyn, man!" Lou shouts and the crowd goes wild. I don't cheer, though. I wouldn't cheer either if Lou said, "Let's hear it for Cuba." Cuba. Planet Cuba. Where the hell is that?

Max's real name is Octavio Schneider. He sings and plays bass and harmonica for the Manichaean Blues Band, a group he started back in San Antonio, where he's from. They do Howlin' Wolf and Muddy Waters and lots of their own songs, mostly hard rock. Sometimes they do back-up for this crazy bluesman, the Reverend Billy Hines, who keeps his eyes shut when he sings. Max says that the reverend was a storefront preacher who played the Panhandle years ago and is attempting a comeback. Max himself had a modest hit in Texas with "Moonlight on Emma," a song about an ex-girlfriend who dumped him and moved to Hollywood.

I met Max at a downtown basement club a few months ago. He came over and started speaking to me in Spanish (his mother is Mexican) as if he'd known me for years. I liked him right away. When I brought him around to meet my parents, Mom took one look at his beaded headband and the braid down his back and said, "Sácalo de aquí." When I told her that Max spoke Spanish, she simply repeated what she said in English: "Take him away."

Dad was cool, though. "What does your band's name mean?" he asked Max.

"The Manichaeans, see, were followers of this Persian guy who lived in the third century. They believed that hedonism was the only way to get rid of their sins."

"Hedonism?"

"Yeah, the Manichaeans liked to party. They had orgies and drank a lot. They got wiped out by other Christians, though."

"Too bad," my father said sympathetically.

Later, Dad looked up the Manichaeans in the encyclopedia and discovered that, contrary to what Max claimed, the Manichaeans believed that the world and all matter were created by nefarious forces, and that the only way to battle them was through asceticism and a pure life. When I told Max about this, he just shrugged and said, "Well, I guess that's okay, too." Max is a tolerant kind of guy.

I just love the way Lou Reed's concerts feel—expectant, uncertain. You never know what he's going to do next. Lou has about twenty-five personalities. I like him because he sings about people no one else sings about—drug addicts, transvestites, the down-and-out. Lou jokes about his alter egos discussing problems at night. I feel like a new me sprouts and dies every day.

I play Lou and Iggy Pop and this new band the Ramones whenever I paint. I love their energy, their violence, their incredible grinding guitars. It's like an artistic form of assault. I try to translate what I hear into colors and volumes and lines that confront people, that say, "Hey, we're here too and what we think matters!" or more often just "Fuck you!" Max is not as crazy about the Ramones as I am. I think he's more of a traditionalist. He has a tough time being rude, even to people who deserve it. Not me. If I don't like someone, I show it. It's the one thing I have in common with my mother.

*

Neither of my parents is very musical. Their entire record collection consists of *Perry Como's Greatest Hits,* two Herb Alpert &
the Tijuana Brass albums, and *Alvin and the Chipmunks Sing Their
Favorite Christmas Carols,* which they bought for me when I was
a kid. Recently, Mom picked up a Jim Nabors album of patriotic
songs in honor of the bicentennial. I mean, after Vietnam and
Watergate, who the hell wants to hear "The Battle Hymn of the
Republic"?

I used to like the Fourth of July okay because of the fireworks.
I'd go down by the East River and watch them flare up from the
tugboats. The girandoles looked like fiery lace in the sky. But
this bicentennial crap is making me crazy. Mom has talked about
nothing else for months. She bought a second bakery and plans
to sell tricolor cupcakes and Uncle Sam marzipan. Apple pies,
too. She's convinced she can fight Communism from behind her
bakery counter.

Last year she joined the local auxiliary police out of some
misplaced sense of civic duty. My mother—all four feet eleven
and a half inches and 217 pounds of her—patrols the streets of
Brooklyn at night in a skintight uniform, clanging with enough
antiriot gear to quash another Attica. She practices twirling her
nightstick in front of the mirror, then smacks it against her palm,
steadily, menacingly, like she's seen cops do on television.
Mom's upset because the police department won't issue her a
gun. Right. She gets a gun and I move out of state fast.

There's other stuff happening with her. For starters, she's been
talking with Abuelo Jorge since he died. He gives her business
advice and tells her who's stealing from her at the bakery. Mom
says that Abuelo spies on me and reports back to her. Like what
is this? The ghost patrol? Mom is afraid that I'm having sex with
Max (which I'm not) and this is her way of trying to keep me
in line.

Max likes Mom, though. He says she suffers from an "imperious disposition."

"You mean she's a frustrated tyrant?" I ask him.

"More like a bitch goddess," he explains.

Max's parents split up before he was born and his mother cleans motel rooms for minimum wage. I guess Mom must seem exotic by comparison.

But she's really not. Mom makes food only people in Ohio eat, like Jell-O molds with miniature marshmallows or recipes she clips from *Family Circle*. And she barbecues anything she can get her hands on. Then we sit around behind the warehouse and stare at each other with nothing to say. Like this is it? We're living the American dream?

The worst is the parades. Mom gets up early and drags us out on Thanksgiving Day loaded with plastic foam coolers, like we're going to starve right there on Fifth Avenue. On New Year's Day, she sits in front of the television and comments on every single float in the Rose Parade. I think she dreams of sponsoring one herself someday. Like maybe a huge burning effigy of El Líder.

Max flatters me but not in a sleazy way. He says he loves my height (I'm five feet eight inches) and my hair (black, down to my waist) and the whiteness of my skin. His mouth is a little sauna, hot and wet. When we slow-dance, he presses himself against me and I feel his hardness against my thighs. He says I would make a good bass player.

Max knows about Abuela Celia in Cuba, about how she used to talk to me late at night and how we've lost touch over the years. Max wants to go to Cuba and track her down, but I tell him what happened four years ago, when I ran away to Florida and my plans to see my grandmother collapsed. I wonder what Abuela Celia is doing right this minute.

Most days Cuba is kind of dead to me. But every once in a

while a wave of longing will hit me and it's all I can do not to hijack a plane to Havana or something. I resent the hell out of the politicians and the generals who force events on us that structure our lives, that dictate the memories we'll have when we're old. Every day Cuba fades a little more inside me, my grandmother fades a little more inside me. And there's only my imagination where our history should be.

It doesn't help that Mom refuses to talk about Abuela Celia. She gets annoyed every time I ask her and she shuts me up quickly, like I'm prying into top secret information. Dad is more open, but he can't tell me what I really want to know, like why Mom hardly speaks to Abuela or why she still keeps her riding crops from Cuba. Most of the time, he's too busy refereeing the fights between us, or else he's just in his own orbit.

Dad feels kind of lost here in Brooklyn. I think he stays in his workshop most of the day because he'd get too depressed or crazy otherwise. Sometimes I think we should have moved to a ranch in Wyoming or Montana. He would have been happy there with his horses and his cows, his land, and a big empty sky overhead. Dad only looks alive when he talks about the past, about Cuba. But we don't discuss that much either lately. Things haven't been the same since I saw him with that blond bombshell. I never said anything to him, but it's like a cut on my tongue that never healed.

*　　*　　*

Mom has decided she wants me to paint a mural for her second Yankee Doodle Bakery.

"I want a big painting like the Mexicans do, but pro-American," she specifies.

"You want to commission *me* to paint something for *you*?"

"*Sí*, Pilar. You're a painter, no? So paint!"

"You've got to be kidding."

"Painting is painting, no?"

"Look, Mom, I don't think you understand. I don't *do* bakeries."

"You're embarrassed? My bakery is not good enough for you?"

"It's not that."

"This bakery paid for your painting classes."

"It has nothing to do with that, either."

"If Michelangelo were alive today, he wouldn't be so proud."

"Mom, believe me, Michelangelo would definitely *not* be painting bakeries."

"Don't be so sure. Most artists are starving. They don't have all the advantages like you. They take heroin to forget."

"Jesus Christ!"

"This could be a good opportunity for you, Pilar. A lot of important people come to my shop. Judges and lawyers from the courts, executives from Brooklyn Union Gas. Maybe they'll see your painting. You could become famous."

My mother talks and talks, but I block out her words. For some reason I think about Jacoba Van Heemskerck, a Dutch expressionist painter I've become interested in lately. Her paintings feel organic to me, like breathing abstractions of color. She refused to title her paintings (much less do patriotic murals for her mother's bakery) and numbered her works instead. I mean, who needs words when colors and lines conjure up their own language? That's what I want to do with my paintings, find a unique language, obliterate the clichés.

I think about all the women artists throughout history who managed to paint despite the odds against them. People still ask where all the important women painters are instead of looking at what they did paint and trying to understand their circumstances. Even supposedly knowledgeable and sensitive people react to good art by a woman as if it were an anomaly, a product of a freak nature or a direct result of her association with a male painter or mentor. Nobody's even heard of feminism in art school. The male teachers and students still call the shots and get the serious attention and the fellowships that further their careers. As for the women, we're supposed to make extra money modeling nude. What kind of bullshit revolution is that?

"*Mira,* Pilar. I'm asking you as a favor. You could paint something simple, something elegant. Like the Statue of Liberty. Is that too much to ask?"

"Okay, okay, I'll paint something," I say deliberately, deciding to play my last card. "But on one condition. You can't see it before the unveiling." This will get her, I think. She'll never agree to this in a million years. She's too much of a control freak.

"That's fine."

"What?"

"I said that's fine, Pilar."

I must be standing there with my mouth open because she pops a macaroon into it and shakes her head as if to say, "See, you always underestimate me." But that's not true. If anything, I overestimate her. It comes from experience. Mom is arbitrary and inconsistent and always believes she's right. It's a pretty irritating combination.

Shit. How did I get into this mess?

Our warehouse is only two blocks from the river, and the Statue of Liberty is visible in the distance. I'd been there once when I was a kid, before we settled in Brooklyn. Mom and Dad took me on a ferry and we climbed up behind Liberty's eyes and looked out over the river, the city, the beginning of things.

A Circle Line tour boat is rounding the tip of Manhattan, optimistic as a wedding cake. There's someone on the top deck with a pair of binoculars aimed at Brooklyn. I can imagine what the tour guide is saying: ". . . and on your left, ladies and gentlemen, is the borough of Brooklyn, former home of the Dodgers and the birthplace of famous 'It' girl Clara Bow. . . ." What they don't say is that nobody ever dies in Brooklyn. It's only the living that die here.

That night, I get to work. But I decide to do a painting instead of a mural. I stretch a twelve-by-eight-foot canvas and wash it with an iridescent blue gouache—like the Virgin Mary's robes in gaudy church paintings. I want the background to glow, to look irradiated, nuked out. It takes me a while to get the right effect.

When the paint dries, I start on Liberty herself. I do a perfect replication of her a bit left of center canvas, changing only two details: first, I make Liberty's torch float slightly beyond her grasp, and second, I paint her right hand reaching over to cover her left breast, as if she's reciting the National Anthem or some other slogan.

The next day, the background still looks off to me, so I take a medium-thick brush and paint black stick figures pulsing in the air around Liberty, thorny scars that look like barbed wire. I want to go all the way with this, to stop mucking around and do what I feel, so at the base of the statue I put my favorite punk rallying cry: I'M A MESS. And then carefully, very carefully, I paint a safety pin through Liberty's nose.

This, I think, sums everything up very nicely. *SL-76.* That'll be my title.

I fuss with Liberty another couple of days, more out of nervousness than anything. I keep getting the feeling that Mom is going to spy on my work. After all, her record doesn't exactly inspire confidence. So, before I leave my studio, I set up a booby trap—two tight rows of paint cans on the floor just inside the door. Mom would trip on them if she managed to open the latch and come creeping around late at night. It would serve her right, too, show her that she can't go breaking her promises and invading my privacy any time she damn well pleases.

I'm usually a heavy sleeper but these last nights every little noise makes me jump out of bed. I'd swear I heard her footsteps, or someone picking the lock on my studio. But when I get up to investigate, I always find my mother sound asleep, looking innocent the way chronically guilty people do sometimes. Then I go to the refrigerator, find something to eat, and stare at the cold stub of her cigar on the kitchen table. In the mornings, my paint cans remain undisturbed and there are no suspicious stains on any of Mom's clothing in the hamper. Jesus, I must really be getting paranoid.

Max helps me set the painting up in the bakery the night before the grand opening, and we drape it with sewn-together sheets. My mother, surprisingly, still hasn't even tried to get a glimpse of the work. I can tell she's proud of the blind faith she's placed in me. She's positively aglow in her magnanimity. When I come home that night, Mom shows me the full-page ad she took out in the *Brooklyn Express*:

YANKEE DOODLE BAKERY

invites

OUR FRIENDS AND NEIGHBORS

to the

GRAND OPENING

of

OUR SECOND STORE

and the

UNVEILING

of a

MAJOR NEW WORK OF ART

for the

200TH BIRTHDAY OF AMERICA

SUNDAY, 12 NOON

(free food and drinks)

Free food and drinks! This is more serious than I thought. Mom doesn't give anything away if she can help it.

Now I can't sleep all night thinking maybe this time I've gone too far. After all, Mom didn't seem to have any ulterior motives, at least none that I can figure. For once, I think she genuinely wanted to give me a break. I try to calm down by reminding myself that *she* was the one that cornered me into doing this painting. What did she expect?

At five in the morning, I go to my parents' room. They're sleeping back to back, like strange doughy twins. I want to warn her: "Look, I wanted to do it straight but I couldn't, I just couldn't. Do you understand?"

She shifts in her sleep, her plump body curling forward. I reach out to touch her but quickly pull back my hand.

"What's wrong? What's the matter?" Mom is suddenly awake, sitting upright. Her nightgown clings to the soft folds of her breasts, her stomach, the creases in her thighs.

"Nothing, Mom. I only wanted . . . I couldn't sleep."

"You're just nervous, Pilar."

"Yeah, well."

"Don't worry, *mi cielo.*" Mom takes my hand and pats it gently. "Go back to bed."

The next morning, the bakery is hung with flags and streamers and a Dixieland band is playing "When the Saints Go Marching

In." Mom is in her new red, white, and blue two-piece suit, a matching handbag stiff on her elbow. She's giving away apple tartlets and brownies and cup after cup of coffee.

"Yes, my daughter created it," I hear her boast, trilling her "r"'s, clipping her vowels even more precisely than usual, as if her accent were partly responsible for the painting. "She is an *artista*. A very brilliant *artista*." Mom is pointing in my direction and I feel the sweat collecting at the small of my back. Someone from the *Brooklyn Express* snaps my picture.

At noon, Mom gingerly balances atop a stepladder on her tiny, size-four feet. The drum rolls endlessly as she pulls on the sheet. There's a stark silence as Liberty, in her full punk glory, glares down at the audience. For a brief moment, I imagine the sound of applause, of people calling my name. But my thoughts stop dead when I hear the hateful buzzing. It's as if the swarm of stick figures have come alive in their background, threatening to fly off the canvas and nest in our hair. The blood has drained from my mother's face and her lips are moving as if she wants to say something but can't form the words. She stands there, immobile, clutching the sheet against her silk blouse, when someone yells in raucous Brooklynese, "Gaaahbage! Whadda piece of gaaah-bage!" A lumpish man charges Liberty with a pocketknife, re-peating his words like a war cry. Before anyone can react, Mom swings her new handbag and clubs the guy cold inches from the painting. Then, as if in slow motion, she tumbles forward, a thrashing avalanche of patriotism and motherhood, crushing three spectators and a table of apple tartlets.

And I, I love my mother very much at that moment.

Baskets of Water

Ivanito

I started learning English from Abuelo Jorge's old grammar textbooks. I found them in Abuela Celia's closet. They date back to 1919, the first year he started working for the American Electric Broom Company. At school, only a few students were allowed to learn English, by special permission. The rest of us had to learn Russian. I liked the curves of the Cyrillic letters, their unexpected sounds. I liked the way my name looked: Иван. I took Russian for nearly two years at school. My teacher, Sergey Mikoyan, praised me highly. He said I had an ear for languages, that if I studied hard I could be a translator for world leaders. It was true I could repeat anything he said, even tongue twisters like *kolokololiteyshchiki perekolotili vikarabkavshihsya vihuholey,* "the church bell casters slaughtered the desmans that had scrambled out." He told me I had a gift, like playing the violin or mastering chess.

He used to embarrass me in front of the other boys. He'd call me up to the front of the class and ask me to recite a poem we had read only once. I'd pretend I couldn't remember it, but he insisted until I gave in, and I was secretly pleased. The words just came to me, clicked together like so many keys to locks. Afterward my schoolmates would tease me, "Teacher's pet!" "Show-off!" and shove me between them in the halls.

Mr. Mikoyan was a short man with shiny, ruddy cheeks like a baby's. He kept ice in a porcelain bowl on his desk. Every once in a while, he'd twist his handkerchief around a cube and press it to his temple. "The most civilized countries are the coldest ones," he told us many times. "Too much heat addles the brain."

I used to stay after class and wipe the blackboard for him with a wet rag. He'd talk of winter sleigh rides in the countryside, of lakes frozen solid enough to jump on and snow that fell like crystal from the sky. He'd tell me stories of the Tsarevitch in St. Petersburg, weak with hemophilia, his fate controlled by wicked forces. All the while, the ice would crackle in his bowl, as if to confirm his words.

I felt that I was meant to live in this colder world, a world that preserved history. In Cuba, everything seemed temporal, distorted by the sun.

Then Mr. Mikoyan would read me quotes from Tolstoy, whom he considered the greatest of all Russian authors, to copy onto the blackboard. My favorite was the first line in *Anna Karenina*: "Happy families are all alike; every unhappy family is unhappy in its own way."

"Perfect, it is perfect!" Mr. Mikoyan would say. He'd clap his hands, happy with Tolstoy and my perfect spelling. I liked to please him, to see his small, milky-marble teeth. He told me his wife was a chemist who worked with Cuban scientists on top-secret projects developing products from sugarcane. They had no children.

One afternoon, as I was wiping the blackboard, Mr. Mikoyan stood close behind me and told me that he was returning to Russia. He said that I would hear vile things about him.

I turned to look at him. His lips were dry and clung to each other as he spoke. I felt his sour little bursts of breath on my face. He looked as if he wanted to say something more, but then he clasped me to him suddenly and smoothed my hair, repeating my name. I pulled away from him, accidentally knocking the porcelain bowl from his desk. It shattered into a thousand pieces, and crunched beneath my feet as I ran.

For a long time, I thought about Mr. Mikoyan, about his ruddy baby cheeks and the things he warned me I'd hear. A boy from an upper grade accused him of indiscretions. Everyone spoke of it like murder or treason, with fascination and revulsion. Then the jokes started, more and more cruel. They said I was his favorite, that I'd stayed with him after school. "Go join him in Siberia!" they taunted. "You'll keep each other warm!" I didn't want to understand.

(1978)

The *oddu,* the official *santería* prediction for this year, is mixed. Yes, believers can accomplish many things because the dead are benevolently inclined toward the living. On the other hand, nothing can be taken for granted because what the living desire will require great effort. Felicia del Pino is fortunate in that she knows unequivocally what she wants: another husband. In this respect, at least, she will be twice more blessed.

In the second week of January, Felicia visits a *santero* known for his grace and power in reading the divining shells. Through the mouths of the cowries the gods speak to him in clear, unambiguous voices. The *santero* dips his middle finger in holy water and sprinkles it on the floor to refresh the shells. He begins to pray in Yoruba, asking for the blessings of the *orishas,* whom he honors one by one. Then, with the sixteen cowries, he touches Felicia's forehead, her hands, and her knees so that the gods may learn of the aching between her legs, of the hunger on her lips and the tips of each finger, of her breasts, taut with desire. The gods will tell her what to do.

The *santero* tosses and retosses the shells, but they foretell only misfortune. He enlists the aid of the sacred *ota* stone, as well as the shrunken head of a doll, a ball of powdered eggshell, and the *eggun,* a vertebra from the spine of a goat. But the reading does not change.

"Water cannot be carried in a basket," the *santero* says, shaking his head. "What you wish for, daughter, you cannot keep. It is the will of the gods."

He instructs Felicia to perform a rubbing ritual to cleanse herself of negative influences. This is easily done, he says, by smearing a piece of meat or a soup bone with palm oil, aspersing it with rum, curing it with cigar smoke, then placing it in a paper bag and rubbing herself from head to toe.

"The bag will absorb the evil that clings to you," the *santero* says. "Take it to the gates of the cemetery and leave it there. When you have done this, return to me for a final cleansing."

Felicia has every intention of following the *santero*'s advice. But on her way home she falls in love.

Not everyone would be attracted to Ernesto Brito. His most remarkable feature besides his paleness, a paleness that obliterates any possible expression, is his hair. He combs his flaxen strands meticulously from the lower left side of his head to his right temple, then swirls them round and round on his bald crown, securing them with a greasy pomade. When a stiff wind disarranges his lacquered locks, he looks panic-stricken, like a man who's just seen his own ghost.

Felicia first notices her second husband-to-be when he pedals by her furiously on a clunky Russian bicycle, his hair vertical as a sail.

At the end of the alleyway, Ernesto Brito, nervously attempting a sharp right turn, clatters to the ground.

Felicia approaches the bleached, crumpled heap that will be her husband. He looks like a colorless worm, writhing on his stomach in a synthetic tan suit with precisely matching socks, his steel glasses smashed against the pavement. Felicia is smitten. She helps him up and, without a word, pats his hair until his face flushes the color of beets. She takes him by the hand and leads him to her 1952 De Soto parked a few yards away.

It is late afternoon. There is a jowly woman hanging her wash across the alley with a trolling motion of rope. A bowlegged farmer unloads a crate of country chickens for the butcher. Two young mechanics in loose jumpsuits smoke cigarettes with oil-creased hands. Felicia opens the rear door of her vintage American car and slides across the backseat, gently tugging Ernesto with her. The windows are rolled down and a fly circles and drones above them. She pulls him toward her and it begins to rain, a hard afternoon rain that is rare in winter.

Four days later, before Ernesto can move his belongings from his mother's apartment to the house on Palmas Street, before Felicia's mother, children, and best friend, Herminia, can object to the suddenness of her marriage to Ernesto, before Felicia can heed the directives of the *santero*, whose advice she has not entirely forgotten, before she and her husband can celebrate their union with a clamorous party, Ernesto dies tragically in a grease fire at a seaside hotel.

Ernesto, her gentle Ernesto, had been a restaurant inspector, renowned for his refusal to take bribes (neither money nor pork loins could tempt him) and for his scrupulous campaign against mice feces. At his sparsely attended funeral, Felicia howls like a lonely she-wolf. "You killed him because he was honest!" she screams, tearing her hair. "He wouldn't tolerate a single dropping!"

Felicia relived their brief time together. Ernesto's pallid skin mottled with excitement, his tentative hands that quickly became assured under her encouragement, the way he laid his downy head between her breasts and slept contentedly, like a well-fed baby. Ernesto had been a virgin when Felicia coaxed him to the backseat of her car, and he displayed the profound gratitude of the unburdened. For three days they rocked in each other's arms, voracious and inseparable, speaking few words, but knowing all they needed to know.

After Ernesto died, Felicia learned from his mother that they'd been born minutes apart, on the same day, of the same year.

Felicia writes a letter of protest to El Líder, demanding a full investigation into her husband's death. When she doesn't hear back from him, she becomes certain, with the surety of the white light illuminating her brain, that El Líder is to blame. Yes, he must have ordered her husband's murder personally. Others, too, are involved. They watch her bleary-eyed from behind their square black glasses, signaling to each other with coughs and claps. It is making sense to her now. Of course, it is finally clear. That is why the light is so bright. They refract it through their glasses so she cannot see, so she cannot identify the guilty ones. All the while, they are spectators to her wretchedness.

Felicia knows that Graciela Moreira is one of their spies. That is why she returns to the beauty shop, time and time again, to have her ringlets seared. She, too, wears the glasses. She, too, loves the fire. Felicia will trap her into a confession. She waits until the moon is propitious, then calls Graciela on the telephone, inviting her to the beauty shop for a free permanent.

"It's a special promotion, a new curling gel," Felicia coaxes. "I want you to be my model."

When Graciela appears an hour later, Felicia is prepared for her. She mixes lye with her own menstrual blood into a caustic brown paste, then thickly coats Graciela's head. Over it, she fastens a clear plastic bag with six evenly spaced hairpins, and waits. Felicia imagines the mixture melting through Graciela's frail scalp, penetrating the roots and bones of her skull until it eats her vicious brain like acid. Graciela cries out and pulls on the cap, hardened now like a helmet, but Felicia clamps it in place with her fists.

"You lying bitch! You killed him, didn't you?" Felicia shouts and knocks Graciela's glasses from her face.

That is the last thing Felicia remembers for many months.

*   *   *

Felicia notices the outdated calendars first, each month taped neatly to the ceiling. She is lying on her back in a bed that's not her own, in a room she doesn't recognize.

In the center of the ceiling, affixed with yellowed tape, is January 1959, the first month of the revolution. The glossy pages of succeeding months blossom around it: landscapes of fluted mountains for 1964; a curious collection of Irish setters and pugs in 1969; twelve varieties of jasmine for each month of 1973. The pages rustle slightly in the breeze. Felicia raises her head from the pillow. Three swivel-neck fans scan her with air. The sun glares through the paper window shades. Suddenly, the room vibrates with a deafening rattle and the Dopplerized screeches of children. A jingling music starts up and the air around her surges with the ricocheting voices of vendors hawking toasted corn and toy rockets.

It's as if Felicia's senses were clicking on one by one. First sight, then sound, then sight again.

She flaps open a shade and blinks unbelievingly at the carnival below her. The whirl of colors is unbearable, a jagged, unsettling choreography. It is summer and hot and well past noon, that

much she can tell. A teenage boy in a baseball cap grins up at
her nervously, and Felicia realizes she is standing naked in the
window. She drops to her knees, wraps herself with a bed sheet,
and lowers the shade.

A man's work clothes, stiff with dirt, hang oddly ballooned
in the closet. There are two sets of barbells, a burlap sack of
sand, a jump rope with red wooden handles, and a pear-shaped
leather punching bag nailed to the closet ceiling. In the corner,
a neat stack of American magazines features page after page of
luridly sculpted men in contorted poses. In one centerfold, someone named Jack La Lanne tows a rowboat with a rope held between his teeth. The words in the caption look insect bristly.
Felicia cannot understand them.

There's a straw shoulder bag on a hanger, and Felicia digs
with her broken fingernails for clues. She finds eleven encrusted
centavos, a rusted tube of orange lipstick, and, through a tear in
the checkered lining, a soiled prayer card for La Virgen de la
Caridad del Cobre. Nothing to tell her who she is, or where she
is from.

Felicia pulls on the navy trousers. They fit her snugly about
the hips, although the hems come up to her shins. The shirt
billows over her breasts. She tries on a pair of rubber flip-flops
that are just the right size. Felicia decides to fry an egg on a hot
plate in the kitchenette. She eats only the yolk, dabbing it with
a piece of stale bread she finds in the cupboard. Then she peels
a tangerine. There's a gold band on her right ring finger. It's
familiar to her. The whole place, in fact, is familiar, but she can't
say how. She is not afraid, though. It's as if her body had in-
habited this space for a time and pronounced it safe for her mind.

Felicia opens the room's only door and follows the hallway
to a bathroom on the other end. She looks tanned and rested in
the mirror, almost pretty. This reassures her. She combs her hair,
spots a lone gray strand and plucks it with a flourish.

Outside, the air is thick and humid and crowded with noise.

Are people watching her? It's hard for her to tell. She smooths her trousers with both hands and continues walking purposefully, to where she doesn't know.

"Excuse me, please, but where are we?" she asks a pudgy girl.

"*Cienfuegos, Señora.*"

"And what day is it?"

"July 26, 1978," she recites, as if Felicia were a teacher testing her history. "Is that your name?" she asks shyly, pointing to Felicia's left shoulder, where "Otto" is stitched in plain lettering. But Felicia does not answer.

There are many men in navy work clothes like hers. They wave and blow mock kisses from their candy stands and ticket booths and from the bumper-car rink. They all know her name. Felicia smiles wanly, waving back. Toward the far end of the amusement park, the roller coaster hovers above the other less-rhythmic rides. Rattle, rattle, rattle, swoosh. Rattle, rattle, rattle, swoosh.

"Come here, *mi reina,* come here!" a broad-chested man calls to her from behind a toolshed. He has a squeaky, inefficient voice that swallows syllables whole.

Felicia moves toward him, toward his tidy, ursine face. An ellipse of curly black hair is visible between the upper buttons of his shirt.

"You couldn't wait to come out, eh?" He laughs, patting her all over with hands solid and undefined as paws. His hair is frizzy, a woolly frame for his stubble-darkened cheeks. Felicia realizes with a start that he is carpeted with damp fur. She imagines him surviving freezing temperatures without so much as a sweater.

"I meant what I said last night," he says, lowering his voice. "We're going to Minnesota. It's the coldest state in the U.S. We'll open an ice-skating rink. I'll sleep naked on the ice. My own ice!"

He pulls her so close she can feel his hot breath on her throat.

"I spoke with Fernando today and he said he could get us a

boat to share with another family Sunday after next. We'll leave at night from the north coast. It's only ninety miles to Key West. He says they treat Cubans like kings there."

"Where are my clothes?" Felicia interrupts him sharply. She notices the stitching on his sweat-stained uniform, the gold band on his finger that matches hers.

"At the laundry, *mi reina*. Remember you asked me to take everything there? It'll be ready this afternoon. Don't worry, I'll bring them back to you."

During the following week, Felicia begins to assemble bits and pieces of her past. They stack up in her mind, soggily, arbitrarily, and she sorts through them like cherished belongings after a flood. She charts sequences and events with colored pencils, shuffling her diagrams until they start to make sense, a possible narrative. But the people remain faceless, nameless.

One evening right after dinner, as Otto is making love to her, her son's face appears in a vision on the ceiling, superimposed on the most recent calendar month.

"When are you coming home, Mami? When are you coming home?" Ivanito begs her in a wavering voice.

Felicia remembers her son's gangly body, his first stilted dancing steps, and begins to cry. Otto, mistaking his wife's sobs for pleasure, pushes his muscled hips against hers and shudders with relief.

Later that night, after the amusement park closes, Felicia urges her husband toward the roller coaster.

Otto Cruz thinks his wife is crazy and beautiful and mysterious and he will do just about anything she asks. He can't believe his luck in finding her. She was wandering by herself behind the spare-parts warehouse last winter. An angel. Heaven-sent. And he'd only gone to get replacement bolts for the Ferris wheel.

"I'm here," she said simply. Then she shook her dark wavy

hair and began unbuttoning her blouse. Her breasts shone like moon-polished marble. Otto's blood pumped so hard he thought he'd explode.

Otto knew he would never recover from his love for her and married Felicia the next morning. She stared at him innocently whenever he asked her where she came from, or where her family lived. "You're my family now," she'd say. "And I've come for you."

Thinking about the night he met Felicia makes Otto hard again. He turns on the switch for the roller coaster and pushes the first car, painted with laughing clowns, along the well-worn grooves. The platform is high above the ground and the electric generator trills and crackles beneath the winding tracks.

The cars lurch forward and Otto jumps in next to his wife. Her skin is smooth and white against her hair. He slides his hands beneath her gauzy skirt and rubs her warm thighs. The car climbs higher and higher, groaning up the rickety wooden tracks. Otto stands, unzips his pants with a fumbling hand, and pushes himself toward Felicia's lips, toward her miraculous tongue. The car stops for a split second at the peak of the first, the steepest crest. The sky is black, a cloudless blue-black. Below them, the roller coaster is a jumble of angles.

Felicia closes her eyes as the car begins to fall. When she opens them, her husband is gone.

(1978)

The day after Felicia burns Graciela Moreira's scalp with lye, Celia's son returns from Czechoslovakia. Javier arrives before dawn in an unraveling tweed suit, his face sunken to flat angles, and collapses on his mother's back porch.

Celia falls on her son like a lover, kissing his face and his eyes and his broken-knuckled hands. His coarse graying hair is matted with salt air and there's a lump the size of a baseball on the back of his neck. He cries deep soundless cries that make his thin body shiver like leaves in the wind. Celia half drags her son to her bed, the bed in which he was conceived, and for three days he sleeps wrapped in blankets and his father's frayed pajamas. Celia pieces together his story from the torments he relives in delirium, between fevers and chills and a painful catarrh.

This is what Celia learns: that her son returned home from the university to find a note on the kitchen table, that the envelope was a buttery yellow and the handwriting tall, loopy, and confident, that his two pairs of trousers hung pressed with sharp creases in the closet, that his wife had made love to him the night before so he wouldn't get suspicious, that she'd left him for the visiting mathematics professor from Minsk, that the professor was a spindly crane of a man with a shaved head and goatee who liked to impersonate Lenin, that Javier's daughter, his beloved daughter, to whom Spanish was the language of lullabies, had left with her mother for good.

Celia ponders the lump on her son's neck and the curious scar on his back, a pulpy line just below his left shoulder blade. She finds $1,040 worth of U.S. twenty-dollar bills divided evenly among Javier's four pockets, and a receipt for nine cuff links.

In the following weeks, Celia boils mild chicken broths for her son, feeding him one spoonful at a time. He eats instinctively, without comprehension, and she reads him poetry from the clutter of books on her dresser, hoping to console him.

> *Me he perdido muchas veces por el mar*
> *con el oído lleno de flores recién cortadas,*
> *con la lengua llena de amor y de agonía.*

Muchas veces me he perdido por el mar,
como me pierdo en el corazón de algunos niños.

Could her son, Celia wonders, have inherited her habit of ru-
inous passion? Or is passion indiscriminate, incubating haphazardly like a cancer?

Celia hopes that the sea, with its sustaining rhythms and
breezes from distant lands, will ease her son's heart as it once
did hers. Late at night, she rocks on her wicker swing as Javier
sleeps, and wonders why it is so difficult to be happy.

Of her three children, Celia sympathizes most with her son.
Javier's affliction, at least, has a name, even if it has no certain
cure. Celia understands his suffering all too well. Perhaps that
is why she is restless in its presence.

She understands, too, how Javier's anguish attracts the eli-
gible women of Santa Teresa del Mar, who bring him casseroles
covered with starched cloths and look into his night-sky eyes,
imagining themselves as his bright constellations. Even the married women drop by to inquire about Javier's health, to hold his
hands, warm as blood, and comfort him, when all the time they
pray, "Oh to be loved by this beautiful, sad boy!"

Celia remembers how her own eyes were once like her
son's—hollow sockets that attracted despair like a magnet. But
in her case, neighbors had kept their distance, believing she was
destined for an early death and anyone she touched would be
forced to accompany her. They were afraid of her disease as if
it were fatal, like tuberculosis, but worse, much worse.

What they feared even more, Celia realized later, was that
passion might spare them entirely, that they'd die convention-
ally, smug and purposeless, having never savored its blackness.

After two months in his mother's bed, Javier emerges from Celia's room. He dusts off the bottle of rum in the dining-room

cabinet, rinses a glass, chips ice from the freezer, and pours himself a long drink. Then he leans forward in the dining-room chair as if expecting electricity to shoot through it, and finishes the bottle in one sitting.

The next day he dresses in his mended tweed suit, takes a bill from his stash of American money, and buys a bottle of rum from a black-market dealer on the outskirts of town. He visits the dealer frequently, despite the rising prices, and buys one bottle after another after another. Javier can afford to be a drunk, Celia overhears her neighbors gossiping. The price of a liter of rum keeps most of them, with their monthly coupons and meager earnings, stone-cold sober.

As her son's condition deteriorates, Celia reluctantly cuts back on her revolutionary activities. She decides one last case before she resigns as a judge for the People's Court. Simón Córdoba, a boy of fifteen, has written a number of short stories considered to be antirevolutionary. His characters escape from Cuba on rafts of sticks and tires, refuse to harvest grapefruit, dream of singing in a rock and roll band in California. One of Simón's aunts found the stories stuffed under a sofa cushion and informed the neighborhood committee.

Celia suggests to the boy that he put down his pen for six months and work as an apprentice with the Escambray Theater, which educates peasants in the countryside. "I don't want to discourage your creativity, Simón," Celia tells the boy gently. "I just want to reorient it toward the revolution." After all, she thinks, artists have a vital role to play, no? Perhaps later, when the system has matured, more liberal policies may be permitted.

Celia's life resumes a stale, familiar air. She no longer volunteers for the microbrigades, and only guards her stretch of shore one night per month. The rest of the time, she tends to Javier's needs. She hadn't expected her son's illness to take this turn, and she feels helpless and angry, like the times Jorge had bullied Javier as a child. In fact, Javier is a small boy again. Celia helps dress him and combs his hair, reminds him to brush his teeth, and ties his shoelaces. She tucks him into her bed at night, absently stroking his brow. But when she holds her son's face in her hands, Celia sees only an opaque resentment. Is it his, she wonders, or her own?

Despite her care, Javier's skin turns sallow and thins until it looks as if she could strip it away in papery sheets. His knuckles heal poorly and he is clumsy with everything but his tumbler of rum. Since Javier returned home, Celia has hardly thought of Felicia, who has been missing since winter, or of the twins or of Ivanito, away at boarding school, or of the faraway Pilar. Something tells Celia that if she can't save her son she won't be able to save herself, or Felicia, or anyone she loves.

With the help of some microbrigade friends in the capital, Celia tracks down the *santera* from east Havana who had diagnosed her in 1934, when she was dying of love for the Spaniard.

"I knew it was you," the *santera* says, clapping her hands with brittle twig fingers when she finds Celia on her doorstep. Her face is black and puckered and oily now and seems to breathe all at once like an undersea creature. But when she smiles, her skin pulls back like a curtain, stretching her features until they are as lineless as a young woman's.

She places her speckled hands over Celia's heart, and nods solemnly as if to say, "I am here, *hija*. Speak to me." She listens closely to Celia, and they decide to travel together to Santa Teresa del Mar.

The *santera* looks up at the brick-and-cement house, bleached by the sun and the ocean air, and positions herself under the pawpaw tree in the front yard. She prays every Catholic prayer she knows in quick, calm succession. Hail Marys, Our Fathers, the Apostles' Creed. Her body starts to sway, and her clasped hands rock beneath her chin until it seems she is all loose, swinging angles. And then, as Celia watches, the little *santera*'s moist eyes roll back in her dwarfish head until the whites gleam from two pinpricks, and she trembles once, twice, and slides against Celia in a heap on the sidewalk, smoking like a wet fire, sweet and musky, until nothing is left of her but her fringed cotton shawl.

Celia, not knowing what else to do, folds the *santera*'s shawl into her handbag, and enters her home.

She knows by the stillness of the house that Javier is already gone. He'd talked of going to the mountains, of planting coffee on the forested slopes. He said he'd descend to Santiago for carnival and dance to the fifes and the *melé*, to the snare and the *batá* drums, that he'd die (in sequins and feathers) at the head of a conga line in Céspedes Park.

Celia reaches up and feels a lump in her chest, compact as a walnut. A week later, the doctors remove her left breast. In its place they leave a pink, pulpy scar like the one she'd discovered on her son's back.

Celia's Letters: 1950–1955

February 11, 1950

Querido Gustavo,

Even on her deathbed, Berta Arango del Pino cursed me. Last month she got a chest cold that turned into a pneumonia, and before you know it she was dead. Jorge asked me to go with him to Palmas Street because his mother swore she wanted to make her peace with me. But when I arrived, she threw a decanter that shattered at my feet and stained my hem green with absinthe.

"You stole my husband!" she screamed at me, then she reached for Jorge, stretching her arms pathetically, her fingers moving like worms. "Come here, my lover. Come to my bed." Ofelia's mouth dropped wide as a shovel and then her mother turned to her and shrieked, "Whore! What are you looking at?" And with those words Doña Berta fell back on her pillows, her mouth twisted, her eyes bulging like a hanged man's, and died. Poor Jorge has been terribly shaken by all this.

Celia

April 11, 1951

Querido Gustavo,

Are you a good father? I ask you this because of Jorge. There is something harsh, something unyielding about him when it comes to our son. Javier never runs to greet his father like his sisters do because he knows the lessons, the admonishments will begin the minute his father sees him. If you can believe this, Jorge has been forcing our son to study accounting. "For the love of God!" I say. "He's only five years old!"

Even Felicia sticks up for her brother, but Jorge ignores us. He is plagued by dreams of that milk-truck accident years ago and fears we'll be left destitute unless Javier learns to manage the family's money. The splinters of glass embedded in Jorge's spine still cause him great discomfort, but this does not excuse his unreasonableness. I try to make it up to the boy after Jorge leaves, baking *natilla,* his favorite dessert, but Javier senses my weakness and is growing cold toward me, too.

Kiss your sons if you have them, Gustavo. Kiss them goodnight.

Yours,
Celia

March 11, 1952

Mi Gustavo,

That bastard Batista stole the country from us just when it seemed things could finally change. The U.S. wants him in the palace. How else could he have pulled this off? I fear for my son, learning to be a man from such men. You'd be proud of me, *mi amor.* Last month I campaigned for the Orthodox Party. Felicia helped me paste up fliers in the plaza, but people shouted at us and tore the papers in our faces.

Afterward, Felicia took me to her best friend Herminia's house. Her father, Salvador, is a *santería* priest, an unassuming, soft-spoken man, black as the blackest Africans. He surprised me by serving us tea and homemade cookies. I'm not sure what I expected, I'd heard so many frightful stories about him. When I spoke about fighting Batista, he said it was useless, that the scoundrel is under the protection of Changó, god of fire and lightning. Batista's destiny, Salvador told me, is set. He will escape Cuba with a fortune in his suitcase, and die of natural causes.

If what he says is true, there will be no justice for Batista. But for the rest of us, Gustavo, for the rest of us, there may be hope.

Love,
Celia

August 11, 1953

Querido Gustavo,

Yesterday, I took the bus to Havana to join the protesters in front of the palace. We marched for the release of the rebels who survived the attack on Moncada. Their leader is a young lawyer, like you were once, Gustavo, idealistic and self-assured. Jorge called last night from Baracoa, and when Lourdes told him where I'd gone, he became very upset. That girl is a stranger to me. When I approach her, she turns numb, as if she wanted to be dead in my presence. I see how different Lourdes is with her father, so alive and gay, and it hurts me, but I don't know what to do. She still punishes me for the early years.

My love,
Celia

May 11, 1954

Gustavo,

I'm very worried about Felicia. She's left high school and says she wants to work. She takes the bus to Havana every afternoon and doesn't come back until late at night. She tells me she's looking for a job. But there's only one job in the city for fifteen-year-old girls like her.

Felicia is spirited and unpredictable, and this frightens me. I've heard too many stories of young girls destroyed by what passes as tourism in this country. Cuba has become the joke of the Caribbean, a place where everything and everyone is for sale. How did we allow this to happen?

Tu Celia

October 11, 1954

Querido Gustavo,

Javier won the children's national science prize for a genetics experiment. His teachers tell me he's a genius. I'm very proud of him, but I'm not exactly sure for what. Lourdes takes out scientific texts for him from the college library and he locks himself in his room to read for days at a time. Lourdes takes out books for me, too. I'm reading *Madame Bovary* in French now, grievously, very grievously.

Yours always,
Celia

P.S. Felicia got a job selling stationery at El Encanto, where I used to work. All the society girls come and order their wedding invitations there. I don't know how long she'll last, though. Felicia has no patience for such frivolous girls.

April 11, 1955

Mi querido Gustavo,

There was a three-person band in the Parque Central today that played their ballads with such heart that many people lingered to hear them. The singer's voice sounded just like Beny Moré's in his finest years. One song made me cry, and I saw others crying, too, as they tossed their coins in the musicians' hat.

> *Mírame, miénteme, pégame, mátame si quieres*
> *Pero no me dejes. No, no me dejes, nunca jamás . . .*

And this in the park across from the Hotel Inglaterra! Forgive me, Gustavo. It is April, and I am melancholy, and twenty-one years have passed.

Yours always,
Celia

June 11, 1955

Gustavo,

The rebels have been released! Now the revolution is close enough to smell. We'll get rid of Batista the way we did that tyrant Machado. But this time, *mi amor,* we'll make it stick like rice to a pot!

Love,
Celia

A Matrix Light

(1977)

Lourdes Puente welcomes the purity, the hollowness of her
stomach. It's been a month since she stopped eating, and
already she's lost thirty-four pounds. She envisions the muscled
walls of her stomach shrinking, contracting, slickly clean from
the absence of food and the gallons of springwater she drinks.
She feels transparent, as if the hard lines of her hulking form
were disintegrating.

It is dawn, an autumn dawn, and Lourdes is walking. She is
walking mile after mile, pumping her arms furiously, her eyes
fixed determinedly before her. She is walking down Fulton
Street in her mauve velour jogging suit, past the shabby May's
department store with mannequins from another era, past shuttered shops and bus-stop benches draped with sleeping bums.
Lourdes turns and strides past Brooklyn's sooty town hall, past
the state supreme court, where the Son of Sam trial will take
place. Lourdes can't understand what happened with Son of
Sam, only that he exists and that he had a dog that commanded

him to kill. His victims were girls with dark flowing hair, young girls like Pilar. But, no matter what Lourdes said, Pilar refused to pin up her hair or hide it under a knitted cap as other girls did. No, Pilar let her hair swing long and loose, courting danger.

Pilar is away at art school in Rhode Island. She won scholarships to Vassar and Barnard, but instead she chose a school of hippies with no future, delicate men with women's lips and a dissembling in their eyes. The thought of her daughter in bed with these men drives Lourdes to despair, to utter repugnance.

Lourdes was a virgin when she married, and very proud of it. The hip-splitting pain, the blood on the conjugal bed were proof of her virtue. She would gladly have hung out her sheets for everyone to see.

Pilar is like her grandmother, disdainful of rules, of religion, of everything meaningful. Neither of them shows respect for anyone, least of all themselves. Pilar is irresponsible, self-centered, a bad seed. How could this have happened?

Lourdes marches down Montague Street, her elbows jutting behind her like pistons. The Greek diner is open and there's a stoop-shouldered man in the back booth eyeing his bacon and eggs. The yolks are too orange, Lourdes thinks. She imagines their sticky thickness coating the old man's throat. It sickens her.

"One coffee, black," she tells the uniformed waiter, then heads for the public telephone. Lourdes dials her daughter's number in Rhode Island. The phone rings four, five, six times before Pilar answers sleepily.

"I know someone is there with you," Lourdes rasps. "Don't lie to me."

"Mom, not again. Please."

"Tell me his name!" Lourdes squeezes the words out between her teeth. "Whore! Tell me his name!"

"What are you talking about? Mom, it's five in the morning. Just leave me alone, okay?"

"I called you last night and you weren't in."

"I was out."

"Out where? To your lover's bed?"

"Out for a pastrami sandwich."

"Liar! You never eat pastrami!"

"I'm hanging up now, Mom. Nice talking to you, too."

Lourdes slaps two quarters on the counter and leaves the coffee steaming in its thick white mug. She hasn't had relations with Rufino since her father died. It's as if another woman had possessed her in those days, a whore, a life-craving whore who fed on her husband's nauseating clots of yellowish milk.

Lourdes lifts one arm, then the other to her face, sniffing them suspiciously for the scent of grease and toast.

The smell of food repels her. She can't even look at it without her mouth filling with the acrid saliva that precedes vomiting. These days, it's nearly impossible to endure even her own bakeries—the wormy curves of the buttery croissants, the gluey honey buns with fat pecans trapped like roaches in the cinnamon crevices.

Lourdes did not plan to stop eating. It just happened, like the time she gained 118 pounds in the days her father was dying. This time, though, Lourdes longs for a profound emptiness, to be clean and hollow as a flute.

She advances toward the Brooklyn Promenade. The abandoned shipyards display their corrugated roofs like infected scars. The East River, meeting the Hudson near its mouth, is quiet and motionless as the mist. On the other side of the river, the towers of Wall Street reach arrogantly toward the sky. Lourdes paces the quarter-mile-long esplanade eight times. A jogger runs by with a tawny Great Dane at his side. Cars hum on the highway below her, headed for Queens.

There is a moment of each dawn that appears disguised as dusk, Lourdes decides, and for that brief moment the day neither begins nor ends.

*   *   *

Lourdes has lost eighty-two pounds. She is drinking liquid pro-
tein now, a bluish fluid that comes in tubes like astronaut food.
It tastes of chemicals. Lourdes rides her new Sears exercise bicycle until sparks fly from the wheels. She tacks up a full-color
road map of the United States in her bedroom and charts her
mileage daily with a green felt marker. Her goal is to ride to San
Francisco by Thanksgiving, when her daughter will return home
from school. Lourdes pedals and sweats, pedals and sweats until
she pictures rivulets of fat, like the yellow liquid that pours from
roasting chickens and turkeys, oozing from her pores as she
rides through Nebraska.

Jorge del Pino is concerned about his daughter, but Lourdes insists that nothing is wrong. Her father visits her regularly at
twilight, on her evening walks home from the bakery, and whispers to her through the oak and maple trees. His words flutter
at her neck like a baby's lacy breath.

They discuss many topics: the worsening crime on New York
City's streets; the demise of the Mets since their glory seasons
in '69 and '73; day-to-day matters of the bakery. It was her father
who had advised Lourdes to open a second pastry shop.

"Put your name on the sign, too, *hija*, so they know what we
Cubans are up to, that we're not all Puerto Ricans," Jorge del
Pino had insisted.

Lourdes ordered custom-made signs for her bakeries in red,
white, and blue with her name printed at the bottom right-hand
corner: LOURDES PUENTE, PROPRIETOR. She particularly liked the
sound of the last word, the way the "r"'s rolled in her mouth,
the explosion of "p"'s. Lourdes felt a spiritual link to American
moguls, to the immortality of men like Irénée du Pont, whose
Varadero Beach mansion on the north coast of Cuba she had

once visited. She envisioned a chain of Yankee Doodle bakeries stretching across America to St. Louis, Dallas, Los Angeles, her apple pies and cupcakes on main streets and in suburban shopping malls everywhere.

Each store would bear her name, her legacy: LOURDES PUENTE, PROPRIETOR.

Above all, Lourdes and her father continue to denounce the Communist threat to America. Every day they grow more convinced that the dearth of bad news about Cuba is a conspiracy by the leftist media to keep international support for El Líder strong. Why can't the Americans see the Communists in their own backyards, in their universities, bending the malleable minds of the young? The Democrats are to blame, the Democrats and those lying, two-timing Kennedys. What America needs, Lourdes and her father agree, is another Joe McCarthy to set things right again. *He* would never have abandoned them at the Bay of Pigs.

"Why don't you go down and report on Cuba's prisons?" Lourdes taunted the journalists who questioned her last year about the opening-day fracas at the second Yankee Doodle Bakery. "Why are you wasting your time with me?"

Lourdes hadn't approved of Pilar's painting, not at all, but she wouldn't tolerate people telling her what to do on her own property.

"That's how it began in Cuba," Lourdes's father whispered hoarsely through the trees, counseling her. "You must stop the cancer at your front door."

After Pilar left for college, Lourdes stared at her daughter's painting every night before she walked home. If Pilar hadn't put in the safety pin and the bugs in the air, the painting would be almost pretty. Those bugs ruined the background. Without the bugs, the background was a nice blue, a respectable shimmering blue.

Why did Pilar always have to go too far? Lourdes is convinced it is something pathological, something her daughter inherited from her Abuela Celia.

*   *   *

It is Thanksgiving Day. Lourdes has lost 118 pounds. Her metamorphosis is complete. She will eat today for the first time in months. The aroma of food is appealing again, but Lourdes is afraid of its temptations, of straying too far from the blue liquid, from the pitchers of cleansing ice water. There is a purity within her, a careful enzymatic balance she does not wish to disturb.

The day before yesterday, Lourdes bought a red-and-black size-six Chanel suit with gold coin buttons. "You're so lucky you can wear anything!" the salesgirl at Lord & Taylor's had complimented her as she swiveled this way and that before the dressing-room mirror. Lourdes spent a week's profits on the suit. It was worth it, though, to see Pilar's astonishment at her weight loss.

"My God!" Pilar exclaims as she walks through the front door of the warehouse and stares at the fraction of her mother before her. "How did you do it?"

Lourdes beams.

"She starved herself," Rufino interjects irritably. He's wearing a toque like a fat white carnation on his head. Lourdes hushes him with a wave of her newly slender hand.

"I just made up my mind to do it. Willpower. Willpower goes a long way toward getting what you want, Pilar."

Her daughter's face registers suspicion, as if Lourdes is going to launch into a lecture. But Lourdes has nothing of the sort in mind. She ushers her daughter to the table, which is set with hand-painted china and an autumn-leaves centerpiece.

"Your father has been learning to cook since I stopped eating," Lourdes says. "He's been in the kitchen since Sunday, preparing everything."

"Are you going to eat today, Mom?"

"Just a few bites. The doctor says I have to start weaning myself back on food. But if it were up to me, I'd never eat again. I feel pure, absolutely clean. And I have more energy than ever before."

Lourdes begins reminiscing about the instant foods she made when she first came to New York. The mashed potatoes she whipped up from water and ashen powder, the chicken legs she shook in bags of spicy bread crumbs then baked at 350 degrees, the frozen carrots she boiled and served with imitation butter. But soon the potatoes and the chicken and the carrots had all tasted the same to her, blanched and waxen and gray.

"I think migration scrambles the appetite," Pilar says, helping herself to a candied yam. "I may move back to Cuba someday and decide to eat nothing but codfish and chocolate."

Lourdes stares hard at her daughter. She wants to say that nobody but a degenerate would want to move back to that island-prison. But she doesn't. It's a holiday and everyone is supposed to be happy. Instead, Lourdes turns her attention to a sliver of turkey on her plate. She tastes a small chunk. It's juicy and salty and goes straight to her veins. She decides to have another piece.

In a moment her mouth is moving feverishly, like a terrible furnace. She stokes it with more hunks of turkey and whole candied yams. Lourdes helps herself to a mound of creamed spinach, dabbing it with a quickly diminishing loaf of sourdough. The leek-and-mustard pie, with its hint of chives, is next.

"*Mi cielo,* you really outdid yourself!" Lourdes praises her husband between mouthfuls.

For dessert, there's a rhubarb-apple betty topped with cinnamon crème anglaise. Lourdes devours every last morsel.

*

The next morning, Lourdes scours the newspapers for calamities as she dunks sticky buns into her *café con leche*. A twin-engine plane crashed in the umber folds of the Adirondacks. An earthquake in rural China buried thousands in their homes. In the Bronx, a fire consumed a straight-A student and her baby brother, asleep in his crib. There's a photograph of their mother on the front page, ravaged by loss. She'd only gone to the corner store for a pack of cigarettes.

Lourdes grieves for these victims as if they were beloved relatives. Each calamity makes Lourdes feel her own sorrow, keeps her own pain fresh.

Pilar suggests they go to an exhibit at the Frick Museum, so Lourdes wriggles into her Chanel suit, the gold-coin buttons already straining across her middle, and they take the subway to Manhattan. On Fifth Avenue, Lourdes stops to buy hot dogs (with mustard, relish, sauerkraut, fried onions, and ketchup), two chocolate cream sodas, a potato knish, lamb shish kebabs with more onions, a soft pretzel, and a cup of San Marino cherry ice. Lourdes eats, eats, eats, like a Hindu goddess with eight arms, eats, eats, eats, as if famine were imminent.

Inside the museum, the paintings all look alike to Lourdes, smeared and dull. Her daughter guides her to an indoor courtyard, suffused with winter light. They settle on a concrete bench by the reflecting pool. Lourdes is mesmerized by the greenish water, by the sad, sputtering fountain, and a wound inside her reopens. She remembers what the doctors in Cuba had told her. That the baby inside her had died. That they'd have to inject her with a saline solution to expel her baby's remains. That she would have no more children.

Lourdes sees the face of her unborn child, pale and blank as an egg, buoyed by the fountain waters. Her child calls to her, waves a bare little branch in greeting. Lourdes fills her heart to bursting with the sight of him. She reaches out and calls his name, but he disappears before she can rescue him.

Pilar
(1978)

My mother told me that Abuela Celia was an atheist before I even understood what the word meant. I liked the sound of it, the derision with which my mother pronounced it, and knew immediately it was what I wanted to become. I don't know exactly when I stopped believing in God. It wasn't as deliberate as deciding, at age six, to become an atheist, but more like an imperceptible sloughing of layers. One day I noticed there was no more skin to absently peel, just air where there'd been artifice.

A few weeks ago, I found photographs of Abuela Celia in my mother's hosiery drawer. There was a picture of Abuela in 1931, standing under a tree in her T-strap shoes and wearing a flouncy dress with a polka-dotted bow and puffed sleeves. Abuela Celia's fingers were tapered and delicate and rested on her hips. Her hair was parted on the right and came down to her shoulders, accentuating the mole by her lips. There was a tension at the corners of her mouth that could have veered toward sadness or joy. Her eyes told of experience she did not yet possess.

There were other photographs. Abuela Celia in Soroa with an orchid in her hair. In a cream linen suit descending from a train. At the beach with my mother and my aunt. Tía Felicia is in Abuela's arms, a plump, pink-lozenge baby. My mother, unsmiling, skinny and dark from the sun, stands a distance away.

I have a trick to tell someone's public face from their private one. If the person is left-handed, like Abuela Celia, the right side of her face betrays her true feelings. I placed a finger over the left side of my grandmother's face, and in photograph after photograph I saw the truth.

I feel much more connected to Abuela Celia than to Mom, even though I haven't seen my grandmother in seventeen years. We don't speak at night anymore, but she's left me her legacy nonetheless—a love for the sea and the smoothness of pearls, an appreciation of music and words, sympathy for the underdog, and a disregard for boundaries. Even in silence, she gives me the confidence to do what I believe is right, to trust my own perceptions.

This is a constant struggle around my mother, who systematically rewrites history to suit her views of the world. This reshaping of events happens in a dozen ways every day, contesting reality. It's not a matter of premeditated deception. Mom truly believes that her version of events is correct, down to details that I know, for a fact, are wrong. To this day, my mother insists that I ran away from her at the Miami airport after we first left Cuba. But it was *she* who turned and ran when she thought she heard my father's voice. I wandered around lost until a pilot took me to his airline's office and gave me a lollipop.

It's not just our personal history that gets mangled. Mom filters other people's lives through her distorting lens. Maybe it's that wandering eye of hers. It makes her see only what she wants to see instead of what's really there. Like Mr. Paresi, a pimpy Brooklyn lawyer who my mother claims is the number-one criminal defense attorney in New York, complete with an impressive roster of Mafia clients. And this because he comes to her shop every morning and buys two chocolate-frosted donuts for his breakfast.

Mom's embellishments and half-truths usually equip her to tell a good story, though. And her English, her immigrant English, has a touch of otherness that makes it unintentionally precise. Maybe in the end the facts are not as important as the underlying truth she wants to convey. Telling her own truth is *the* truth to her, even if it's at the expense of chipping away our past.

I suppose I'm guilty in my own way of a creative transformation or two. Like my painting of the Statue of Liberty that caused such a commotion at the Yankee Doodle Bakery. It's funny but last year the Sex Pistols ended up doing the same thing with a photograph of Queen Elizabeth on the cover of their *God Save the Queen* single. They put a safety pin through the Queen's nose and the entire country was up in arms. Anarchy in the U.K., I love it.

Mom is fomenting her own brand of anarchy closer to home. Her Yankee Doodle bakeries have become gathering places for these shady Cuban extremists who come all the way from New Jersey and the Bronx to talk their dinosaur politics and drink her killer espressos. Last month they started a cablegram campaign against El Líder. They set up a toll-free hot line so that Cuban exiles could call in and choose from three scathing messages to send directly to the National Palace, demanding El Líder's resignation.

I heard one of my mother's cohorts boasting how last year he'd called in a bomb threat to the Metropolitan Opera House, where Alicia Alonso, the prima ballerina of the National Ballet of Cuba and a supporter of El Líder, was scheduled to dance. "I delayed *Giselle* for seventy-five minutes!" he bragged. If I'd known about it then, I would have sicked the FBI on him.

Just last week, the lot of them were celebrating—with cigars and sparkling cider—the murder of a journalist in Miami who advocated reestablishing ties with Cuba. Those creeps passed around the Spanish newspaper and clapped each other on the back, as if they themselves had struck a big blow against the forces of evil. The front-page photograph showed the reporter's

arm dangling from a poinciana tree on Key Biscayne after the
bomb in his car had exploded.

I wonder how Mom could be Abuela Celia's daughter. And
what I'm doing as my mother's daughter. Something got hor-
ribly scrambled along the way.

*   *   *

Outside, the afternoon light is a dark, moist violet. It's a matrix
light, a recombinant light that disintegrates hard lines and
planes, rearranging objects to their essences. Usually I hate it
when artists get too infatuated with light, but this is special. It's
the light I love to paint in.

Last semester when I was studying in Italy, I found the same
light in Venice at carnival. It surrounded an impossibly tall person cloaked in black and wearing a white eyeless mask. The
person dipped and circled like a bat in a square behind the Piazza
San Marco. I was afraid to stay, but I was more afraid to go.
Finally the light chased him down an alleyway and I was released from his spell.

The light was also in Palermo at dusk on Holy Thursday.
Slaughtered lambs, skinned and transparent as baby flesh, hung
evenly on rusted hooks. They were beautiful, and I longed to
stretch out next to them and display myself in the light. When
I returned to Florence, I began to model nude at my art school,
something I'd vowed I'd never do. As I posed, I thought of the
transparent lambs in the violet light.

Sometimes I ask myself if my adventures, such as they are,
equal experience. I think of Flaubert, who spent most of his adult
life in the same French village, or Emily Dickinson, whose
poems echoed the cadence of the local church bells. I wonder if
the farthest distance I have to travel isn't inside my own head.
But then I think of Gauguin or D. H. Lawrence or Ernest Hem-

ingway, who, incidentally, used to go fishing with my Abuelo Guillermo in Cuba, and I become convinced that you have to live in the world to say anything meaningful about it.

Everything up until this very minute, as I sit at my desk on the second floor of Barnard library, looking out over a rectangle of dead grass, and beyond that, to the cars racing down Broadway, feels like a preparation for something. For what, I don't know. I'm still waiting for my life to begin.

My boyfriend, Rubén Florín, is Peruvian and his family, like mine, is divided over politics. His aunts and uncles, parents and grandparents align themselves against one another. Rubén moved to New York with his parents when he was two, like me. The difference is that at least he can go back to Lima anytime he wants. This makes me ache for the same possibility.

Rubén has a recurring dream of me. I'm in aqua robes threaded with gold, stepping through trapezoidal doors into the sun. Nothing happens to me, he says, but I look unhappy, very unhappy. "Keep sleeping," I tell him, but his dream never goes any further.

I met Rubén my first day at Barnard. I'd transferred here after a semester of art school in Rhode Island and another semester in Florence. I couldn't face going back to Providence after Italy, so I decided to give mainstream academia a try. Art school was getting to be a drag anyway, cutthroat and backbiting, with everyone seeking praise from the instructors. I didn't want to end up being dependent on people I didn't respect much, so here I am majoring in anthropology instead.

Rubén wants to join the Foreign Service after he graduates from Columbia and bounce around the Third World. I like being with him. We don't show off like other couples on campus, always pawing at each other or exchanging hungry looks. We take our deep satisfactions for granted. I like it in the early evenings

best, when I'm just tired enough from the day to appreciate
Rubén's slow mouth and hands. We speak in Spanish when we
make love. English seems an impossible language for intimacy.

Thinking about Rubén this way makes me pack my books,
run a brush through my hair, and cross Broadway. It's rush hour
and people are pouring out of the 116th Street subway station
as if it's on fire. Someone's playing a guitar on the steps of Low
Library, a folk song, but nobody's listening. People here react
negatively to any overt displays of soulfulness. Besides, he could
be a Moonie. There're a lot of them on campus these days.

I want to surprise Rubén, get to his room before he returns
from his late class, but instead I find him fucking the Dutch exchange student he introduced me to last week. She's a pale, big-
bosomed woman with enormous pink nipples. I keep staring at
her nipples as Rubén talks. She doesn't even pull the sheet over
herself. I get the feeling she's displaying herself, giving me a
chance to size up the competition. She feels that certain of her
charms. I don't understand a word Rubén says. I must be standing there a long time because he runs out of things to say and
the woman starts coughing delicately into her hand. Her breasts
wobble as she coughs, like sunflowers in a breeze.

"Maybe you should leave," Rubén tells me weakly in Spanish.
And I do.

An hour later, I'm on my sixth cup of coffee at the Hungarian
pastry shop on Amsterdam Avenue. I'm browsing through the
Village Voice personals, the real kinky ones like: "Bisexual Am-
azon wanted for straight professional couple. Serious inquiries
only." Reading the ads is hardly getting my mind off what
Rubén and that milkmaid were doing back at his room. I heard
a psychologist on a radio talk show once describe the four stages
of grief. I forget whether revenge is a stage or not. I'm probably
out of sequence anyway.

A misplaced ad catches my attention. Under WOMEN SEEKING
WOMEN, I see "Acoustic bass for sale. Student desperate for cash.

$300 obo. Mick. 674–9981." I think about how my old boyfriend Max used to tell me I'd make a good bass player, and things start getting clearer. I call the number. It's on Bleecker Street and I make it down there in a half hour flat.

A scrawny guy wearing a flannel shirt over his sweatpants counts my cash and pushes the bass at me. It's a piece of furniture, a fucking *huge* piece of furniture. It's like I'm buying my own heirloom. I struggle uptown with it in a kind of trance.

My whole body is aching by the time I get back to my room, but I don't waste any time. I flip straight to the album I want— *The Velvet Underground & Nico.* I peel off Andy Warhol's banana sticker and put on the good, thumping, straight-ahead rock and roll. The thick strings vibrate through my fingers, up my arms, down my chest. I don't know what I'm doing but I start thumping that old spruce dresser of an instrument for all it's worth, thumping and thumping, until I feel my life begin.

God's Will

Herminia Delgado
(1980)

I met Felicia on the beach when we were both six years old. She was filling a pail with cowries and bleeding tooth. Felicia used to collect seashells, then rearrange them on the beach before going home because her mother wouldn't allow them in their house. Felicia designed great circles of overlapping shells on the sand, as if someone on the moon, or farther still, might read their significance. I told her that at my house we had many shells, that they told the future and were the special favorites of Yemayá, goddess of the seas. Felicia listened closely, then handed me her pail.

"Will you save me?" she asked me. Her eyes were wide and curious.

"Sure," I answered. How could I realize then what my promise would entail?

Felicia's parents were afraid of my father. He was a *babalawo,* a high priest of *santería,* and greeted the sun each morning with outstretched arms. His godchildren came from many miles on his saint's day, and brought him kola nuts and black hens.

The people in Santa Teresa del Mar told evil lies about my father. They said he used to rip the heads off goats with his teeth and fillet blue-eyed babies before dawn. I got into fights at school. The other children shunned me and called me *bruja*. They made fun of my hair, oiled and plaited in neat rows, and of my skin, black as my father's. But Felicia defended me. I'll always be grateful to her for that.

Felicia was forbidden to visit my house but she did anyway. Once she saw my father use the *obi*, the divining coconut, to answer the questions of a godchild who had come to consult him. I remember the pattern of rinds fell in *ellife*, two white sides and two brown, a definite yes. The godchild left very pleased, and Felicia's fascination with coconuts began that day.

I never doubted Felicia's love. Or her loyalty. When my oldest son died in Angola, Felicia didn't leave my side for a month. She cooked me *carne asada* and read me the collected plays of Molière, which she borrowed from her mother. Felicia arranged for Joaquín's remains to be brought home for a decent burial, and then she stayed with me until I could laugh again at silly things.

Felicia could be very stubborn, too, but she had a gift that offset her stubbornness, a gift I admired very much. I guess you could say she adapted to her grief with imagination. Felicia stayed on the fringe of life because it was free of everyday malice. It was more dignified there.

There is something else, something very important. Felicia is the only person I've known who didn't see color. There are white people who know how to act politely to blacks, but deep down you know they're uncomfortable. They're worse, more dangerous than those who speak their minds, because they don't know what they're capable of.

For many years in Cuba, nobody spoke of the problem between blacks and whites. It was considered too disagreeable to discuss. But my father spoke to me clearly so that I would understand what happened to his father and his uncles during the Little War of 1912, so that I would know how our men were hunted down day and night like animals, and finally hung by their genitals from the lampposts in Guáimaro. The war that killed my grandfather and great-uncles and thousands of other blacks is only a footnote in our history books. Why, then, should I trust anything I read? I trust only what I see, what I know with my heart, nothing more.

Things have gotten better under the revolution, that much I can say. In the old days, when voting time came, the politicians would tell us we were all the same, one happy family. Every day, though, it was another story. The whiter you were, the better off you were. Anybody could see that. There's more respect these days. I've been at the battery factory almost twenty years now, since right after the revolution, and I supervise forty-two women. It's not much, maybe, but it's better than mopping floors or taking care of another woman's children instead of my own.

One thing hasn't changed: the men are still in charge. Fixing that is going to take a lot longer than twenty years.

But let me begin again. After all, this story is about Felicia, not me.

Felicia returned to our religion with great eagerness after her disappearance in 1978. She showed up at my house one day, slim and tanned, as if she'd just returned from a vacation at a fancy foreign spa. "Take me to La Madrina," she told me, and I did. Then, during a holy trance, Felicia spoke of her days in a far-off town. She said she'd married a bearish man in an amusement park and that he'd planned to escape Cuba, to take a fishing boat north and go ice skating. I don't know if this part is true, but Felicia said that she'd pushed this man, her third husband, from the top of a roller coaster and watched him die on a bed of high-voltage wires. Felicia said his body turned to gray ash, and then the wind blew him north, just as he'd wished.

She never spoke of this again.

Within a week, Felicia had her old job back at the beauty shop. She worked hard to regain the confidence of her former customers, except, of course, for Graciela Moreira, who'd taken to wearing synthetic wigs imported from Hungary. I sent Felicia a few customers myself from the factory. Those girls *needed* manicures after assembling batteries all day long.

At night, Felicia attended our ceremonies. She didn't miss a single one. For her, they were a kind of poetry that connected her to larger worlds, worlds alive and infinite. Our rituals healed her, made her believe again. My father used to say that there are forces in the universe that can transform our lives if only we'd surrender ourselves. Felicia surrendered, and found her fulfillment.

Felicia's mother discouraged her devotion to the gods. Celia had only vague notions about spiritual possession and animal sacrifice, and suspected that our rites had caused her daughter's mysterious disappearance. Celia revered El Líder and wanted Felicia to give herself entirely to the revolution, believing that this alone would save her daughter. But Felicia would not be dissuaded from the *orishas*. She had a true vocation to the supernatural.

Before long, La Madrina initiated Felicia into the *elekes* and gave her the necklaces of the saints that would protect her from evil. They weren't easy to make. Since the revolution, it's been difficult to obtain the right beads. La Madrina told me she had to fashion Felicia's necklaces from the beaded curtains of a restaurant in Old Havana.

Many initiations followed, but I was not allowed to Felicia's last one, her *asiento*. This ritual has been done in secret since the first slaves worked the sugarcane fields on this island. But Felicia told me what she could.

Sixteen days before the *asiento,* Felicia went to live with La

Madrina, who had procured seven white dresses for her, seven sets of underwear and nightclothes, seven sets of bedding, seven towels, large and small, and other special items, all white.

Felicia changed every day to stay pure.

On the morning of her initiation, sixteen *santeras* tore Felicia's clothes to shreds until she stood naked, then they bathed her in river water, rubbing her with soap wrapped in vegetable fibers until her skin glowed. The women dressed Felicia in a fresh white gown and combed and braided her hair, treating her like a newborn child.

That night, after a purifying coconut shampoo, Felicia was guided to a windowless room, where she sat for many hours, alone on a stool. La Madrina slipped the sacred necklace of Obatalá around Felicia's neck. Felicia told me she grew sleepy, and felt as though she were drifting through the heavens, that she was a planet looking at herself from one of her moons.

After many more rituals and a final bath in the *omiero,* the *santeras* led Felicia to Obatalá's throne. The diviner of shells shaved her head as everyone chanted in the language of the Yoruba. They painted circles and dots on her head and cheeks—white for Obatalá, reds and yellows and blues for the other gods—and crowned her with the sacred stones. It was then Felicia lost consciousness, falling into an emptiness without history or future.

She learned later that she'd walked purposefully around the room, possessed by Obatalá. The *santeras* had made eight cuts on her tongue with a razor blade so that the god could speak, but Felicia could not divulge his words. When Obatalá finally left her body, she opened her eyes and emerged from the void.

Once more Felicia was led to the throne. The goats to be sacrificed were marched in one by one, arrayed in silks and gold braids. Felicia smeared their eyes, ears, and foreheads with the coconut and pepper she chewed before the *babalawo* slit their throats. She tasted the goats' blood and spit it toward the ceiling, then she sampled the blood of many more creatures.

Four hours later, the *babalawo,* drenched in sweat and count-less immolations, lowered his head near hers.

"Eroko ashé," he whispered. It is done, with the blessings of the gods.

When I visited Felicia the following day, she was dressed in her coronation gown, her crown, and all her necklaces. She sat on a throne surrounded by gardenias, her face serene as a goddess's. I believe to this day she'd finally found her peace.

But when Felicia returned to Palmas Street with her sacred stones and her tureen, her seashells and the implements of her saint, neither her mother nor her children were there to greet her. Felicia was crestfallen, but she was certain that the gods were testing her. She wanted to prove to the *orishas* that she was a true believer, serious and worthy of serving them, so she con-tinued her rituals.

Felicia did everything she was supposed to as a novice *san-tera.* She dressed only in white, and didn't wear makeup or cut her hair. She never touched the forbidden foods—coco-nuts, corn, or anything red—and covered the one mirror in her house with a sheet, as she was prohibited from seeing her own image.

When I came to visit her, we settled on the warping floor-boards, where Felicia ate her meals with a serving spoon. As she spoke, Felicia rolled the spoon between her palms and watched its clumsy, twirling shadow on the wall.

"Have you spoken with them?" she asked me, referring to her mother, her daughters, her son.

"Your mother says they're frightened, like the summer of co-conuts."

"But this is completely different. I have a clarity now. You can see the sun enters here." Felicia indicated the dusty shafts of light. "Did you tell her that even El Líder is initiated? That he's the son of Elleguá?"

I shook my head, saying nothing. Felicia covered her face with her hands. A rash erupted on her neck and cheeks. I noticed the imprint her fingers made on her forehead, the delicate chain of bloodless flesh.

Then Felicia spoke of our faith, of her final healing, and held my hands in hers.

"You've been more than a sister to me, Herminia. You saved me, like you promised on the beach."

That night, I dreamt of Felicia in her bathing suit with her pail of cowries and bleeding tooth.

"Will you save me?" she asked me.

"Sure," I answered, again and again.

I've seen other *santeras* during their first year. They are radiant. Their eyes are moist and clear, their skin is smoothed of wrinkles, and their nails grow strong. When you make a saint, the saint takes good care of you. But Felicia showed none of these blessings. Her eyes dried out like an old woman's and her fingers curled like claws until she could hardly pick up her spoon. Even her hair, which had been as black as a crow's, grew colorless in scruffy patches on her skull. Whenever she spoke, her lips blurred to a dull line in her face.

Over the next weeks, all of us from the *casa de santo* took turns visiting Felicia. We wrapped her wrists with beaded bracelets, gave her castor-oil enemas, packed hot cactus compresses on her brow. We boiled *yerba buena* teas and left yams and swatches of cotton on Obatalá's altar. But nothing seemed to help. Felicia's eyesight dimmed until she could perceive only shadows, and the right side of her head swelled with mushroomy lumps.

La Madrina was beside herself with worry. She performed sacrifices every day in Felicia's behalf. Some of us traveled with our offerings to the mountains, where Obatalá is said to live, and placed white flags around the house on Palmas Street to attract peace.

But each time La Madrina threw the shells, the omen was the same. *Ikú*. Death.

A group of *babalawos* tried a *panaldo*, an exorcism, and thought they had trapped an evil spirit in the rooster they buried in a knotted cloth. But Felicia continued to grow worse. The *babalawos* consulted the oracles with all their powers of divination. The *opelé*. The table of Ifá. Even the *ikin*, the sacred palm nuts. Still, the omen did not change.

"It is the will of the gods," they concluded. "It will be resolved by the spirits of the dead."

Just as the *babalawos* were about to leave, Felicia's mother entered the house on Palmas Street. She was wild-eyed, like a woman who gives birth to an unwanted child.

"Witch doctors! Murderers! Get out, all of you!" she cried, and swept the image of Obatalá off its altar.

We pulled back, afraid of the god's response.

Celia overturned the tureen with the sacred stones and crushed Felicia's seashells under the heels of her leather pumps. Suddenly, she removed her shoes and began stamping on the shells in her bare feet, slowly at first, then faster and faster in a mad flamenco, her arms thrown up in the air.

Then just as suddenly she stopped. She made no sound as she wept, as she bent to kiss Felicia's eyes, her forehead, her swollen, hairless skull. Celia lay with her torn, bleeding feet beside her daughter and held her, rocking and rocking her in the blue gypsy dusk until she died.

Ivanito

The night is pitch-black. I aim my radio at the farthest point in the sky and click it on. It pops and sputters like my mother's old car. I turn and turn the dial, half expecting to hear Mom singing in her deep-throated way, singing the sad words of her Beny Moré song.

After my mother's funeral, I found a package addressed to me on the front steps of Abuela Celia's house. Inside I found this radio wrapped in shredded newspapers. I think my father may have sent it to me, I don't know why. Maybe he understood how alone I felt. People who knew him say I look like him, skinny and gangly, all arms and legs. I've grown six inches since last summer. My clothes don't fit me anymore, so at school they gave me the uniform of a senior who'd hanged himself from a tree the year before.

I return to the beach whenever I can. My mother never speaks to me, but sometimes I sidestep along the beach until I pick up radio stations in Key West. I'm learning more English this way but it's a lot different from Abuelo Jorge's grammar books. If I'm lucky, I can tune in the Wolfman Jack show on Sunday nights. Sometimes I want to be like the Wolfman and talk to a million people at once.

Daughters of Changó

(1979)

By the fall of 1979, Jorge del Pino speaks less and less with his daughter on her evening walks home from the bakeries. He complains of an energy waning within him, and is convinced that the time he's stolen between death and oblivion is coming to an end. His voice crackles softly, like the peeling of an eggshell, and Lourdes has to stand perfectly still to hear his words. Trees and buildings interfere with her reception, so Lourdes seeks quiet, open places to speak with her father—the limestone plazas of a younger Brooklyn, the expanse of lawn in front of the post office, the path by the river where the Navarro boy jumped to his death.

"My knowledge is no greater dead than alive," Jorge del Pino tells his daughter. It is the first day of November, nearly dusk, and he is speaking in morbid riddles again.

"What are you saying?" Lourdes asks.

"That we can see and understand everything just as well alive as dead, only when we're alive we don't have the time, or the peace of mind, or the inclination to see and understand what we could. We're too busy rushing to our graves."

"How many days do we have left, Papi?"

"I couldn't say precisely."

"A year? A month?"

"Not that long.."

Lourdes sits on a bench overlooking the river. It is a dull moving metal, incapable of reflection. Only on a night with an exceptional moon can the river rightfully claim its light or any other subtlety. Now it offers Lourdes a bitterness she can taste. Her father is dying all over again, and her grief is worse than the first time.

"Ask me, *hija*. I am here."

"Why did you leave Cuba, Papi?"

"Because I was sick. You know that."

"Yes, but why?"

"Those doctors were butchers, poorly trained."

Lourdes waits.

"And your mother. I couldn't bear to watch her. She had fallen in love again. She thought only of the revolution. There was nothing I could do but eat my own sour guts."

"Did you love her? Did you love Mamá?" Lourdes asks tentatively. The remnants of the day's light tangle in the sky. Lourdes studies the colors wrestling to unravel, flaring like certain male species of birds. She thinks of how singular yet familiar they are.

"Yes, *mi hija,* I loved her."

"And did she love you?"

"I believe she did, in her way."

*   *   *

"I thought you had left me for good," Lourdes tells her father as she walks on the wooden-planked tier of the Brooklyn Bridge. It is a Sunday afternoon in winter, so clear it appears hard glazed. Lourdes has not heard from her father in over a month.

She watches as two gulls circle a pier, rotating a wheel of air. They stir the near-absent blue.

"I can't return anymore," her father answers ruefully.

Lourdes looks up through the steel lattice of the bridge coated black with exhaust. Through one elongated triangle she sees a clean patch of cloud. The black outlines it, defines it.

"I've come to tell you a few last things. About myself. About your mother. So you'll understand."

"I know too much already."

"You haven't even begun to understand, Lourdes."

Jorge del Pino is silent for a long time.

"Your mother loved you," he says finally.

The bridge's planks reverberate with the cars passing below. Down the river, a train crosses another bridge with the sound of a dragging chain. Lourdes wants to slow it down, to examine the faces in the streaming windows before they disappear into the tunnel on the other side.

"After we were married, I left her with my mother and my sister. I knew what it would do to her. A part of me wanted to punish her. For the Spaniard. I tried to kill her, Lourdes. I wanted to kill her. I left on a long trip after you were born. I wanted to break her, may God forgive me. When I returned, it was done. She held you out to me by one leg and told me she would not remember your name."

Lourdes follows a tugboat moving toward the sea. It seems to pull the city behind it. She finds it difficult to breathe.

"I left her in an asylum. I told the doctors to make her forget. They used electricity. They fed her pills. I used to visit her every Sunday. She told me to turn on my electric brooms and then laughed in my face. She told me that geometry would strangle nature. She made a friend there who had murdered her husband, and I became afraid. Her hands were always so still."

Jorge del Pino stops; his voice softens.

"The doctors told me that her health was delicate, that she

must live by the sea to complete her forgetting. I bought her a piano like her aunt's. I wanted to see her hands move. I was afraid they'd lie still in her lap, threatening me. I kept traveling, Lourdes. I couldn't bear her gentleness, her kind indifference. I took you from her while you were still a part of her. I wanted to own you for myself. And you've always been mine, *hija*."

Lourdes stands and circles the desolate bridge tower. She thinks of how the most accidental gestures can lead to precise conclusions.

"Your mother loved you," Jorge del Pino repeats urgently.

"She loved me," Lourdes echoes.

The colors drain from the sky until the air seems more sand than light. Lourdes feels its texture on her fingertips. Everything, it seems, has slowed to its constituent elements.

"There is something else I must tell you," Jorge del Pino says. "Your sister has died. She was sad when she died. She spoke your name and mine."

"Felicia? How?"

"You must go to them."

"I can't go back. It's impossible."

"There are things you must do, things you will only know when you get there."

"You don't understand," Lourdes cries and searches the breeze above her. She smells the brilliantined hair, feels the scraping blade, the web of scars it left on her stomach.

"I know about the soldier, Lourdes. I've known all these years," her father says evenly. "But your mother never knew, I swear it."

"And you? Who told you?" Lourdes collapses on the walkway, her lungs swelling with air.

"Nobody. I just knew."

Lourdes rests on the wooden planks. She breathes deeply, until the air courses through her chest without effort. She looks up and sees faint lights in the sky—the sun, the moon, the other planets. Perhaps they are farther than anyone thinks.

"Please return and tell your mother everything, tell her I'm sorry. I love you, *mi hija.*"

Lourdes imagines white azaleas and an altar set for high mass on an April Sunday. She sings in a high, pure voice, carefully pronouncing each word. She remembers she likes April. It is her favorite month.

Pilar
(1980)

I'm browsing in the remainders bins outside a record shop on Amsterdam Avenue when two men call to me halfheartedly from across the street, more out of habit than desire. I sift through old 78 polkas with beribboned women smiling at me from the album covers. There's something grotesque about their grins, fixed for thirty years. Maybe I'd do them a favor by buying their records and breaking them in two. Maybe it'd release them from some terrible Romanian spell.

I find a Herb Alpert record, the one with the woman in whipped cream on the cover. It looks so tame to me now. I read somewhere that the woman who posed for it was three months pregnant at the time and that it was shaving cream, not whipped cream, she was suggestively dipping into her mouth.

In the last bin, I find an old Beny Moré album. Two of the cuts are scratched but I buy it anyway for fifty cents. The cashier's features are compressed beneath a bulbous forehead. When I thank him in Spanish, he's surprised and wants to chat. We talk about Celia Cruz and how she hasn't changed a hair or a vocal note in forty years. She's been fiftyish, it seems, since the Spanish-American War.

Then we get to talking about Lou Reed. It's funny how his fans can sniff each other out. We agree that his sexually ambiguous days—when he wore white face and black nail polish— were his best. It's hard to believe that Lou came out of a suburban home on Long Island and went to college in upstate New York. He should have been a lawyer or an accountant or somebody's father by now. I wonder if his mother thinks he's dangerous.

The cashier, Franco, puts on the *Take No Prisoners* album. I was at the Bottom Line the night they recorded it. How many lifetimes ago was that? I think about all that great early punk and the raucous paintings I used to do.

Shit, I'm only twenty-one years old. How can I be nostalgic for my youth?

Midterms are in a week and I can't seem to concentrate on anything. The only thing that helps is my bass. I've taught myself to play the thing these last two years and I'm not half bad. There's a group at Columbia that meets Sunday afternoons to jam on this punky fake jazz everyone's into. When things are cooking, me and my bass just move the whole damn floor.

Still, I feel something's dried up inside me, something a strong wind could blow out of me for good. That scares me. I guess I'm not so sure what I should be fighting for anymore. Without confines, I'm damn near reasonable. That's something I never wanted to become.

Franco and I commiserate about how St. Mark's Place is a zoo these days with the bridge-and-tunnel crowd wearing fuchsia mohawks and safety pins through their cheeks. Everybody wants to be part of the freak show for a day. Anything halfway interesting gets co-opted, mainstreamed. We'll all be doing car commercials soon.

It used to be you could see the Ramones in the East Village

for five bucks. Nowadays you have to pay $12.50 to see them with five thousand bellowing skinheads who don't even let you hear the music. Count me out.

I enter a *botánica* on upper Park Avenue. I've passed the place before but I've never gone inside. Today, it seems, there's nowhere else for me to go. Dried snakeskins and *ouanga* bags hang from the walls. Painted wooden saints with severe mouths stand alongside plastic plug-in Virgins with sixty-watt bulbs. Iridescent oils are displayed with amulets, talismans, incense. There are sweet-smelling soaps and bottled bathwater, love perfumes and potions promising money and luck. Apothecary jars labeled in childish block letters are filled with pungent spices.

I'm not religious but I get the feeling that it's the simplest rituals, the ones that are integrated with the earth and its seasons, that are the most profound. It makes more sense to me than the more abstract forms of worship.

The owner of the shop is an elderly man who wears a white tunic and cotton fez. For a young woman with cropped hair, he prescribes a statuette of La Virgen de la Caridad del Cobre, a yellow candle, and five special oils: *amor* (love), *sígueme* (follow me), *yo puedo y tú no* (I can and you can't), *ven conmigo* (come with me), and *dominante* (dominant).

"Carve his name on the candle five times and anoint it with these oils," he instructs. "Do you have a picture of your intended?"

The woman nods.

"*Bueno,* put it on a dessert plate and coat it with honey. Then arrange five fishhooks on the picture and light the candle. Rest assured, he will be yours in two Sundays."

I envy this woman's passion, her determination to get what she knows is hers. I felt that way once, when I ran away to Miami. But I never made it to Cuba to see Abuela Celia. After that, I felt like my destiny was not my own, that men who had nothing to do with me had the power to rupture my dreams, to separate me from my grandmother.

I examine the beaded necklaces near the register. Most have five strands and come in two colors. I select a red-and-white one and place it over my head. I lift an ebony staff carved with the head of a woman balancing a double-edged ax.

"Ah, a daughter of Changó," the elderly man says and places a hand on my shoulder.

I say nothing but I notice that his eyes are the same almond color as his skin, that they're centuries older than his face.

"You must finish what you began," he says.

I rub the beads in my left hand and feel a warm current drifting up my arm, across my shoulders, down between my breasts.

"When?" I ask him.

"The moon after next."

I watch as he moves through the store. His back is long and straight, as if his ancestors were royal palms. He gathers herbs from various jars, then reaches for a white votive candle and a bottle of holy water.

"Begin with a bitter bath," he says, lining up the ingredients on the counter. "Bathe with these herbs for nine consecutive nights. Add the holy water and a drop of ammonia, then light the candle. On the last day, you will know what to do."

I reach in my jeans to pay him but he holds up his palm.

"This is a gift from our father Changó."

I can't wait to get back to my room and fill up the bathtub so I take a shortcut through Morningside Park. I feel shielded by the herbs, by the man with the straight spine and starched cotton fez. An elm tree seems to shade the world with its aerial roots. It begins to rain and I pick up my pace. The herbs shift rhythmically in my sack like the seeds of a maraca.

I remember the nannies in Cuba with their leaves and rattling beads. They prayed over me, sprinkled cinnamon in my bath, massaged my stomach with olive oil. They covered me with squares of flannel in the dead heat of summer.

The nannies told my mother that I stole their shadows, that I made their hair fall out and drove their husbands to other women. But my mother didn't believe them. She fired the nannies without an extra day's pay.

One night there was a furious thunderstorm. Lightning hit the royal palm outside my window. From my crib, I heard it snap and fall. The fronds whined in the wind. The aviary shattered. The toucans and cockatoos circled in confusion before flying north.

My new nanny wasn't afraid. She told me that it was only the temperamental Changó, god of fire and lightning. Changó, she said, once asked a young lizard to take a gift to the lover of a rival god. The lizard put the present in its mouth and scurried to the lady's house but it tripped and fell, swallowing the precious trinket.

When Changó found out, he tracked down his inept accomplice to the foot of a palm tree. The terrified reptile, unable to speak, ran up the tree and hid among the fronds, the gift still lodged in its throat. Changó, who believed the lizard was mocking him, aimed a lightning bolt at the tree, intending to scorch the sorry creature dead.

Since then, Lucila explained, Changó often takes out his rage on innocent palm trees, and to this day the lizard's throat is swollen and mute with the god's gift.

Three boys surround me suddenly in the park, locking me between their bodies. Their eyes are like fireflies, hot and erased of memory. The rain beads in their hair. They can't be more than eleven years old.

The tallest one presses a blade to my throat. Its edge is a scar, another border to cross.

A boy with a high, square forehead grabs the sack with the dried herbs and throws my Beny Moré album like a Frisbee against the elm. It doesn't break and I'm reassured. I imagine picking up the record, feeling each groove with my fingertips.

The boys push me under the elm, where it's somehow still dry. They pull off my sweater and carefully unbutton my blouse. With the knife still at my throat, they take turns suckling my breasts. They're children, I tell myself, trying to contain my fear. Incredibly, I hear the five-note pounding of Lou Reed's "Street Hassle," that crazy cello with its low, dying voice.

I watch as the last boy pinches some of the herb and arranges it on a rectangle of paper in his palm. He shapes it into a narrow cylinder then rolls the paper, licking the edge with the delicacy of a preening cat.

"Who's got a match?" he demands and the boy with the square forehead offers him a flame from a red plastic lighter. The boy takes a deep breath and holds it in his lungs. Then he passes it to the others.

I press my back against the base of the elm and close my eyes. I can feel the pulsing of its great taproot, the howling cello in its trunk. I know the sun sears its branches to hot wires. I don't know how long I sit against the elm, but when I open my eyes, the boys are gone. I button my blouse, gather up my herbs and my album, and run back to the university.

In the library, nothing makes sense. The fluorescent lights transmit conversations from passing cars on Broadway. Someone's ordering a bucket of chicken wings on 103rd Street. The chairman of the linguistics department is fucking a graduate student named Betsy. Gandhi was a carnivore. He came of age in Samoa. He traversed a subcontinent in blue suede shoes. Maybe this is the truth.

I buy apples and bananas in the cafeteria and eat them furtively in my room. I'd prefer a cave, a desert, a more complete solitude.

I light my candle. The bath turns a clear green from the herbs. It has the sharp scent of an open field in spring. When I pour it on my hair, I feel a sticky cold like dry ice, then a soporific heat. I'm walking naked as a beam of light along brick paths and squares of grass, phosphorescent and clean.

At midnight, I awake and paint a large canvas ignited with reds and whites, each color betraying the other. I do this for eight more nights.

On the ninth day of my baths, I call my mother and tell her we're going to Cuba.

Celia's Letters: 1956–1958

February 11, 1956

Mi querido Gustavo,

Lourdes is seeing a young man I like very much. His name is Rufino Puente, and despite the fact that he comes from one of the wealthiest families in Havana, he's a modest young man. Lourdes says he shows up to classes in overalls and reeks of manure from his father's ranch. I'm pleased that he's not afraid to work, to get his hands dirty, unlike so many men from his circle. In the evenings, Rufino comes to court Lourdes, impeccably dressed, and brings us juicy steaks to grill. He's a funny-looking boy, too, with wavy reddish hair.

Jorge is so jealous that he acts like a stubborn child. He refuses to shake Rufino's hand and then he locks himself in our bedroom, sulking until Rufino leaves. Jorge complains incessantly about him, finding faults where there are none. This is the first time I've ever seen Lourdes cross with her father.

Last Saturday, I chaperoned a dance at the university and

Rufino spent the entire evening talking with me. Lourdes is quite a dancer but Rufino's feet are put on backward. He can barely make it through the simplest merengue without bruising the dancers around him. His awkwardness makes him very endearing, although it's clear my daughter prefers more refined dancers. Lourdes was wearing an organdy dress that cinched her waist. I was astonished to see how popular she is, how much of a woman she's become.

Celia

April 11, 1956

Gustavo,

Spring again. What happened to us, Gustavo? We used to stay up whole nights, there was so much to learn about each other. Then the morning after I finally slept, I awoke with only your scent on my skin. When I opened the shutters of our room, I saw you rushing across the plaza. There was a crowd protesting I don't know what, shaking placards in the air. I called out to you but you couldn't hear me. That was the last I saw of you.

I've asked myself many times whether this was better than watching you grow old and indifferent beside me.

I remember when I applied for a job at El Encanto, the director wanted me to be a model, to walk up and down the aisles in gowns and hats draped with chiffon. The salesmen bought me perfume and invited me to lunch. But they couldn't talk to me about why families of *guajiros* slept in the city's parks under flashing Coca-Cola signs. Those men only murmured sweet nonsense to me, trying in vain to flatter me.

You were different, *mi amor*. You expected much more of me. That is why I loved you.

Yours as always,
Celia

September 11, 1956

Querido Gustavo,

Lourdes will marry Rufino in three months. Jorge blames himself for traveling so much during her childhood. Felicia is sullen and envious and barely speaks to her sister. Even Javier is unsettled by all the emotion.

Two weeks ago, we had dinner with Rufino's parents. Don Guillermo looked like an oafish policeman, right down to his elephantine ears and the brass buttons on his cuffs. He spoke the entire evening of the importance of maintaining good relations with the Americans and insisted that they are the key to our future. When I reminded him of the Platt Amendment, of the way the Americans have interfered in our affairs from the very beginning, he waved his fat, jeweled hand dismissively and turned to Jorge, continuing his pontifications.

Everyone knows that the Mafia runs Don Guillermo's casinos and that he lunches with Batista on Thursdays at the Havana Yacht Club. People say that Batista had to pay a million dollars to become a member because his skin is not light enough. Don Guillermo fears the rebels, although he pretends not to. This gives me great pleasure.

His wife, Doña Zaida, is no better. During dinner, I heard cries as if there were a cat trapped above our heads. Later I learned that Zaida keeps her mother, La Muñeca, locked upstairs. Lourdes told me that La Muñeca is as Indian as they come, from Costa Rica. She refuses to wear shoes and used to carry her children and grandchildren in slings on her back. For this, Zaida keeps her mother a prisoner. How Rufino survived such horrid parents is a mystery to me.

Love,
Celia

October 11, 1956

Querido Gustavo,

I awoke one night startled and aroused. I touched Jorge tenderly and he sat upright with fear. That's how long it's been between us. I told him I wanted to be with him again and he began to cry. I held him for a long time and then we made love slowly, with discovery. He told me that I've never been more beautiful, and I almost believed him.

Celia

November 11, 1956

Mi querido Gustavo,

Zaida Puente changed all my plans for Lourdes's wedding and arranged a spectacle instead at the Tropicana Club. She's invited hundreds of society people whom she doesn't even know, and insists that the food be French— pheasants and eels and God knows what else. Not a suckling pig in sight! Then she has the nerve to tell me that my plain taffeta dress is *unsuitable* for the Tropicana. That woman is a snake, an insufferable snake!

Love,
Celia

December 11, 1956

Gustavo,

The rebels attacked again, this time in Oriente. They're hiding in the Sierra Maestra. People say the rebel leader sleeps in his uniform and olive cap, that his hair and beard are one, like a bear's, and his eyes are just as fearless. The tension here is unbearable. Everyone wants Batista out.

Jorge is afraid that if the rebels win they'll throw out the Americans and that he'll lose his job before he can get his pension. But I tell him that there'll be *more* jobs for everyone when they throw that thief out of the palace.

Love,
Celia

P.S. The wedding was a circus, as I expected. The Tropicana was like a brothel, red lights everywhere, making me dizzy. The navy commander's wife, unaccustomed to the rich foods and the imported champagne, vomited on the ballroom floor. And in the confusion, Silvio Arroyo Pedros, a retired Spanish matador (have you heard of him?), and a devotee of Havana's most notorious fleshpots, broke his clavicle dancing with the widow Doña Victoria del Paso. They say that poor Doña Victoria dipped him too deeply in a moment of long-repressed passion. The ordeal lasted until morning when skinny women in sequined bodices served us scrambled eggs and bacon. Lourdes and Rufino appeared dazed but not unhappy. Zaida Puente, of course, had her picture in all the newspapers the next day, posing in her plum moiré gown like a would-be queen. She'll be among the first to hang, no doubt.

June 11, 1958

Querido Gustavo,

I took a walk on the beach late this afternoon. The moon appeared early, absorbing the lingering light. Each shell echoed a song my bones could hear. I have something to celebrate, Gustavo. I'm going to be a grandmother.

Tu Celia

THE LANGUAGES LOST

(1980)

Six Days in April

It is long past midnight. Celia searches the cardboard box containing the few articles Felicia left behind and finds her daughter's black bathing suit. None of the foam or the underwire remains in the pointed brassière, and the seat is worn to near obscenity.

Celia remembers Felicia in another bathing suit, a tiny lemon-yellow one she wore the year the sea retreated beyond the horizon, the year the archaeology of the ocean floor revealed itself—catacombs of ancient coral, lunar rocks exposed to the sun. Felicia squatted, examining the shells as if they were unexpected gems, then rearranged them on the sand. Around her, neighbors scrambled with wooden buckets, looting the beach for stranded fish and crabs. The sun baked their footsteps hard as fossils. Then the tidal wave hit, wiping their traces from shore.

The day before the funeral, Celia had taken the morning bus from Santa Teresa del Mar to the house on Palmas Street. She no longer hitchhiked. She gathered up Felicia's nightgown with the blue roses, Tía Alicia's tarnished peacock brooch (which Celia had given to Felicia for her fifteenth birthday), a stump of orange lipstick, two unraveling stretch shorts, and her daughter's *santería* clothing.

Celia found unused ration cards permitting Felicia one and a half pounds of chicken per month, two ounces of coffee every fifteen days, two packs of cigarettes per week, and four meters of cloth per year. Her daughter had had little use for these provisions during the last months of her life.

Felicia had left a note with Herminia saying she wanted to be buried as a *santera,* and Celia could not refuse her daughter's last request. In the mortuary, her friends from the *casa de santo* dressed Felicia in her initiation gown, her crown, and her necklaces. They arranged a pouch of seashells on her breast together with morsels of smoked fish and a few grains of corn. Into a large gourd they placed her cut hair and head dyes, okra, ashes, and wisps of dried corn silks. They covered the gourd with crossed cloths, then killed a black chicken and laid it over the offerings.

Later, they passed colorful handkerchiefs over Felicia's body, all the while grieving in low voices to purify her corpse. By the time they finished, the terrible lumps on Felicia's head had disappeared, and her skin was as smooth as the pink lining of a conch. Her eyes, too, had regained their original green.

After they removed the coffin to the street, the *santeros* broke a clay urn behind Felicia's old De Soto, the funeral car, and sprinkled it with cold water to refresh her for the final journey. A block before the cemetery, the car broke down and Felicia's coffin had to be carried the rest of the way by eight pallbearers in white.

At the entrance to the cemetery, a tall man stood in shreds and patches, his face slackly wrapped in scarves. He stood perfectly still and seemed to breathe through the dark open slit by his eyes, sucking sorrow from the air like venom.

*

Celia undresses noiselessly in the dark. She opens the closet door and studies her image in the speckled mirror. She feels a stain descend within her, like water through a plaster wall. It spreads, slow and sodden, loosening her teeth, weighing down her limbs, darkening the scar on her withered chest. Celia's remaining breast droops by her elbow, the indifferent nipple facing downward. Her abdomen, though, is as unmarred as a childless woman's. Between her legs, sparse hair clings to a swell of flesh.

She examines her hands next, bloated and twisted as driftwood, but she cannot reclaim them. Her legs, too, are unrecognizable—the enlarged knees, the calf muscles shorter and more angular than in her youth, her wounded feet. Her face, at least, is familiar. The faded mole by her lips holds the folds of thin flesh in place like a flat black button. And her drop pearl earrings still hang stiffly from her lobes.

Celia slips on Felicia's sheer bathing suit. Outside, a crescent moon mocks her from its perch. She strides toward the water, and swims with brisk strokes far out to sea. The sky is dimmed of stars and Celia cannot identify their milky lights, their waning conclusions.

Pilar

My mother and I pass billboards advertising the revolution as if it were a new brand of cigarette. We drive by the Plaza de la Revolución, where, the taxi driver explains, El Líder holds his biggest rallies. He tells us that there's more trouble for El Líder, that a busload of people seeking asylum crashed the gates of the Peruvian embassy early this morning. Mom hardly listens. She seems to be in her own world. The driver takes a detour along the Malecón, pointing out La Punta Fortress, and the Morro

Castle across the harbor. All Mom says is that the buildings in Havana are completely decayed, held up by elaborate configurations of wooden planks. What I notice most are the balconies.

The driver turns onto Palmas Street. The houses are painted a garish yellow. They're chipped and flaking and look smeared with confetti. We stop in front of Tía Felicia's house, the house in which Abuelo Jorge grew up. The windows are shuttered tight and the square of front yard is littered with broken pottery and soiled flags. My mother says there used to be sparrows in the tamarind tree, heavy once with fat clusters of pods.

Mom doesn't bother to get out of the car or ask the neighbors what happened to her sister. She says she's expected this since Abuelo Jorge spoke to her on the Brooklyn Bridge. As for me, I'm not sure what to expect, only that I'll see Abuela Celia again, like I learned after my ninth herbal bath.

Since that day in Morningside Park, I can hear fragments of people's thoughts, glimpse scraps of the future. It's nothing I can control. The perceptions come without warnings or explanations, erratic as lightning.

"Take us to Santa Teresa del Mar," Mom orders the driver. She closes her eyes. I think it's less painful for her than looking out the window.

We take the coastal highway to my grandmother's house. I look at the sea I once planned to cross by fishing boat. Trade winds roll the water in great masses. A hurricane is submerged. There are dolphins and parrotfish, hawksbill turtles and shovelnose sharks. There's a shipwreck in the Gulf of Mexico filled with ingots and doubloons. Men in wet suits will find the galleon three years from now. They will celebrate with champagne and murder.

Four fresh bodies are floating in the Straits of Florida. It's a family from Cárdenas. They stole a boat from a fisherman. It collapsed in the current early this morning. A boatload of Haitians will leave Gonaïves next Thursday. They will carry the phone numbers of friends in Miami and the life savings of relatives. They will sail to the Tropic of Cancer and sink into the sea.

I've brought a sketchbook with me and a toolbox of brushes and paints, mostly watercolors. I wanted to bring my bass along but Mom said there'd be no room. She's crammed every inch of our suitcases with cheap sneakers and tacky clothing from the Latino stores on Fourteenth Street. I want to do a few sketches of Abuela Celia, maybe even a formal portrait of her on her wicker swing. I think she'd like that.

Mom jumps from the taxi in her sling-back pumps and runs past the giant bird of paradise bushes, past the rotting pawpaw tree, and up the three front steps of Abuela Celia's house. I follow her. The cement shows through the floor where the tiles are missing. It's a patterned tile, with pastel buds and climbing vines. It hasn't been mopped for months. A faded mantilla, soft as a moth, is draped over the sofa. There's a chalk-white piano and a refrigerator, a bulk of rust, against the far wall.

My mother inspects the bedroom she used to share with Tía Felicia, vacant now except for a frilly party dress hanging in the closet. She crosses the hallway to Abuela's room. A lace tablecloth is spread on the bed. A photograph of El Líder is on the night table. Mom turns from it in disgust.

I find Abuela sitting motionless on her wicker swing, wearing a worn bathing suit, her hair stuck haphazardly to her skull, her feet strangely lacerated. I kneel before her and press my cheek to hers, still salty from the sea. We hold each other close.

"*Dios mío,* what happened to you?" Mom screams when she finds us. She scurries about preparing a hot bath with water boiled on the stove.

Abuela is missing a breast. There's a scar like a purple zipper on her chest. Mom holds a finger to her lips and flashes me a look that warns, "Pretend not to notice."

We wash Abuela's hair and rinse it with conditioner, then we pat her dry with towels as if this could somehow heal her. Abuela says nothing. She submits to my mother like a solemn novitiate. Mom untangles Abuela's hair with a wide-toothed comb. "You could have died of pneumonia!" she insists, and plugs in a Conair dryer that blows out the lights in the living room.

I notice Abuela Celia's drop pearl earrings, the intricate settings, the fine gold strands looping through her lobes. There's a cache of blue shadows in the pearls, a coolness in the smooth surfaces. When I was a baby, I bounced those pearls with my fingertips and heard the rhythm of my grandmother's thoughts.

"I went for a swim last night," Abuela Celia whispers to me alone. She looks through the arched window above the piano as if searching the waves to find the precise spot. Then she squeezes my hand. "I'm glad you remember, Pilar. I always knew you would."

Mom replaces Abuela's bedding with fresh sheets and a lamb's wool blanket we brought from home. I help Abuela into a new flannel nightgown while Mom prepares bouillon and instant tapioca pudding. Abuela Celia tastes a spoonful of each, swallows a vitamin C tablet, and falls into a deep sleep.

I pull the covers over Abuela's shoulders, searching her face for a hint of my own. Her hair turned gray since I last saw her. Her black mole has faded. Her hands are stamped with faint liver spots.

I know what my grandmother dreams. Of massacres in distant countries, pregnant women dismembered in the squares. Abuela Celia walks among them mute and invisible. The thatched roofs steam in the morning air.

"Can you believe this *mierda?*" My mother snatches the picture of El Líder off Abuela's night table. It's framed in antique silver, wedged over the face of Abuelo Jorge, whose blue eye peers out from behind El Líder's army cap. Mom walks to the edge of the ocean in her silk dress and stockings, her pleated skirt ballooning like a spinnaker, and flings the picture into the sea. Two sea gulls dive for it but surface with empty beaks. The horizon shifts like a bright line of buoys.

I wonder about the voyages to old colonies. Ocean liners gliding toward Africa and India. The women on board wore black elbow-length gloves. They drank from porcelain teacups, longed for moist earth to eat. They lingered with their impulses against the railings.

Perhaps my mother should have approached Havana by sea. Boarded a ship in Shanghai and crossed the Pacific wave by wave. Rounded Cape Horn, the coast of Brazil, stopped for carnival in Port-of-Spain.

Cuba is a peculiar exile, I think, an island-colony. We can reach it by a thirty-minute charter flight from Miami, yet never reach it all.

*   *   *

Later, while Abuela still sleeps, my mother and I walk to the corner of Calle Madrid. Mom stops a *guajiro* selling a few stalks of sugarcane. She chooses one and he removes the woody husk for her with a machete. Mom chews the cane until she tastes the *guarapo,* the sticky syrup inside.

"Try some, Pilar, but it's not as sweet as I remember."

Mom tells me how she used to stand on this corner and tell tourists that her mother was dead. They felt sorry for her and bought her ice cream. They patted her head. I try to picture my mother as a dark skinny girl, but all I can envision is a miniature

version of her today, an obese woman in a beige dress with
matching pumps, and a look fearsome enough to stop the Lex-
ington Avenue express in its tracks.

Suddenly, I want to know how I'll die. I think I'd prefer self-
immolation, on a stage perhaps, with all my paintings. I'd definitely want to go before I got too old, before anyone would
have to wipe my ass or push me around in a wheelchair. I don't
want *my* granddaughter to have to take out my teeth and put
them in a glass of water fizzing with tablets like I did with Abuelo
Jorge.

My mother keeps talking but I'm only half listening. I have
this image of Abuela Celia underwater, standing on a reef with
tiny chrome fish darting by her face like flashes of light. Her hair
is waving in the tide and her eyes are wide open. She calls to
me but I can't hear her. Is she talking to me from her dreams?

"You'd think they could make a few decent solid colors in
this place," my mother complains loudly so everyone can hear.

I look around me. The women on Calle Madrid are bare-
armed in tight, sleeveless blouses. They wear stretch pants and
pañuelos, match polka dots with stripes, plaids with flower prints.
There's a man in goggles pumping his sharpening wheel, a dull
ax shrieking against its surface. A pair of frayed trousers stick
out from beneath a '55 Plymouth. Magnificent finned automo-
biles cruise grandly down the street like parade floats. I feel like
we're back in time, in a kind of Cuban version of an earlier
America.

I think about the *Granma,* the American yacht El Líder took
from Mexico to Cuba in 1956 on his second attempt to topple
Batista. Some boat owner in Florida misspells "Grandma" and
look what happens: a myth is born, a province is renamed, a
Communist party newspaper is launched. What if the boat had
been called *Barbara Ann* or *Sweetie Pie* or *Daisy?* Would history
be different? We're all tied to the past by flukes. Look at me, I
got my name from Hemingway's fishing boat.

Mom is talking louder and louder. My mouth goes dry, like the times I've gone with her to department stores with merchandise to return. Four or five people gather at a safe distance. It's all the audience she needs.

"Look at those old American cars. They're held together with rubber bands and paper clips and *still* work better than the new Russian ones. *Oye!*" she calls out to the bystanders. "You could have Cadillacs with leather interiors! Air conditioning! Automatic windows! You wouldn't have to move your arms in the heat!" Then she turns to me, her face indignant. "Look how they laugh, Pilar! Like idiots! They can't understand a word I'm saying! Their heads are filled with too much *compañero* this and *compañera* that! They're brainwashed, that's what they are!"

I pull my mother from the growing crowd. The language she speaks is lost to them. It's another idiom entirely.

*   *   *

I'm lying on Tía Felicia's childhood bed. My breathing falls in time with my mother's, with the tempo of the waves outside. When I was a kid, Mom slept in air thin and nervous as a magnetic field, attracting small disturbances. She tossed and turned all night, as if she were wrestling ghosts in her dreams. Sometimes she'd wake up crying, clutching her stomach and moaning from deep inside a place I couldn't understand. Dad would stroke her forehead until she fell asleep again.

My mother told me once that I slept just like her sister, with my mouth open wide enough to catch flies. I think Mom envied me my rest. But tonight it's different. I'm the one who can't sleep.

Abuela Celia is in her wicker swing looking out to sea. I settle in beside her. There's a comforting wilderness to Abuela's hands, to the odd-shaped calluses, the split skin on her thumb.

"When I was a girl, I used to dry tobacco leaves one at a time," she begins in a quiet voice. "They stained my hands, my face, the rags on my body. One day, my mother bathed me in a tin tub behind our house and rubbed me with straw until my skin bled. I put on the ruffled dress she had made, a hat with ribbons, and patent-leather shoes, the first I ever wore. My feet felt precious, tied up like shiny parcels. Then she left me on a train and walked away."

As I listen, I feel my grandmother's life passing to me through her hands. It's a steady electricity, humming and true.

"There was a man before your grandfather. A man I loved very much. But I made a promise to myself before your mother was born not to abandon her to this life, to train her as if for war. Your grandfather took me to an asylum after your mother was born. I told him all about you. He said it was impossible for me to remember the future. I grieved when your mother took you away. I begged her to let you stay."

There's a wrinkled hand in the window next door. The curtain drops, the shadow recedes. The gardenia tree fills the night with its scent. Women who outlive their daughters are orphans, Abuela tells me. Only their granddaughters can save them, guard their knowledge like the first fire.

Lourdes

Every way Lourdes turns there is more destruction, more decay. *Socialismo o muerte*. The words pain her as if they were knitted into her skin with thick needles and yarn. She wants to change the "o" to "e"'s on every billboard with a bucket of red paint. *Socialismo es muerte*, she'd write over and over again until the people believed it, until they rose up and reclaimed their country from that tyrant.

Last night, she was shocked to see how her nephew devoured his food at the tourist hotel in Boca Ciega. Ivanito refilled his plate six times with *palomilla* steak, grilled shrimp, *yuca* in garlic sauce, and hearts of palm salad. Ivanito told her that they didn't get such good food at his boarding school, that it's always chicken with rice or potatoes. They don't do much to disguise it. Lourdes knows that Cuba saves its prime food for tourists or for export to Russia. Degradation, she thinks, goes hand in hand with the certainty of deprivation.

At the next table, a group of sunburnt French Canadians were enjoying baked lobsters and getting drunk on Cuba libres. Lourdes overheard one woman remarking on a Cuban boy who had flirted with her on the beach. So these were El Líder's supporters overseas? Odious armchair socialists! *They* didn't need coupons to eat! *They* didn't have to wait three hours for a pitiful can of crabmeat! It had taken all of Lourdes's resolve to remain calmly in her seat.

Celia picked at her food, not saying much. She ordered two dishes of coconut ice cream and ate them slowly with a soup spoon.

Was it true, Lourdes wonders, that the older you get the less you can savor and that sweetness is the last taste left on the tongue? Had her mother really aged so much? Could so much time have passed?

She is a complete stranger to me, Lourdes thinks. Papi was wrong. Some things can never change.

Her nieces look nothing like Felicia or the pictures Lourdes has seen of their father. Luz and Milagro are plain and squat, with wide noses, and appear to be a mixture of black and Indian. Could Felicia have slept with someone besides Hugo? It wouldn't have surprised Lourdes. Nothing Felicia ever did surprised her. Since they were children, her sister would do any-thing to be the center of attention, even take off her blouse in front of the neighborhood boys and charge them a nickel apiece to touch her breasts. Felicia used to burst in on conversations between Lourdes and her father, whining and stamping her feet until they included her. Of course they never spoke of anything important while she was present.

Pilar looked so clumsy last night dancing with Ivanito. The band was playing a cha-cha-chá, and Pilar moved jerkily, off the beat, sloppy and distracted. She dances like an American. Ivan-ito, though, is a wonderful dancer. His hips shift evenly, and his feet keep precise time to the music. He glides through his turns as if he were ice-skating.

When Lourdes finally danced with her nephew, she felt be-holden to the congas, to a powerful longing to dance. Her body remembered what her mind had forgotten. Suddenly, she wanted to show her daughter the artistry of *true* dancing. Lourdes exaggerated her steps, flawless and lilting, teasing the rhythm seductively. She held the notes in her hips and her thighs, in the graceful arch of her back. Ivanito intuited her movements, dipping her with such reluctant fluidity that the mu-sic ached and blossomed around them. The crowd gradually pulled back to watch their unlikely elegance. Then someone clapped, and in an instant the room rumbled with applause as Lourdes spun and spun and spun across the polished dance floor.

This morning, Ivanito told Lourdes that dancing with her had reminded him of his mother. He'd meant it as a compliment, but his words ruined the spell of the dance for her, ruined its very memory. But Lourdes said nothing. Yesterday was Ivanito's birthday. He is thirteen years old. What, Lourdes asks herself, does the boy have to look forward to in this country?

Lourdes is driving along the north highway to Varadero in the black Oldsmobile she rented from a neighbor. She admires the sea, a calm, brilliant turquoise to her left, and the familiar pattern of royal palms dotting the landscape. She remembers the summer vacation she spent crisscrossing the island with her father, stopping in the plazas and main streets of every town and village from here to Guantánamo. He used to straighten his tie and adjust the angle of his hat in the rearview mirror before pulling his sample fans and electric brooms from the trunk. Lourdes waited patiently for him in the front seat, and each time he returned with an order she'd throw her arms around him and kiss him on the cheek. Her father would blush with pleasure.

Lourdes drives through the city of Matanzas along its famous bay. It was her favorite stopover that summer because of the Bellamar caves nearby. It seemed the coolest, most magical place on the island. Her wandering eye would transform the stalagmites and stalactites into sculptures of hanging alligators, witches' claws, or the face of her hated history teacher.

As she reaches the narrow Hicacos peninsula, Lourdes searches for the outline of the Hotel Internacional at the far end of Varadero Beach. She and her husband had spent their honeymoon at the hotel. She remembers the men in white tuxedos, the women encased in their strapless gowns, rubies fastened to their ears. There were no views of the moon or the peninsula of powdery sand from the gambling rooms, only the lights of the chandeliers enticing them to stay. One night, Lourdes won six hundred dollars at the roulette table.

Today, the town is fallen to pieces. Only the du Pont mansion has been somewhat maintained. Lourdes wishes Ivanito were with her so she could point out the opulence—the nine-hole golf course, the landing dock for the seaplane, the Carrara marble floors. It's impossible, Lourdes thinks, for failure to argue with success.

She climbs to the top-floor ballroom, with its panoramic view of the bay. The shadowed waters conceal a coral reef offshore. Lourdes remembers paddling gently over the reefs with Rufino the day after their wedding night. Once the first pain subsided, it was as if a rainstorm were falling between her legs, flooding her entire body. She would have willingly drowned.

It's an hour south to the Puente *finca*. The red clay earth reminds Lourdes of Rufino's mud-caked overalls. He used to arrive late to their accounting class with singular excuses—a cow's lack of appetite, the difficult birth of two foals. Their teacher, a delicate Jesuit with forgiving eyes, would simply point him to a seat in the back row.

Lourdes learned to appreciate Rufino's humble ways. He was the opposite of his flashy brothers, who drove Cadillac convertibles and fraternized with the shapely waitresses and cigarette girls employed at their father's casinos. Rufino's mother, Doña Zaida, encouraged her sons' philandering. As long as her sons didn't get too serious about any one girl, they belonged to her.

When Doña Zaida realized she couldn't dissuade Rufino from marrying Lourdes, she took control of the wedding instead. Lourdes remembers the day Doña Zaida appeared at the little brick-and-cement house in her chauffeured limousine.

"My dear Celia, I cannot have my son getting married at a picnic on the beach," Doña Zaida patiently explained, as if Lourdes's mother were an imbecile. "After all, we have a reputation to uphold in the capital."

After Lourdes and Rufino got married, his brothers followed in quick succession, marrying pretty, dull-eyed girls from families approved by Doña Zaida herself. Doña Zaida had decided she couldn't risk another Lourdes in the family.

Lourdes turns up the main driveway of the old ranch. She recognizes the poinciana at the gate. In two months, it will be ablaze with purplish pink blossoms. She walks behind the villa to the patio. The pool is filled with concrete, the fountain is dry. A redheaded woman pushes another in a wheelchair. Both wear nylon robes. They execute a precise rectangle then switch places and repeat the maneuver.

A blind man sits alone on the rim of the fountain. His bleeding fingers pick absently at the tiles. His blank eyes appear fixed on the women and their unerring choreography.

Lourdes's thoughts come sniffing like underfed dogs. She remembers the night the lightning hit the royal palm, how the birds circled in confusion before scattering north.

She lost her second child in this place. A baby boy. A boy she would have named Jorge, after her father. A boy, Lourdes recalls, a boy in a soft clot of blood at her feet.

She remembers a story she read once about Guam, about how brown snakes were introduced by Americans. The snakes strangled the native birds one by one. They ate the eggs from the nests until the jungle had no voice.

What she fears most is this: that her rape, her baby's death were absorbed quietly by the earth, that they are ultimately no more meaningful than falling leaves on an autumn day. She hungers for a violence of nature, terrible and permanent, to record the evil. Nothing less would satisfy her.

Lourdes circles back to the front of the villa on unsteady legs. The sculpted mahogany doors have been replaced by unvarnished plywood. She follows a nurse across the portal into the bare foyer. Lourdes studies the checkered linoleum, longs to dig for her bones like a dog, claim them from the black-hooded earth, the scraping blade.

A petite nurse stands before Lourdes, tilting her head like a parakeet. There's a minute scar on her cheek.

"May I help you?" she asks, startled by Lourdes's drifting eye.

But Lourdes cannot answer.

Ivanito

Everything is mixed up, as if parts of me are turning in different directions at once. I wake up exhausted, not knowing why, as though I'm working hard in my sleep, moving my thoughts like so many stones in the dark.

Last night I dreamt I visited my sisters at their boarding school and they took me horseback riding in the woods. It had just rained and the horses gleamed in the wet air. I rode with one hand on the pommel and the other goading my horse with a switch. We came upon a clearing where other horses were grazing. I galloped hard, inciting a stampede. I galloped like a thunderstorm across the field and disappeared into the woods on the other side. I didn't know where I was going, only that I must not stop.

I talk and talk to my cousin Pilar late at night on the beach. I tell her about Mom's devotions, about the summer of coconuts and how we'd spoken in green. I tell her about my Russian teacher, Mr. Mikoyan, and what the boys at school said, and about the time I saw my father with the black-masked whore, his sex hard with purple veins. I tell her about Mom's funeral, and how the colors all melted together like on summer days, and the radio on Abuela's doorstep addressed to me. I tell her about the Wolfman. I didn't know I had so much to say.

Pilar has this book, a Chinese oracle, that predicts the future. Today, she gathers everyone in the living room and encourages each of us to ask it a question. Luz and Milagro exchange a glance that says, "Oh no, not another *loca* in the family!" and refuse to ask anything. They've been oddly subdued around Tía

Lourdes and Pilar, and barely speak to them, or to me. I'm glad they're going back to boarding school tomorrow. I don't like the way they follow me with their eyes, indicting me, as if being close to Pilar or Tía will somehow contaminate me.

Pilar has tried to talk to the twins, but they answer her in monosyllables. Their world is a tight sealed box. Luz and Milagro are afraid of letting anyone inside. They're afraid of Pilar's curiosity as if it were a stick of dynamite that could blow apart their lives. I know as long as they have each other they'll survive. But what about me?

I think about a suitable question for the *I Ching*, but I'm too afraid to ask what I really want to know. Tía Lourdes doesn't want to ask anything at first, calling it "Chinese mumbo-jumbo," but she finally gives in.

"Will I see justice done?" Tía demands angrily, as if the oracle will betray her. But then she looks at me kindly, slaps the three coins back and forth between her hands like a piece of dough, and throws them on the table.

Tía Lourdes has taken a special liking to me since we danced that first night at the hotel. She watches me when she thinks I'm not looking and hugs me tightly for no reason. Tía seems concerned that I spend so much time with Pilar, and finds excuses to pull me away. "Show me the new dances, Ivanito!" she coaxes. Or "Come here, Ivanito, I have a surprise for you!" She buys me treats at the tourist shop—chocolate bars with hazelnuts, German swimming trunks, and more underwear than I could possibly use. I tell her it's too much, that she shouldn't spend her money this way, but she insists, pressing the gifts into my arms. "You're my sweet boy, Ivanito. You deserve this," she says and kisses me again and again.

Tía tells me stories about America, things she thinks I'd like to hear. Like the farm boy who grew up to be a billionaire or the paperboy who now has a dozen satellites in space. "Anything is possible if you work hard enough, *mi hijito*." Tía says she plans to open hundreds of bakeries from coast to coast. She wants to be rich, like her idol du Pont, but she needs help. I tell her I want to be a translator for world leaders, that I speak good Russian, but I don't think she hears me. Instead, Tía looks right through me and describes a Christmas show at Rockefeller Center with an indoor parade of camels. I don't want to hurt her feelings so I say nothing more.

Pilar runs her finger up and down the Chinese chart, interpreting the symbols, then she shakes her head warily and begins to read. She tells Tía Lourdes that "the times demand an alignment with the flow of the cosmos," and that adjustments have to be made before any further action can be taken. "Examine your motives," Pilar reads from her book, translating into Spanish as she goes along. "They will be the cause of your problems."

Tía Lourdes gets upset and says it's like a horoscope, that it means nothing unless you want it to, that it's a complete waste of time. "It's like the newspapers here in Cuba! Not even good for toilet paper!"

"What about you, Abuela?" Pilar says, ignoring her mother. "You can ask it whatever you want. You can ask about your future."

Abuela Celia considers this for a moment, then looks up, smiling. I haven't seen her so happy since before Mom died. She and Pilar sit for hours on the wicker swing, passing the afternoons. Pilar is painting our grandmother's portrait. She says she's used up most of her blue already, and has to mix in other colors to make it last. I'm worried about what will happen after she leaves. Abuela keeps saying, "Everything will be better now that Pilar is here," even though she knows Pilar and Tía will be in Cuba only a week. Before my cousin arrived, I thought my grandmother would die soon. But Pilar has brought her back to life.

"Should I give myself to passion?" Abuela asks, surprising everyone.

But the message is uncertain. Pilar says the pattern of coins reveals something called "Ta Kuo," critical mass. She says it's like having a piece of wood suspended between two chairs, but piled in the middle with too many heavy objects. The pressure will eventually break it. "You may have to act alone and firmly during the onslaught of these weighted times," Pilar reads hesitantly.

Abuela doesn't seem to mind, though, and goes off to take a nap.

Afterward, Pilar pulls me aside and asks me to take her to Herminia Delgado's house. She says she wants to learn the truth about my mother, to learn the truth about herself.

"I need to know more than you can tell me, Ivanito," she explains.

I've never actually been to Herminia's house, but everyone in town knows where she lives. It's a white house with red shutters, and has a giant acacia in the front yard. Herminia welcomes Pilar and me as if she's been expecting us, and serves us *guayaba* juice in tall glasses. It's peaceful inside. There are velvet pillows with tassels on the sofa and a ceiling fan that cools us.

Herminia settles down next to us and holds Pilar's hands in hers. She's wearing a turban layered high on her head, and she sits very straight. A bunch of red and white beaded necklaces click together in her lap as she speaks.

We listen to stories about my mother as a child, about her marriages to my father and to other men, about the secret ceremonies of her religion and, because Pilar insists on every detail, about my mother's final rite, and her last months on Palmas Street.

When she finishes, Herminia closes her eyes for a moment, then guides Pilar to a back room lit with candles. There's an ebony statue of a female saint in the corner, and a tureen on an altar crowded with apples and bananas and dishes of offerings I can't identify.

"*Bienvenida, hija,*" Herminia says and embraces Pilar. Then she draws me to them, and I breathe in the sweet, weary fragrance of my mother.

Pilar

"So tell me how you want to be remembered," I tease Abuela Celia. It's very early in the morning and the light is a transparent blue. "I can paint you any way you like."

"You don't have to do that, *hija*. I just want to sit here with you." She settles into her wicker swing and pats the cushion by her thigh. Abuela is wearing her faded jade housedress and a brand-new pair of sneakers with thick cotton socks. Suddenly she leans toward me. "Did you say any way I like?"

"*Sí*, Abuela. You name it."

"Even younger? Much younger?"

"Or older, if you prefer." I laugh. She laughs, too, and her drop pearl earrings dance from her lobes.

"Well, I've always envisioned myself in a flared red skirt like the flamenco dancers wear. Maybe with a few carnations."

"Red ones?"

"Yes, red ones. Many red ones."

"Anything else?" I joke around, feigning a flamenco. But Abuela doesn't laugh. There's a sadness in her expression tempered by hope.

"Are you going to stay with me, Pilar? Are you going to stay with me this time?"

*

I paint a series of watercolor sketches of my grandmother. I'm out of practice, though. Abstract painting is more up my alley. I feel more comfortable with it, more directly connected to my emotions. In a few of the sketches, I paint Abuela Celia just the way she wants—dancing flamenco with whirling red skirts and castanets and a tight satin bodice. Abuela likes these paintings best, and even ventures a few suggestions. "Can't you make my hair a little darker, Pilar? My waist a little more slender? *Por Dios,* I look like an old woman!"

Mostly, though, I paint her in blue. Until I returned to Cuba, I never realized how many blues exist. The aquamarines near the shoreline, the azures of deeper waters, the eggshell blues beneath by grandmother's eyes, the fragile indigos tracking her hands. There's a blue, too, in the curves of the palms, and the edges of the words we speak, a blue tinge to the sand and the seashells and the plump gulls on the beach. The mole by Abuela's mouth is also blue, a vanishing blue.

"These are very beautiful, Pilar. But do I really look so unhappy?"

Abuela talks to me as I paint. She tells me that before the revolution Cuba was a pathetic place, a parody of a country. There was one product, sugar, and all the profits went to a few Cubans, and, of course, to the Americans. Many people worked only in winter, harvesting the sugarcane. In the summer it was the *tiempo muerto,* the dead time, and the *campesinos* barely escaped starvation. Abuela says she was saved because her parents sent her to live with her great-aunt in Havana, who raised her with progressive ideas. Freedom, Abuela tells me, is nothing more than the right to a decent life.

Mom eavesdrops on Abuela and me then lambastes us with one of her sixty-odd diatribes when she doesn't like what she hears. Her favorite is the plight of the *plantados,* the political prisoners who've been in jail here almost twenty years. "What were their crimes?" she shouts at us, pushing her face close to ours. Or the question of retribution. "Who will repay us for our homes, for the lands the Communists stole from us?" And religion. "Catholics are persecuted, treated like dogs!" But Abuela doesn't argue with Mom. She just lets her talk and talk. When Mom starts to go too haywire, Abuela gets up from her swing and walks away.

We've been in Cuba four days and Mom has done nothing but complain and chain-smoke her cigars late at night. She argues with Abuela's neighbors, picks fights with waiters, berates the man who sells ice cones on the beach. She asks everyone how much they earn, and no matter what they tell her, she says, "You can make ten times as much in Miami!" With her, money is the bottom line. Mom also tries to catch workers stealing so she can say, "See! *That's* their loyalty to the revolution!"

The Committee for the Defense of the Revolution has started hassling Abuela about Mom, but Abuela tells them to be patient, that she'll only be here a week. I want to stay longer, but Mom refuses because she doesn't want to give Cuba any more hard currency, as if our contributions will make or break the economy. (Mom is apoplectic because she has to pay for a hotel room and three meals a day even though we're staying with relatives.) "Their pesos are worthless! They let us visit because they need us, not the other way around!" Why did they let my mother in here, anyway? Don't these Cubans do their homework?

I keep thinking Mom is going to have a heart attack any minute. Abuela tells me it's been unusually hot for April. Mom is taking several showers a day, then rinsing her clothes in the sink and putting them on damp to cool herself off. Abuela doesn't get any hot water at her house. The ocean is warmer than what comes out of her pipes, but I'm getting used to cold showers. The food is another story, though, greasy as hell. If I stay much longer, I'll need to get a pair of those neon stretch pants all the Cuban women wear. I have to admit it's much tougher here than

I expected, but at least everyone seems to have the bare necessities.

I wonder how different my life would have been if I'd stayed with my grandmother. I think about how I'm probably the only ex-punk on the island, how no one else has their ears pierced in three places. It's hard to imagine existing without Lou Reed. I ask Abuela if I can paint whatever I want in Cuba and she says yes, as long as I don't attack the state. Cuba is still developing, she tells me, and can't afford the luxury of dissent. Then she quotes me something El Líder said in the early years, before they started arresting poets. "Within the revolution, everything; against the revolution, nothing." I wonder what El Líder would think of my paintings. Art, I'd tell him, is the ultimate revolution.

Abuela gives me a box of letters she wrote to her onetime lover in Spain, but never sent. She shows me his photograph, too. It's very well preserved. He'd be good-looking by today's standards, well built with a full beard and kind eyes, almost professorial. He wore a crisp linen suit and a boater tilted slightly to the left. Abuela tells me she took the picture herself one Sunday on the Malecón.

She also gives me a book of poems she's had since 1930, when she heard García Lorca read at the Principal de la Comedia Theater. Abuela knows each poem by heart, and recites them quite dramatically.

I've started dreaming in Spanish, which has never happened before. I wake up feeling different, like something inside me is changing, something chemical and irreversible. There's a magic here working its way through my veins. There's something about the vegetation, too, that I respond to instinctively—the stunning bougainvillea, the flamboyants and jacarandas, the orchids growing from the trunks of the mysterious ceiba trees. And I love Havana, its noise and decay and painted ladyness. I could happily sit on one of those wrought-iron balconies for days, or keep my grandmother company on her porch, with its ringside view of the sea. I'm afraid to lose all this, to lose Abuela Celia again. But sooner or later I'd have to return to New York. I know now it's where I belong—not *instead* of here, but *more* than here. How can I tell my grandmother this?

Lourdes

When Lourdes learns that dozens of people have taken refuge in the Peruvian embassy, she rushes to Havana to investigate. It's sweltering in the capital, and Lourdes wipes her brow repeatedly with a moist cloth she keeps on the seat beside her. A crowd is milling outside the embassy gates, but no one dares to enter. A Jeep rounds the corner and a knot of young men chase it, calling a familiar name. Others scatter, averting their faces or hiding behind their sleeves.

The Jeep pulls up to the embassy and a barrel-chested man steps out. He's wearing an olive cap and army fatigues, and his curly, graying beard floats below his chin, elongating his tired features. He looks much older than her mother's photograph, the one that replaced her father's face, the one Lourdes flung into the sea. He looks smaller, too, more vulnerable, a caricature of himself.

Long ago, Lourdes had prepared a curse for him but today her tongue is flat and dry, an acre of desert. She follows El Líder inside the compound. The defectors in the courtyard are nervous in his presence. They run their fingers under their collars and scan the walls for cameras and rifles.

Lourdes realizes she is close enough to kill him. She imagines seizing El Líder's pistol, pressing it to his temple, squeezing the trigger until he hears the decisive click. She wants him to see her face, to remember her eyes and the hatred in them. Most of all, Lourdes wants him to be afraid.

Suddenly she thinks of Francisco Mestre, a Cuban exile and freedom fighter who launched a commando raid on Cuba in 1966. He had fought until he had no ammunition left, and vowing that he'd never be taken alive, detonated a grenade that blinded and crippled him. He survived, and returned to Miami a hero. Lourdes wants to follow in his footsteps.

She takes a deep breath and concentrates on extracting a phrase from the reeling in her brain.

"*Asesino!*" she shouts abruptly, startling everyone in the courtyard.

Several soldiers move toward her but El Líder waves them still. Then, ignoring her, he turns to the defectors and in the voice he reserves for his longest speeches declares: "You are free to emigrate to whatever country will accept you! We won't hold you here against your will!" And before Lourdes or the soldiers or the unshaven defectors can respond, El Líder stalks to his Jeep and drives away.

*　　*　　*

The sea is at low tide and mournful as a bassoon. Celia is walking along the shore with Pilar and Ivanito. Lourdes removes her shoes and walks barefoot to the water's edge. The sea recedes for a moment, exposing a family of silvery crabs. Ivanito lifts the smallest one and watches its claws dig the air. Its relatives flee recklessly into the surf.

Lourdes returns to the little brick-and-cement house without saying anything. She removes her gold bracelets, her sheer stockings, her pink rayon dress with the faux-pearl buttons, and lies on her childhood bed. Old sentences lurk beneath the mattress, in the rusted coils beneath her back. She thinks of her father and his endless destinations, his suitcase filled with rag dolls and oranges, his voice soothing as leaves. Lourdes lights a cigar, and rolls the dry, tart smoke on her tongue. She knows that she cannot keep her promise to her father, to tell her mother that he was sorry, sorry for sending her away, sorry for her silent hands. The words refuse to form in her mouth. Instead, like a brutal punishment, Lourdes feels the grip of her mother's hand on her bare infant leg, hears her mother's words before she left for the asylum: "I will not remember her name."

That night, Lourdes dreams of thousands of defectors fleeing Cuba. Their neighbors attack them with baseball bats and machetes. Many wear signs saying, SOY UN GUSANO, "I am a worm." They board ferries and cabin cruisers, rafts and fishermen's boats. The homes they leave behind are scrawled with obscenities. Rogelio Ugarte, the former postmaster of Santa Teresa del Mar, is beaten to death with chains on the corner of Calle Madrid, a visa in his pocket. Ilda Limón, too, is hoarse from screaming. She found a man face down in a pool of night rain in her yard and swears it's Javier del Pino, although her eyesight is no longer so good. Her neighbors tell Ilda she's crazy, that it's not Javier but just a poor wretch who tripped on the roots of her gardenia tree and drowned.

Before dawn, Lourdes wakes Ivanito, motioning him to stay quiet. "Come, I've packed you a bag." Lourdes has laid out his new clothes from New York—jeans with cross-stitched pockets, a striped jersey, white canvas sneakers. She hands him a glass of watery lemonade. "This is all we have time for now. I don't want to wake your grandmother."

Lourdes speeds along the highway to Havana. The earth is stained black from the morning rains. By the time they reach the embassy, hundreds of people are pushing their way through the gate. They're carrying boxes and cardboard suitcases tied with rope and belts. Lourdes remembers her own exodus, the watercolor landscape she wrapped in brown paper, her wedding veil and riding crops and the sack of birdseed. Pilar had fled through the crowds in her crinoline dress, escaping, always escaping.

Ivanito is silent as Lourdes hands him an envelope with two hundred dollars and a statement neatly printed in English: "MY NAME IS IVAN VILLAVERDE. I AM A POLITICAL REFUGEE FROM CUBA. MY AUNT, LOURDES PUENTE, OF 2212 LINDEN AVENUE, BROOKLYN, NEW YORK, WILL SPONSOR ME. PLEASE CALL HER AT (212) 834–4071 OR (212) 63-CAKES."

"Try to get on the first plane out, Ivanito. Don't leave the embassy no matter what. When you get to Peru or wherever they send you, call me. I'll come pick you up, *mi hijito.* I'll bring you back to Brooklyn. We'll go to Disney World this summer."

"*Y Abuela?*" Ivanito asks.

"Go, *mi cielo,* go!"

Pilar

Everyone in Santa Teresa del Mar has been talking about the trouble at the Peruvian embassy. The lady next door, Ilda Limón, came over last night and told us that she'd heard that El Líder announced that anyone who wished to leave the country was free to do so. She insisted that El Líder hasn't been himself since his mistress died in January. "He's depressed and it's clouding his judgment," she said. Mom was suspiciously restrained during the entire discussion and I should've known then that she was up to something. She'd been driving God knows where all day in that rented Oldsmobile of hers, and refused to say where she'd been. I knew it'd be only a matter of time before she pulled some crazy stunt.

This morning, when Abuela came to my room and told me

that Mom and Ivanito were missing, I assumed the worst.
Abuela told me that Ilda had seen the two of them leave before
dawn. She said Ivanito was dressed in new clothes and carried
a flight bag with AIR FLORIDA in big letters. "Shit!" I thought.
"Shit! I can't believe this!" I ran to Herminia's house and borrowed her new Russian Lada.

Abuela Celia looks straight ahead as I drive. Her hands stretch
like she's doing piano exercises, but then they crumple in her
lap like injured fans. I can see each twisted vein in her hands as
if light flowed through them, rivers of light.

"We have no loyalty to our origins," Abuela tells me wearily.
"Families used to stay in one village reliving the same disillu-
sions. They buried their dead side by side."

I take Abuela's hands in one of mine, feel the age in her stiffened fingers, the porous joints. She turns toward the ocean, a
horizon of blue.

"For me, the sea was a great comfort, Pilar. But it made my
children restless. It exists now so we can call and wave from
opposite shores." Then she sighs, waiting for her next words to
form. "*Ay, mi cielo,* what do all the years and the separation mean
except a more significant betrayal?"

My thoughts feel like broken glass in my head. I can't understand what my grandmother tells me. All I hear is her voice,
thickened with pain.

In Havana, the traffic is jammed in every direction. We leave
the car in an alley and walk the rest of the way to the Peruvian
embassy. Policemen have thrown a cordon around the compound to prevent new arrivals from entering. The defectors are
perched in the trees like overgrown turkeys. They jeer at the
police, cursing them violently, and shout encouragement to
those trying to break in. Abuela and I search the branches, the

roof, the high cement walls for a sign of Ivanito. But we don't see him anywhere.

A fight breaks out by the gate. A policeman swings his club and shatters someone's skull. It spatters the mob with blood and bone. A rock slams into my forehead. I don't feel anything at first, only the warm, sticky blood filling my eye. But then my head ignites with pain. Abuela is knocked aside when the crowd surges forward, but I'm carried high on the back of the beast as it forces its way through the gate. A moment later, it's over. The gate closes behind us. The mob holds together another instant, reluctant to lose its power.

"They're sending another plane to Lima," I overhear a fleshy woman with a Mickey Mouse T-shirt say. "The ones who got here this morning already left."

I think about climbing a tree, but I can't get close enough to one to hoist myself up. My head is aching and feels twice its normal size. My forehead sticks out like a ledge. I have to balance it carefully to walk. People look at me and turn away. They've got too many troubles of their own.

"They'll round us up and shoot us like pigs! They'll send us to the work camps with the *maricones!*" a mule-faced man shouts. He's got a chartreuse tattoo of the Virgin Mary on his forearm. Next to him, a wiry man in a tattered suit juggles two oranges and a grapefruit. He taps his foot to a rhythm in his knee.

Nothing can record this, I think. Not words, not paintings, not photographs.

I squeeze myself through the crowd, looking for Ivanito. For a minute, I can't remember his face. He's just a name, an impulse that keeps me moving, but then his image returns to me, his hazel eyes, his lanky body, his oversized hands and feet. At last I see him straight ahead, and then he turns and spots me, too. "Crraaaazzzzy!" Ivanito shouts at the sky, talking to a million people at once. I pull him toward me, hold him by the waist. I can feel my cousin's heart through his back. I can feel a rapid uncoiling inside us both.

*   *   *

"I couldn't find him," I lie to Abuela. My grandmother, too, is bruised, her shins are scraped and bleeding. She's been waiting for me for over an hour. "Somebody told me a plane left for Lima this morning. Ivanito must have been on it."

Abuela stares at the smooth-ringed trunk of a royal palm. I know what she is thinking: of upright men in homburg hats, of black silk umbrellas and the corrupting rains of northern latitudes. Jesus, what have I done? She turns to me once more.

"You looked everywhere, *mi hija?* Are you sure?" she asks me sadly. "Are you absolutely sure?"

"*Sí,* Abuela." I press my face into my grandmother's neck. But there's no scent of salt or violet water hidden in its creases.

Celia

Celia del Pino descends the three front steps of her house as if from a great height. She walks past the pawpaw tree, past the rows of gangly bird of paradise, past the house of her neighbor, Ilda Limón, and down a sandy path skirting the beach. There is jasmine in the breeze, and the aroma of distant citrus trees. The sea beckons with its blue waves of light.

I remember my first day in Havana. I arrived precisely at noon and the air rang with a thousand church bells. My Tía Alicia was waiting for me in her wide skirt and petticoats, the peacock brooch at her throat. She comforted me after my long train ride from the countryside. She taught me how to play piano, to make each note distinct from the others yet part of the whole.

Celia removes her leather pumps and walks toward the sea. The sand's cool moisture astonishes her. She buries her feet in the sand until she is planted, rooted as the palms, rooted as the gnarled gardenia tree. Her stained housedress billows in the wind, then is still.

The duende, *her head thrown back in throaty seduction, called to me through the poet. Her black sounds charmed me, and she wove her black ribbons as the rain hammered assent.*

> *The field*
> *of olives*
> *opens and shuts*
> *like a fan.*
> *Over the olive grove*
> *in a sunken sky*
> *and a dark rain*
> *of cold evening stars.*

It occurs to Celia that she has never been farther than a hundred yards off the coast of Cuba. She considers her dream of sailing to Spain, to Granada, of striding through the night with nothing but a tambourine and too many carnations.

Sing with me, the duende *cries, sing for the black sea that awaits your voice.*

Celia steps into the ocean and imagines she's a soldier on a mission—for the moon, or the palms, or El Líder. The water rises quickly around her. It submerges her throat and her nose, her open eyes that do not perceive salt. Her hair floats loosely from her skull and waves above her in the tide. She breathes through her skin, she breathes through her wounds.

Sing, Celia, sing . . .

Celia reaches up to her left earlobe and releases her drop pearl earring to the sea. She feels its absence between her thumb and forefinger. Then she unfastens the tiny clasp in her right ear and surrenders the other pearl. Celia closes her eyes and imagines it drifting as a firefly through the darkened seas, imagines its slow extinguishing.

Celia's Letter: 1959

My dearest Gustavo,

The revolution is eleven days old. My granddaughter, Pilar Puente del Pino, was born today. It is also my birthday. I am fifty years old. I will no longer write to you, *mi amor*. She will remember everything.

My love always,
Celia

A NOTE ABOUT THE AUTHOR

Cristina Garcia was born in Havana, Cuba, in 1958, and grew up in
New York City. She attended Barnard College and the Johns Hopkins
University School of Advanced International Studies. Ms. Garcia has
worked as a correspondent for *Time* magazine in San Francisco,
Miami, and Los Angeles, where she currently lives with her husband,
Scott Brown, and their English bulldog. *Dreaming in Cuban* is her first
novel.

A NOTE ON THE TYPE

This book was set in Fournier, a type face named for Pierre Simon
Fournier, a celebrated type designer in eighteenth-century France.
Fournier's type is considered transitional in that it drew its inspiration
from the old style yet was ingeniously innovational, providing for an
elegant yet legible appearance. For some time after his death in 1768,
Fournier was remembered primarily as the author of a famous manual
of typography and as a pioneer of the point system. However, in
1925, his reputation was enhanced when The Monotype Corporation
of London revived Fournier's roman and italic.

Designed by George J. McKeon

Composed by Brevis Press,
Bethany, Connecticut

Printed and bound by Fairfield Graphics,
Fairfield, Pennsylvania